PRAISE FOR
SHADOWBRIDGE

"One of fantasy's most challenging thinkers, who also knows how to tell a top-notch story."
—KAREN TRAVIS, *New York Times* #1 bestselling author of *City of Pearl*

"*Shadowbridge* is a compelling work which ends appropriately in a cliff-hanger, but it's emphatically not for the faint of heart."
—FAREN MILLER, *Locus*

"One of the best reads of the year and this is just the beginning."
—JAY TOMIO, FantasyBookSpot

"Leodora's journey is filled with the brilliant details of Frost's masterful world building. . . . [He] has created a world containing all manner of fantastic story and the promise of a fascinating history as Leodora moves into her destiny and the unknown future."
—REGINA SCHROEDER, *Booklist* (starred review)

"Frost draws richly detailed human characters and embellishes his multilayered stories with intriguing creatures—benevolent sea dragons, trickster foxes, death-eating snakes and capricious gods—that make this fantasy a sparkling gem of mythic invention and wonder."   —*Publisher's Weekly*

"For all its painterly beauty, *Shadowbridge* is a tough-minded novel that confronts some disturbing issues, and that is remarkably efficient in the telling."
—GARY K. WOLFE, *Locus*

"Frost immediately pulls the reader into a world of stories within stories with the tale of Leodora."   —BookPage

"The prose has an exotic, even ethereal feel."
—*San Diego Union-Tribune*

BY GREGORY FROST

Lyrec

Tain

Remscela

The Pure Cold Light

Fitcher's Brides

Attack of the Jazz Giants & Other Stories

Shadowbridge

Lord Tophet

LORD TOPHET

To Larry —
The final bend of the spiral.
Best.
Gregory Frost

LORD TOPHET

A SHADOWBRIDGE NOVEL

GREGORY FROST

BALLANTINE BOOKS / NEW YORK

A Del Rey Books Trade Paperback Original

Published in the United States by Del Rey Books, an imprint of The Random House Publishing Group, a division of Random House, Inc., New York.

DEL REY is a registered trademark and the Del Rey colophon is a trademark of Random House, Inc.

LIBRARY OF CONGRESS CATALOGING-IN-PUBLICATION DATA
Frost, Gregory.
Lord Tophet : a Shadowbridge novel / Gregory Frost.
p. cm.
ISBN 978-0-345-49759-8 (pbk.)
1. Women storytellers—Fiction. 2. Puppeteers—Fiction. I. Title.
PS3556.R59815L67 2008
813'.54—dc22   2008006642

Printed in the United States of America

www.delreybooks.com

2 4 6 8 9 7 5 3 1

Book design by Casey Hampton

*For Terri Windling, who long ago (though she didn't know it then)
started me down this path*

ACKNOWLEDGMENTS

Numerous people gave of their time and wisdom in providing feedback on this book as it grew. I want to thank especially Fran Grote, who argued against the most obdurate resistance in the world—mine; Oz Whiston, for her blade-edged criticism; Janine Latus, a superb writer and canny reader; and my editor, Keith Clayton, who caught every single thing that everybody else missed and then some. Thanks to Shana Cohen, my agent, for keeping everything on track, including me. Once again a special thanks to M. Swanwick and the M. C. Porter Endowment for the Arts for the long-term chivvying they provided; and to Barbara for weathering it all. Finally, my thanks to the great shadow puppeteer Richard Bradshaw, who once upon a time let me have a peek into his world.

LORD TOPHET

I

THE BLIGHT OF COLEMAIGNE

ONE

"Everything has its own vortex," said a deep male voice.

Whoever spoke must have been right at her back. Leodora glanced behind herself but saw only a great expanding gyre, a white-scorched tunnel stretching all the way back to the span of Colemaigne—to the hexagonal Dragon Bowl on which she stood . . . still stood, surely. Diverus and Soter must be there even now, and all of this a dream. Someone else's dream that had scooped her up and carried her off. "Wake up," she said, but nothing changed, and she wondered if anyone could hear her.

She had no sense of motion; she hadn't taken a single step, and yet the Dragon Bowl shrank until it was like a pinhole at the far end of the gyre, so she had to be moving, carried, transported . . . somewhere. She looked down at herself—at her legs stretched a thousand wyrths down the tunnel, as long as a full spiral's length from one coiled end to the other, which was farther even than she had traveled with Soter from Bouyan to Colemaigne. She kicked her feet but they were so distant in this dream that she couldn't see them, or her ankles. The view of her impossible legs fascinated her.

The disembodied voice spoke again, solemnly, beside her now. "The Traveler thro' Eternity has passed that first Vortex. She enters another."

She glanced up, facing the source, but once again no one was there.

As if cooling, the tunnel surface lost its white-hot glow, and the duller orange light left in its wake revealed the walls of the structure: intricately linked geometric shapes in a state of constant flux. She rushed along beside the bright geometries, diminutive satellites whirling in interlocked orbits. "I'm past the world," she said.

"Thus is heaven a vortex passed already," replied the voice.

"I must get back," she told it.

"You haven't *been* anywhere yet," the voice answered her.

"And where is it I'm going?" She thought she sounded remarkably calm.

The voice didn't reply. Behind her now the tunnel appeared to have no end point, unspooling forever. Her legs, however, had come unstuck from the distortion and had returned to their proper proportions. *At least I am myself again*, she thought.

Slowly, a vinegary stink stole upon her, a foulness as of a few unwashed bodies that grew until it was like the stench of a crowd, as if a mob coated in filth pressed in against the glowing tunnel. Her eyes watered, it was so noisome. She put out a hand as though to repel the odor, and her palm penetrated the spinning geometries and brushed something solid, moving. Alive. Another's hand tried to grasp at her fingers, but she snatched them free of the greasy grip. This motion propelled her away from the stink and the unseen thing and through the tunnel wall of spinning stars and globes, triangles and trapezoids, which washed over her body without sensation, passed through her like ghosts—like the bizarre phantoms that had paraded with her across the span of Hyakiyako and toward the end of time, the end of everything.

It had never occurred to her before to wonder what the end of everything might look like, how different it might be from the infinite bridge spirals of Shadowbridge. Perhaps that was where she was now, and this wasn't a dream. Had she, perhaps, died?

Outside the tunnel, separated from it, she stood on solid ground and watched it twist snake-like, as if alive, away from her. The glow of its spinning geometries dimmed like a cooling ember, until it was a golden thread of beaded sparks that finally flickered out, much like the red lamps on the black, silent ship that had passed hers on her way to Colemaigne and so terrified Soter. She must remember to ask him about it, when she returned. Or woke up. Or . . . where exactly was she?

A thick fog swirled out of the blackness to enclose her. Beneath her bare feet lay an unseen and uneven ground of hard rough stones. It was cold, and she wished that before she'd started walking through Colemaigne she'd put on her boots or the sandals Tastion had given her back on Bouyan.

The putrid stench still hovered, near but less intense, blended as it was with an odor of food, of something meaty frying with onions. And distantly, or else close but muffled by the fog, she heard a rhythmic knocking noise of something hard upon the stones, getting louder as she focused on it, a *clop*-clop-*clop*-clop that drew her to it, louder and louder every second and behind it, beneath it, a growing roar. The noise swelled, almost on top of her. She raised a defensive hand as a monstrous dark shape erupted out of the fog, giving her not even time to scream as it bore down on her. In that instant something grabbed hold of the hood at her neck and yanked her to one side. The fog roiled where she'd been and a huge creature with a great snout and a black glass eye surged past her so closely that she could see the sheen of its coat. Behind it came a large black carriage with curtained windows and skinny, wiry wheels thundering over the rough ground. Animal and carriage swept by and were swallowed in the fog as quickly as they appeared.

"Do you *want* to be squished?" asked the voice as Leodora's hood was released.

She turned about. The figure stood behind her. He was tall, and the fog abstracted his features until they were smudges, like the features of the Coral Man that lay in her puppet case back on Colemaigne.

"What *was* that thing?" she asked.

"Your demise if you don't learn to get out of the way. Standing in the middle of the road is never a good idea. You can be knocked down from *both* directions. As for what that was—surely you know."

"A palanquin, yes, but what monster led it?"

"Oh, no monsters here. Then again, *here* is itself monstrous to you. We're quite the world apart."

"This is Edgeworld, then?" Briefly she glimpsed wet gray paving stones under her feet.

"I think it most unusual that you've transported here. That's not how it's done generally. Seems your gift wasn't determined. I can't recall the last time that happened . . . at least, not at *our* particular terminus. Who can say *what's* gone on in Babylon? May-my, that could be a song title."

She tried to steal nearer the speaker. "Do you write songs?"

"I'm thinking about taking it up. 'Oh, what's gone on in Babylon,' late Enkidu inquired. 'For I've been dead,' is what he said, 'and missed . . . ' Drat, I have no idea how to complete that rhyme."

"I would offer to help, but I don't know the story."

"Don't *know* it? How Enkidu died and the hero Gilgamesh went into the underworld and brought him back?"

She shook her head, then realized he probably couldn't see the gesture any better than she could see him. "No," she replied.

"Well, there's a wonder. What are they teaching you in . . . where were you just now?"

"Colemaigne."

"Oh. Never mind, then, they don't teach anything there. Others build moments, minutes, hours. Not Colemaigne, not ever. Land of honey and surfeit."

"What happened to it?"

"Hmm? Oh. Not surfeited anymore, is it? Blighted by Tophet, was Colemaigne. He, in the guise of Chaos, placed one hand upon the wall of a building, and from his imperishable fingers spread the web of decay. Sum and substance cracked and spilled out bitterness, in shoals of torment."

"Who is Tophet?"

"More like, *what* is Tophet, if you're going to ask. He's done away with the *who*. For Colemaigne, he was the Destroyer, come from the far side of the world seeking vengeance."

"But he didn't destroy all of it."

"Yes, and lucky the span was, too. He became distracted. Else it would have been a silent place forever."

"What distracted him?"

"Something. Something to do with *you*, it was. Something to do with death."

"Me?" She edged still nearer. "But it happened before I was born."

"True. And false."

She puzzled at that. "*You* know, though, don't you?" she said.

"Goes without saying, dear heart, goes without saying."

"Then why can't you explain it clearly?"

"Why? Because. It's necessary for you to find the answers to the larger puzzles of life yourself. They can't be handed out, providing information that would change the pattern you have to walk. The maze. The labyrinth. It's yours, I can't go about altering its shape just as a *courtesy*. Your mettle is to be tested and no one's to interfere in that. Besides, you won't remember a thing I say."

As he spoke, gesturing with caped arms, she stole ever closer, and before he noticed she'd slipped up beside him. When he looked down, she saw him clearly.

It was Soter's face.

"Taking a peek at eternity, are you?" he asked, amused.

"You're—"

"No, I'm not. This is a false body, an incrustation over my immortal spirit." He winked. "For *your* benefit, I should add."

From deeper in the fog came wailing, as if a chorus stood beyond the limit of her vision, responding to his words, answering or lamenting.

"Terrible time, this, terrible. But then what time isn't, hmm? We all wear the mind-forged manacles in this world to bring forth your own."

"I don't understand at all," she answered.

"Stories—yours and others'—they're the products of disenchantment. Without it, no telling would be necessary. All would be harmony. But it never is, save in memory where the disharmonious is excised as with a scalpel, and 'Oh, for the Golden Days of Old' becomes the Song of Delusion, when no such days ever have been or will be. Joys impregnate. Sorrows bring forth."

Leodora shook her head. His words danced along the edge of comprehension, as if his meaning, like the chorus, lay just outside the wall of fog, attainable if only she could penetrate it. To delve into the fog, however, meant to move away and lose sight of him, which seemed to her a great risk.

The chorus sounded again, in doleful harmony with her dilemma. They were nearer, right behind him, as if they or the street were moving, sliding.

The rhythmic clop and clatter of another carriage approached, and this time she drew back as it neared, well before his hand grabbed her, so that this time she pulled *him* away. The fog parted as though fleeing her, and there stood the chorus in a half circle around a low stone wall upon which perched a large, long-haired cat. The cat's fur ran through a rainbow of colors, as bright as if a beam of sunlight were somehow penetrating the fog bank and striking the creature. One of the members reached out and ran a grubby hand the length of the cat, smoothing its fur. Its mouth opened, and a weird music floated out. The chorus listened to the notes and then as a group repeated them. Their dissonant chants had nothing to do with her songwriter after all.

"Beast knows all the tunes," he said.

She became aware that the latest coach had slowed and come to a halt behind them, and she turned back.

"It's for us," said the songwriter. His hand at her elbow gently impelled her. His gaze—Soter's gaze—was benign.

"Where are we going?"

"That I cannot say. It's *your* journey, and you must tell the carriage where to go, when to stop."

In the mist behind him, the cat lit up in colors and let forth another musical refrain of gliding notes that the crowd tried to emulate immediately, producing a caterwaul of conflicting voices. Had she been any nearer, she would have winced.

"How can I know where to stop when I can't see anything?" she asked him.

"Perhaps," he suggested, "it's not something you do with your eyes?"

"I'm not used to this. I'm not ready."

"No one ever is. Nor will you be here long enough to adapt. Not that you'd want to. The stink of old Londinium would win in the end. The blackened churches, the sighs like blood running down the walls. Not for you." He held open the door of the carriage and reached out, his palm up. "Come into my hand," he said, which she found stranger even than what he'd said previously.

She took his palm and let him lift her forward and up into the carriage, which rocked back and forth as she took her seat. He got in behind her and closed the door. Then, with a walking stick she hadn't noticed previously, he rapped twice on the ceiling.

The carriage lurched, and he said, "Off we go."

She studied him now. In the shadowy confines of the carriage she could make him out more clearly than in the fog. It was Soter's face, all right, but with a thick shock of hair wild about his head, and much less dissolution across the terrain of his cheeks—a Soter who hadn't drowned his every trouble in tuns of wine.

Under her scrutiny, he commented, "The maiden forgets her fear."

She sat back. "How is this my journey?" she asked.

"You walked the pattern, although it wasn't visible any longer. That's an impressive enough feat for almost anyone. You traveled though you never left the spot. Now you choose the thing that returns with you, which might be important, or superfluous—but you do choose it."

"Does everyone?"

"Does everyone choose? May-my, yes, everyone who comes here, though none—including you—remembers. Nothing I've told you will you remember."

"Diverus, then. He chose his gift."

"I assume that is the name of someone who came before you? If so, then yes. I didn't meet him, but what are the odds of two who know each other arriving in my care in my moment? Surely astronomical. Your look tells me that you remain confused, which is as it must be, and no matter, for you'll lose this conversation shortly. The ride, the smells, the caterwauls, the beast that draws us—all will fall away. For now . . . you have but to choose."

"But what am I choosing?"

"What everyone chooses. What your Diverus chose."

Frustrated, she folded her arms. He shifted on the seat and his forehead furrowed, giving her the impression that if he had known more, he *would* have told her, but the larger picture was as obscure to him as it was to her.

She asked, "How do I make the choice?"

"You say *stop*. The carriage stops. You pick your prize, whatever it might be, and this all comes to an end."

Leodora said, "I see," although she didn't. His explanation explained nothing. She was to decide without knowing. How could Diverus have chosen when he had no mind to think with? And yet he had—had chosen the divine gift of music. There really wasn't anything she wanted, except perhaps shoes for her feet, which had almost gone numb on the pavement. If Diverus had taken this same carriage ride, how would he have known when he'd arrived at the thing he wanted? Or had they healed him first? There seemed to be no point in asking if she wasn't going to remember the answers anyway.

She closed her eyes and listened to the carriage, the creak of wood and leather. The roll and jounce traveled through her, the steady rhythm of the hooves of the beast pulling her down into reverie or dream, a senseless state that was neither alertness nor slumber.

Then all at once she cried "Stop!" and the carriage drew to a halt so fast that she lurched out of her seat and back again.

Her companion, his eyes half lidded, remarked, "Excellent choice."

"What?" She *had* said stop. She *had* come alert. But she had no idea what had provoked the response.

"Go," he said, and opened the carriage door. "Quickly now. Once you choose, you've only a brief time to retrieve."

"Don't you—"

"No, I do not," he answered as if he had known her question before she even spoke. "I give you a golden string, but I await you here."

He gestured with the stick, and she climbed down from the carriage. The humid fog was as thick as before, the bricks of the street slick and fetid. She stepped up onto a raised walk, which proved smoother underfoot. Crossing it, she came upon wide steps going up and, beside them, a smaller set that descended beneath the level of the walk.

Up or down? She'd called out, chosen this spot, but didn't know why nor how to proceed. Up or down? It would matter. It must. Yet how was she to proceed when she didn't know what had prompted her, what compelled her now? Up or down?

She stared at the arrangement of the stairs, railings, the wide blank doors just visible at the top of the steps. Uncertainly, she started up, her hand on the cold iron rail. She looked over the side of it. The lower stairwell curved beneath the steps, leading to a doorway that was upside down as she viewed it. The arrangement reminded her of the inverted world she'd glimpsed under Colemaigne and of the underworld of Vijnagar. There were secret worlds enfolded in her world. And Diverus was from the secret world, sent to it after he'd stood upon the Dragon Bowl. These thoughts, notions, observations interlaced, although why they should she couldn't say. She had to operate on instinct and nothing more. Instinct instructed her to descend, just as it urged her to hurry.

She ran down the lower steps, which were black and worn as from a thousand years of use. Inset in the wall to her right was a window, its other side framed in lace. She peered in upon a chamber beneath the sidewalk where a rose-red lamp glowed warmly. Farther back in the room were people—a family, two parents and three children. They looked happy, contented, affection-ate, oblivious of her presence, though she must have blotted out the light as she pressed to the glass. Tenderness for them consumed her—a longing to be in that room, part of that family, to be so loved. The ache of that desire drove her from the view and down the last two steps.

She stood before a door, surely the door that led to that room, that family. It was green, wet with mist, and embellished with a large brass knocker in the shape of a lion's head that held the knurled ring in its mouth.

Leodora reached up, grabbed the ring, and swung it hard against the door. The sound of it thundered, echoed as along endless hollow corridors. The lion's brass head opened golden eyes and stared down at her.

"The choice is made!" said the voice of her companion, and she jolted upright in her carriage seat, then glanced about herself in disorientation.

Across the carriage, Soter-but-not-Soter leaned toward her and said, "What is now proved was once only imagined." He offered her his walking stick, and the head of it was the lion's head of the door knocker. Had it been thus earlier? She hadn't looked closely enough. But she closed her fingers over it.

"Good-bye, Leodora," said the songwriter, and through her hand, be-tween her fingers, the geometrics she'd stepped through before came swirling. They spun about her, twisted into a cylindrical blur that drew her upright and held her with her arms extended to the side, fingers skimming the patterns as she descended, flowed through the dream, sliding down the golden string, which settled her gently back within the hexagonal bowl. As her toes touched, the bowl reignited with so bright a light that it seemed to burn straight through her as though she were no thicker than the hammered skin of a shadow puppet. She looked at her hands glowing red from the blood within, and then all at once brighter still. In a burst that consumed her, she became light, and as the blaze faded all that remained was the thread of gold, which she followed downward into darkness.

Diverus maintained that he had slept through the visitation of the gods to the Dragon Bowl in which he'd been chained. He'd gone to sleep an idiot and waked a whole and reasoning being with no memory of the event that linked the two, which presumed that the event *had* been a visitation—that gods *had* descended in the night, driving mad all who saw them. Now that he had stared into the milky wasting eyes of soul-drinking afrits and been transported to some other place or time at acute cost to his life, he could well imagine being driven mad at the sight of beings divine and horrible.

Whatever he had envisioned of that missing time, it had been dark and subtle, nothing like a flash of light bright and powerful enough to knock him down in the sea-lane, dazzling him where he sprawled. His senses returned, a moment or an hour later. Along the rail and the bollards beside him a bluish fire scurried, crackling like grinding glass. It edged the building behind him, too, and sparked off Soter, who still lay stretched out in the lane. Rising up, Diverus saw his own hands, arms, and torso defined by the dancing fire, like an illusion, with no hint of sensation. As he got to his feet, this flame flickered and leapt as if willfully to the rail, abandoning him and merging with the glow there as though it shunned anyone conscious. Beam and Dragon Bowl both pulsed with the blue fire. The bowl stood empty. Leodora had vanished.

Now people appeared, out of doorways and from between buildings. People in cloaks and vests and some in careless dishabille looked, saw, came running along the narrow lane. Wherever they brushed the blue glow, it sparked and crackled but seemed to harm no one. They ran to him, to Soter, to the space in the railing where the dragon beam projected.

Soter climbed unsteadily to his feet and had to be held up. His head had a gash, a crooked line of blood over one eye. With a dull expression, he focused on Diverus, and his eyes went wide. "Lea!" he said, and with sudden ferocity he wrestled free of helpful supportive arms and hands while Diverus, already panicked by the sight of the empty bowl, plunged onto the dragon beam ahead of him.

The length of the beam had been repaired. Before the blast of light, the retaining walls had been nothing but crumbling remains. Now they were smooth and waist-high on both sides of a brown-tiled walkway. So, too, the wall around the bowl, sparking with blue fire, had been rebuilt. It shone hard and glossy. People in the lane were crying, "Lookit, lookit!" but only one or two were willing to step onto the beam so long as that blue fire burned.

The beam curved around to the outside of the bowl, entering it, as was the tradition, from seaward. Diverus ran, looking, seeing only an unoccupied bowl. With each step his anxiousness swelled.

The brown tiles continued as a motif into the refurbished bowl, circling it in a pattern that Diverus recognized immediately as a maze. And lying in the depressed center of the maze was Leodora, on her back with her red hair fanned out like blood around her head.

He ran across, unheedful of the maze pattern: He wasn't entering the bowl to capture the gods' goodwill; he didn't care.

He slid to his knees beside her. Her face was flushed or sunburned. He touched her, and she was warm as with a fever. Warm, which meant alive. He rejoiced, at the same time trying to recall if he had been similarly affected, but all he could remember of it was confusion upon awaking.

Behind him at the entrance to the bowl, Soter collapsed—peripherally Diverus saw the old man spiral into a heap like a broken puppet clinging in anguish to the wall. Soter's crust of pomposity fell away and revealed his true concern for Leodora. With a sharp stab of pity, Diverus said to him gently, "She's only sleeping." Soter glanced sharply up. The agony in his expression was slow to allow hope.

"It lit up," he said, "the gods—"

"The gods have favored her," Diverus replied, adding, "At least, if they haven't driven her mad, they have." He recalled that not one of the others who'd been in the Dragon Bowl with him had walked away sane.

"And if they have?" Soter asked, clinging to his misery.

Diverus had no answer for that, saying only, "We should move her off the beam before that crowd comes out here and picks her apart. They will, as soon as the blue fire dies, and they won't be reasonable." Already the strange fire was dwindling.

Soter cast him a peculiar look, and it was only then that he realized he was explaining situations, giving orders. Where the information came from, he had no idea. There had been no blue flame when he'd been in the Dragon Bowl of Vijnagar. Why would he possess such authority and fore-knowledge? Right now there was no time to ponder it.

Quickly, then, they each took one of her arms and placed it over their shoulders, supporting Leodora between them. Diverus, as he did this, saw a chain dangling from her loosely closed hand. He tugged gently upon it, and a gold object slipped from between her fingers. In the same instant her eyes opened and gazed blankly at him, closing again almost as fast. Soter could not have seen it. He took a step up the bowl, but Diverus cried, "Wait!"

"What is it?"

"I think we have to walk the pattern out of here."

Soter seemed to consider the maze for the first time. "Did she walk it coming in?"

"I don't know. But I think we have to if we're to take her out, to protect her. The gods embedded it, we have to assume it applies." He glanced toward Colemaigne; the blue glow along the rail was flickering out. "And we'd best hurry."

Supporting Leodora between them, they walked the brown-tiled maze from the center out, around and around the bowl, out to the edge but looping in closer to the center again. Finally, on the fifth tier of lines, they arrived at the lip where the brown tiles led onto the dragon beam. Before they could even step onto the beam, the first and most daring of the citizens blocked their way, not menacing but anxious. "Is anything in the bowl—she have anything on her?"

"No," Diverus lied. "But the pattern has appeared, you see?"

"Then . . . oh, my."

"You should walk it," Soter suggested, but the man wasn't staring into the bowl. He was gaping at the view beyond it, at the span itself. Soter and Diverus craned their heads to follow his gaze, discovering that the row of buildings lining the sea-lane, all of which had been ruins before the blast of light, now stood whole and gleaming, newly formed.

"The gods did come! We're blessed again!" the man cried, and leapt past them into the Dragon Bowl. Disregarding Diverus's advice, he charged into the center of it across the lines of the maze.

Soter and Diverus wasted no more time, but carried their unconscious friend along the curved beam. So narrow was the space that they had to crab sideways with her. As others started out onto the beam, Soter snarled, "Back, back, the lot of you, or I'll stamp you flat!"

Diverus smiled at the effect that threat had on the crowd. They skittered timidly off the beam. Then he happened to glance off to the side, and he saw in the darkness beneath the span's surface what he took at first to be a reflection of the new buildings above, cast upon still water . . . until a door opened in one of them and a figure walked out upside down, went to the rail, and stared across right at Diverus. Above, upright in the newly recast lane, there was no corresponding figure. The upside-down man, as blue as lapis, lifted one hand, and it seemed that he waved, and Diverus answered with a wave of his free hand, swinging the gold chain and, on the end of it, a medallion in the shape of a broad face.

When he looked up again, the man had turned and gone back inside the impossible upside-down house. They were nearing the end of the beam then, and the edge of the span gradually cut off the vision. One of the citizens, unable to wait, jumped up and perilously walked the retainer wall to get around them. He glowered at Leodora and Diverus as he edged by and then leapt onto the brown tiles and ran, crying out, "Gods, I'm here, your devoted servant is here!" With raised hands, he rushed into the bowl, turning in circles, face to the sky, until the one who'd preceded him struck him down from behind. *It's starting,* Diverus thought, and quickly pocketed the medallion.

They reached the end of the beam, and the people there opened a space, not from courtesy so much as to get them out of the way. The moment Diverus stepped down, the nearest ones knocked him aside in their surge up the curving beam.

Someone asked, "What did she get, what did she see?" and Soter replied, "We don't know, do we? She's unconscious yet." A few eyed her as she was carried past, obviously weighing the desire to wait and find out what had happened to the girl against the immediate lure of the Dragon Bowl itself. They all chose the latter. Some slid by. Others touched her reverently as she was carried past. When from one jarring movement her head lolled, someone said, "Why, she's dead," and Soter growled, "No, she's not, you fool. The gods dazzled her, the same as they would have anyone. Same as they will you." That acted as an invitation to the speaker, who bounded toward the beam.

"They were really here? The gods really came?" asked the next man. Behind him a veiled woman with aristocratic poise reached forward and touched the man's shoulder. She silently directed his attention to the front of the house beside him—to the hard, slick coating that edged it. The man licked a finger and reached across Leodora to run the finger along it. He licked his finger again. Then he covered his mouth with both hands and hurried toward the beam, all but knocking Diverus off his feet.

That left the veiled woman, their two undaya cases, the satchel full of Diverus's instruments, and their wardrobe.

Behind the woman, two tall thin men with oddly shallow features beneath their cowls waited stiffly like servants. She, dressed in an embroidered ocher chemise and green overtunic, pressed a finger to Leodora's sunburned cheek. "Oh, my. She was in the bowl when it happened?"

"Yes," Soter replied with what seemed to Diverus an odd inflection of uncertainty.

"A blessing or a curse then, when she awakens."

Diverus frowned at her air of mystical superiority. "Sometimes it's both, and sometimes not worth anything to anyone," he said, holding her gaze to make her understand that he spoke from experience.

Rather than being intimidated, the woman raised her head. He could feel her considering him.

"Diverus, can we lay her down on one of the cases?" Soter asked. "I can't hold her up any longer."

They lifted her onto the nearest undaya case, where she lay as if napping. Soter collapsed beside her. In setting Leodora down, Diverus noted the veiled woman's gold sandals, her painted toes.

"You're a troupe, are you not," she said, and Soter nodded without looking up. "And what do you do?"

"We tell stories," Diverus replied, still annoyed by her superior airs.

"Well," she said, "it appears you've now become a story. At least, in Colemaigne." She pointed to the crowd in the Dragon Bowl, many of them with their arms raised, some jumping up and down, others reciting, others jostling.

Just then another group edged around them in the lane and hurried to the crowded beam.

"Yes, quite a story," the woman muttered. "You are performers. In the manner of Bardsham, no doubt." Soter's brows arched, but he said nothing. "If so, coming here may prove difficult for you—at least I would have said so until today, as there is a law here that bans all such theater. Did you not know?"

"What?" Soter looked up at her. "That can't be! This was the greatest venue—"

"Not since Bardsham's *final* performance have any been allowed here. He was the last. Disorder followed so close upon his heel that the one became tied to the other. He got off this span, but we could not. So either you don't travel this spiral of the Great Bridge very often, or you were last here with him."

"How are those two things of necessity mutually exclusive?" asked Soter, and Diverus thought, *He's angered by her, too.*

Overlooking Leodora, the woman replied, "I very much doubt they're different at all." She raised her face, and through the veil Diverus caught a glimpse of her features: austere, handsome, and hard, though her eyes betrayed some tenderness. "She needs somewhere to rest, and I expect you do, as well. Please come with me—bring her with you, and my men will carry your puppets."

Soter's brow furrowed. "How do you—"

"A long story, dear sir, which I'll willingly relate to you later—after you've settled in."

"Settled in?" Diverus and Soter exchanged a look.

"I own a theater. Like so much of Colemaigne, it was long ago blighted. Yet this very day and, I suspect, with thanks to this girl, it has been resurrected. If there's to be a performance, you will of course make your debut there."

"Who are you, madam?" Soter asked, clearly troubled. Diverus likewise could not figure out the cause of his own ire.

"For the moment, your benefactress. Please, bring her." She turned with a dramatic flourish and led the way back along the cramped lane. Her servants stepped aside to let her pass.

Soter and Diverus lifted Leodora from the black case. She was indeed as limp as if dead. Diverus wrapped his arms around her legs and led the way.

As they shuffled clumsily past, the servants melted into the shadows of a doorway, standing strangely still. Soter slowed to stare at them until Diverus almost pulled Leodora out of his grip. Ahead, the woman had rounded a corner and disappeared.

Hastily, they hobbled after her.

Soter said to Diverus, "How long did you sleep when it happened to you?"

"I don't know," Diverus replied over his shoulder. "I was asleep before, and never did awaken till after. I don't know how long was the time between. Hours, I thought, but it *might* have been days. I was very confounded."

"Mmmm." Soter huffed along a moment before asking more quietly, "What was the thing you found in the bowl?"

Diverus glanced back. "A pendant, on a chain. It was beside her, in her hand. It might be what they gave her, the gods." As he spoke he was recalling all the containers strewn in the bowl on Vijnagar when he'd awakened, and the madness they had seemed to induce in those who handled them. Of course the scrambling magpies in that Dragon Bowl so long ago might well have been mad already. He kept the woman in sight and tried not to worry that Leodora might never be herself again.

The woman led them to a wider avenue that angled away from the seawall lane and into the center of Colemaigne. Odd spade-shaped trees grew in pots along the middle of the avenue. The area bustled with life. There were carts and strollers, and outdoor tables; but the throng had gathered loosely in the avenue in front of certain buildings. They stared up, gestured, as if at holy shrines.

All the buildings were well appointed—not just the ones at which people gawked. The façades looked freshly polished, ornamented with colorful bright new awnings, umbrellas, and penants. Some had half-round balconies above the shops, of which every variety was represented—markets, tailors, boot makers, drapers, cafés, and more within the short distance Diverus and Soter walked. The woman soon turned into a narrower street.

They were moving deeper into the core of Colemaigne. Unlike the few spans Diverus had known so far, here the buildings were packed tightly together, with the result that a state of perpetual dusk hung over the street. The tight intersecting alleys looked darker still.

The woman led them toward the end of the street and a building distinct from the others they'd seen. For one thing it was round. And immense. A wide door, barred and locked, faced the street, but the woman walked past this and into the shadows beside the building.

Diverus scanned the walls, which rose up for two stories before opening into what appeared to be a roofed gallery—at least in the front. Farther back, the gallery became a third story with small windows. As with the buildings on the main thoroughfare, it looked as if it had been painted and polished just this morning. An adjacent blind alley in the rear led into a still-darker space, and that was where the woman directed them. It smelled vaguely foul, the closed-off space no doubt trapping vapors from out of the sewer grates instead of allowing them to disperse. There, at the very back of the circuit, the woman unlocked a chain and flung open a small and insignificant door. She waved them inside. A different smell—like the fusty odor of old clothes—unfolded from the interior, and it was a compelling and welcoming scent, as if the old place had been awaiting them. Despite doubts traded in glances, they carefully lifted Leodora through the doorway and inside. The two servants arrived soon after and pushed through with the cases and instruments, walking immediately deeper into the darkness while Soter and Diverus gathered their breath and waited for the woman to tell them what to do next.

Diverus's eyes adjusted slowly to the dim bluish light, most of which came through a row of tiny windows and bathed the interior in what seemed like moonlight.

A long broad table occupied the center of the room. At the far end he could just make out the black recess of a hearth large enough to stand in. Open doorways bracketed it on both sides. One of the odd servants who'd carried the undaya cases knelt before the hearth with a bellows and began pumping air at the ashes, which soon glowed.

The woman spoke from behind, startling him. "This is my home," she said. As he turned about, she closed the door through which they'd entered. She stood in front of a full rack of clothing that appeared to run the rest of the room's length and even along the far wall. She said, "Put it on the table, Bois," and Diverus glanced back to see the servant place a small oil lamp on the table beside the undaya case he'd set down there. The lamp was shaped like a slipper with a curled toe.

"Go on, then," said the woman. "I know you both want to explore." The two servants nodded vigorously and without a word went through one of the doors by the hearth.

"Explore?" asked Soter.

"Yes," she replied. She removed her veil and picked up the lamp. "Follow me and we'll put your friend somewhere she can rest, meanwhile." She crossed to the doorway on the far side of the hearth. It led to a flight of steps.

The stairwell proved difficult to navigate with Leodora between them, as they couldn't all three fit on a step together, and Diverus in the lead with her legs had to go up one step and wait for Soter before moving up another.

"It might be easier if one of you simply slung her over his shoulder," their hostess suggested. She was probably right, but now in the stairwell they could only crab their way up as they'd begun. "Explore," she explained as if Soter had asked again, "because until an hour ago the theater wall we circled coming in here did not exist. It collapsed years ago, after . . . after the calamity." She turned and stared down past Diverus at Soter as she said it.

Out of the stairwell, she led them a short way down a corridor with more doors on either side. She opened the first one and said, "Put her in here."

It was a small room, hardly larger than the narrow mattress on the floor. The ceiling slanted, a dormer. They lowered Leodora onto the bed, and Soter banged his head as he stepped back. Diverus knelt with her and carefully slipped the pendant out of his pocket, tucking it underneath her.

"The rear of the theater is full of tiny chambers like this," the woman was saying.

"It's where the players change," Soter stated.

"Where they used to, yes. Your friend may sleep for days, you know. Or never wake up at all."

"Never wake?" asked Diverus, as he stood. The possibility hadn't occurred to him. It was a matter of when, not if.

"In stories, on occasion," she reassured him. "She was touched by gods, and that hasn't happened here in so long that no one's going to recall what is *supposed* to happen."

"*He* should," Soter said as he stepped out of the room. He pointed at Diverus. "He's been touched, himself."

"That is gratifyingly improbable," she answered. "You will both surely be hungry. Let me have something prepared for you. Bois!"

When nothing happened, Soter said, "You sent them off to explore, madam."

"Well, that was ill planned, then."

Footsteps sounded at the far end of the hallway, and a servant entered from one of the side doors there. He came up beside Diverus and stopped, awaiting her orders. While she directed him what to prepare, Diverus got his first close look at her manservant.

He had a hard, chiseled face, and eyes that seemed almost painted on. Bois, sensing the scrutiny, turned his head and Diverus shyly lowered his gaze . . . and saw Bois's hand. The fingers were articulated, each joint hinged, very much like Leodora's shadow puppets.

Soter seemed utterly unaware of the strangeness of Bois. He was too intent upon ensuring that there would be wine to drink with their meal.

Bois shambled past them and clumped down the stairs they'd come up. Staring after him, Diverus missed the next thing the woman said, coming alert only to Soter's reply of "By all means." The two—Soter and the hostess— started off along the corridor. Diverus glanced in again at the sleeping Leodora, attempting to convince himself that she was safe and that the oddness of this place, much less of the whole span itself, was not a threat, or at least no more of one than the parade of monsters had been on Hyakiyako. They'd come through that just fine, hadn't they?

He made up his mind that he could leave her, and turned just as Soter and the woman exited through one of the doorways up the hall. Hurrying after them then, he found that the doorway led to a short descending ramp ending in a curtain, which wasn't quite closed. Light spilled through the center seam. He hastened down the ramp and stepped through the curtain into daylight again.

He stood in an open balcony. Drapery hung on each side, ornately decorated with flowers and vines. Cushions had been strewn about the floor, but Soter and the hostess remained standing at the rail, overlooking the circular theater. Diverus moved quietly up beside them.

It was magnificent. Below, a broad, bare stage projected out and wide to either side of the balcony. The remaining servant walked about on it, pausing, opening his arms as if declaiming, but never making a sound; then setting off again, he suddenly struck a regal pose, sprang from it, capered, stopped and stood humbly, demure and shy, trying on one character after another before a nonexistent audience.

The theater was empty. The main floor—deep enough that the stage stood at waist height above it—contained huge semicircular benches layered in amphitheater fashion away from the stage. The curved rear walls comprised a series of niches, of draped private boxes similar to this balcony. Overhead, thatched roofing extended to perhaps the first row of seats.

"It's a wonder," said Soter.

"Indeed, it is," their hostess replied. "A miracle. Only yesterday this and the two balconies to our right were misshapen holes in the wall, the floorboards below were rotted, the drapery in tatters. The interior walls across there with the boxes for patrons—those had all fallen in, a heap of crumbled stucco and stone. No glassine upon any of it at all. The thatch of that roof was black and rotten, a home for vermin, and had been thus for more than a decade."

"This is because of Leodora, all this change?" asked Diverus. "But you can't even *see* the Dragon Bowl from here."

"Nevertheless, look about you and marvel," she replied.

"And what is *he* doing?" Soter asked her, with a nod to the stage.

"Glaise is remembering. Reenacting. Once, we had a company, and they played to a thousand people in a night. Do *you* remember?" she asked carefully, looking sidewise at Soter, and he tensed, his face pinched as at some unpleasant recollection.

"I . . . of course I do."

"I thought perhaps the gods had snatched away your past, Soter, as happened to so many others."

He twitched when she said his name and responded in kind. "No, not the gods, Orinda. No gods came for *me*."

A brief smile crossed her lips at the mention of her name. Diverus eyed them both warily, attempting to fathom the meaning interlacing the words. "He died, you know, right after."

Soter rubbed his hand along his jaw. "I recall he was ill. He kept it from us but even so, I knew. Bardsham saw it first, the way he winced when he stood. He was a grand actor but sometimes in the pain, he would forget, his expression failed him, or else it was too excruciating to mask."

She nodded solemnly. "It spared him having to endure the ruin of the theater for so long. That would have destroyed him just as certainly, but it would have worn him to nothing first." She slid her arm along the railing and covered Soter's hand with her own. "How did you lose the tips of these fingers?"

"Storyfish bit 'em off," he quickly replied; it was the same response he'd given Diverus when he'd asked.

"Of course," answered Orinda, and Diverus could tell she didn't believe him. "That child, then—she's Bardsham's daughter." When he didn't reply, she said, "How fitting that she should repair our span."

"She is her mother in spirit."

"And will she bring destruction upon us, too? That *was* a gift you left Colemaigne."

Although Soter didn't move, it was as if his body twisted tight before Diverus's eyes. He said finally, "They don't know about her."

"If they learn of her here, history will rerun its course."

Squirming even more, Soter shifted the subject. "I must tell you, I've hardly a real recollection of you, Orinda. No solid memory beyond . . ."

"You would have dealt with *him*," she answered, taking no offense. "I was busy with our troupe. What would the play have been, I wonder. It was the end of—*Cardenio*, yes, they were rehearsing *Cardenio*. Never performed it. It's lost to the ages, along with its author."

"I'm sorry for both. But surely now you can revive the troupe?"

"Revive. What an appropriate word. I would have to. Revive them, that is."

"What, they've all died?"

She leaned farther over the glistering balcony. "You don't know, do you? You've no idea what happened here."

Soter looked fearful. "Apparently not," he answered.

Orinda glanced back at Diverus, who could only express his own puzzle-ment. As if to him, she replied, "What they did to punish us for harboring Bardsham. The horror they wrought. Not just the buildings suffered. You un-derstand?"

Diverus, without knowing details, comprehended the enormity she im-plied. He'd seen enough pain dispensed in his short life. He nodded, and the woman brushed his cheek tenderly.

She continued to focus upon Diverus as she asked, "Did they ever catch you, Soter?"

Beyond her fall of hair, Diverus could see Soter's awful face, the eyes looking inward, at what horrible memory he couldn't imagine. Softly, Soter replied, "They found us."

She rubbed the tips of his foreshortened fingers. "I thought as much. No one ever heard of Bardsham again, anywhere."

Soter tilted back his head and sighed. "But you, your husband— Colemaigne never harbored us. We'd no idea that trouble came here. We thought you'd been spared. We'd moved on, after all, far away. A different spi-ral. That's what a traveling troupe *does.*"

"It was what we maintained, as well, but that wasn't what they wanted to hear. What they wished to believe. When your captors have an answer in mind, it doesn't always matter that you tell them the truth."

"I . . . no, I suppose not."

"Innocence was not one of our choices."

"So it would be better if we left, then."

"Left?" she asked incredulously. She dropped her hand from his and turned. "If that girl has a mote of the talent her father had, she must perform for us. Here. This theater—this *span*—needs its stories back."

"She's better than him," said Diverus. Soter glared at him. "Well, *you* told her she was."

The woman regarded them both in apparent disbelief, until Soter with strange reluctance said, "It's true."

Diverus found himself watching the figure on the stage. Suddenly he put the performance together with what she had said. "Was Glaise a member of your troupe?" he asked. When both Soter and the woman regarded him in surprise, he added nervously, "I mean, he's not human, is he? Neither of them. They're—"

"*Pinottos.* Both of them, yes." The admission appeared to pain her. At her back Soter fumed with anger as though Diverus had committed the most terrible violation of etiquette. As if the answer had slammed the door on discussion, Orinda stated, "Your meal will be ready by now," and walked back through the curtain.

Soter scowled and, shaking his head, went after her, calling, "Orinda, please!"

Left alone on the balcony, Diverus muttered, "No one tells me anything, and then they blame me when I have to guess." Finally he decided that he wanted something to eat, too, and parted the curtains again.

The mute *pinotto* continued to perform for the emptiness.

TWO

Leodora awoke. The space around her was dark and sounded fearfully close; for a moment she imagined she was inside one of the undaya cases, transformed into a puppet, locked in with the Coral Man. She reached up with both hands and swept them back and forth through the air. Her fingertips touched nothing and she realized she was in a larger space, a room. The sound of it might have been dull and tight, but it was not a puppet case.

Something was poking at the ribs of her right side. She reached under herself, fingers digging, snaring a length of fine chain. As she tugged at it, the chain made a slithery sound, uncurling against something else metal that was vaguely oval, its surface a symmetrical raised design. Her fingertips couldn't identify what the design was, but it was nothing she owned, nothing she knew. It forced her to try to remember where she'd been last before awakening here.

She had walked—yes, that was right—walked out onto the decrepit dragon beam of Colemaigne. She'd done it on a dare, as a taunt to Diverus. She must have gone into the bowl itself, but squeezing her memory brought forth only a view of inverted buildings that might have been a reflection in a rain puddle, some odd music that tinkled like glass breaking, a few other disjunct and incoherent images, a few swirls of clarity in a fog bank of forgetfulness and beyond that, nothing. She might be anywhere save in the belly of a ship, for the room wasn't rocking in the slightest. That wasn't much, but it was *some* small knowledge. Diverus and Soter must surely be near.

"How do I choose?" she heard herself ask. The words seemed to die as they left her mouth. She said it aloud again to hear her voice, dry and muffled against the close walls: "How do I choose?"

In the darkness beside her, a different voice answered, "That *is* a challenge without more information about the choices proposed."

Leodora sat up. The voice spoke from so near that the speaker must have been right at the edge of the bed. Her eyes strained the darkness for any hint of a shape, a body, a face. Finally she let go of the pendant chain and reached out. Her splayed fingers found nothing.

She wondered for a moment if she might be hearing the voice of the Coral Man: She had heard it, she thought, in dreams, though they seemed so removed now that she couldn't be certain he'd ever spoken, nor could she recall now anything he had said—just the sound of it, like humming. This voice didn't resonate in her head. It was separate from her, the voice of someone else, even if that someone else proved to be a phantom.

"How do I . . . get more information?" she asked.

"You could simply get up and leave the room," the voice suggested.

"Will that work?"

"If it's not as dark as a crow in a mine everywhere else."

"*Is* it that dark everywhere else?"

"Oh, my, yes. Just now it is. It's night outside, and cloudy, and moonless, so there's no cast light, either."

"You've been outside."

The voice didn't answer.

"How do you know what it's like outside if you haven't been outside?" she asked, slightly peeved by its reticence.

"It's just something I know."

"Who are you, then?"

"I? I can't say."

"Why not?"

"No self-awareness," the voice explained.

She could not help laughing. "That's absurd."

The voice said nothing, and she was sure she had offended the person behind it. "You can speak to me, but you don't know that you exist? You're a figment, then. I must have made you up. Otherwise how can you talk to me and have no self-awareness?"

"I'm a counselor. You ask. I counsel."

"A ghost counsel. You're certainly not the one who visits me in my *sleep*." Upon the last word she lunged and waved both hands in the air this time, all around. She touched nothing until she strained so far that her fingers brushed a wall. No one was there. She realized that she would have sensed movement, heard a rustling if the other had moved. She'd heard nothing. It really *was* a ghost.

Now that she'd touched one wall, she rose. She sensed the slope of the ceiling just before her head brushed it. Close to the wall, everything smelled musty. She slid her palms down the slope to the vertical wall and along it, around a corner and on, until her hands brushed against a door. It rattled slightly and she snatched her hands back, afraid to make noise. Then with care she touched it again, patting as lightly as a butterfly, down until she felt against her wrist a cold bar, the handle. It was small, and she felt all around it, trying to picture what she was feeling, an image in her head of the mechanism. The bar was on a spring, and a pin projected from it that she could pull on to slide it back. Slowly she drew it back; the door swung toward her as on well-oiled hinges.

She glanced outside. Like the room, it proved to be featureless, dark, but some distance away on her left, a hint of illumination—no more than a dull glow—suggested an opening. She stuck her head back into the room and whispered, "Will you come with me?" but the voice of the counselor didn't answer. "Can you hear?" she asked, to no avail. He had apparently evaporated, and she shook her head as if to rid herself of the notion that it had been anything other than imaginary, her befuddled mind's creation after the . . . the events.

Out of the room again she moved toward the wan light, her hands out and to the sides. Her fingers brushed against walls on each side as she shuffled cautiously along. It was a narrow hallway. As she went, her balance seemed to tip, the light ahead wanting to tilt. She turned, pressing both palms to one wall, to a rough, solid coolness that anchored her and stabilized the hall. She hung her head and breathed deep lungfuls of air. She realized what must have happened in the Dragon Bowl.

Like Diverus she had no memory of it, but that didn't shake her belief; rather, it reinforced it. Sounds, smells, where she'd gone or what had come to her—these things lingered in the back of her mind, tantalizingly unreachable. She knew no more of them than of where she was at this moment. Had she been transported? Could she even now be in Edgeworld? Instinct maintained that she wasn't, although she could hardly express why.

She needed to find Diverus. She thought that if she insisted he try to remember Edgeworld, anything he might recall would help her to recollect her own experience—assuming that they were in the same place.

Pressed to the wall, she shuffled along. The nearer she got to the light, the more details she saw in the corridor: other doors, sconces for lamps, and finally an oval of lighter color where the wall had been patched but not painted.

The light shone through a split curtain. Behind it lay a short ramp that ended in a second, heavier drape below. She crept down the ramp to the drapery. With two fingers, she eased one side of it open, revealing a balcony railing that overlooked a large theater space.

She could see tiers of curved benches beneath a distant wall lined with similar small enclosed balconies. The source of the light remained out of view below the balcony, but it threw shadows that moved, accompanied by soft footfalls and a creak of floorboards.

She pushed her head through the curtain and discovered that hers was one of three balconies projecting from the back wall of a stage, each with elaborately wrought moldings. High above the balconies, a large thatched roof covered the stage area, held up by a framework that must have been attached from above. A higher, larger box-like balcony projected out beneath it.

On the stage below, two figures dressed identically in brown vests and trousers strode the boards. They faced each other and gestured as if in a pantomime of declaiming, of demanding. Transfixed, she watched the curious performance. After a while one of them gestured as if putting on shoes while the other mimed the act of writing on a small tablet. "It's 'The Tale of the Two Brothers'!" She thought she said this only to herself, but the twins halted their enactment and turned to look up at her. They didn't move after that. They seemed to be waiting for a response from her.

"I know your story," she called down.

One of the two took a few steps toward her, gesturing excitedly for her to come down to the stage.

She raised her hands. "How?" she asked.

He pointed a finger around the rear of the stage, through the balconies, directing her back into the hall and beyond the room from where she'd emerged, then effected jagged movements signifying stairs. She nodded that she understood and then retraced her steps back into the dark corridor, where she felt her way along the wall. As he'd indicated, stairs began but a short distance beyond her room.

From then on she navigated by instinct, approximating the location of the stage and feeling her way in search of an entrance. She touched a heavy curtain and, pushing it aside, entered a dark area to one side of the stage, hidden from the audience, but with part of the stage itself visible.

The two figures had stopped their pantomime and awaited her, still as statues. Leodora walked out onto the stage. Four of the lights along the front of it had been lit. Past them she could see the empty theater space that threw back echoes of her footsteps.

Drawing nearer, she found that *statues* was not an unreasonable comparison to the two men. They were like clockwork creatures that had wound down. Bodies motionless, they watched her approach. Their eyes were alive, though shallowly set; but their mouths were painted on, their chins defined by vertical lines as though separately inserted and hinged. So, too, their fingers had three distinct joints.

Looking from one to the other, she asked, "Am I still in Edgeworld?"

The two faced each other, their expressions changing to show confusion, their painted mouths pursing. Then together they turned back to her and shook their heads. "I'm in Colemaigne, then?"

This time they nodded without prior consultation.

"So my companions, they're here, too? In this theater?"

One figure nodded; the other pressed his hands together and placed them against his cheek, closing his eyes.

"Yes, I understand," she said with relief. It was night. They were asleep. Everything would be fine. Until they awoke, she was in no position to learn what had happened to her, so she might as well explore on her own.

The two inhuman men waited for her to say something.

"I know the story you were performing. I perform it, too. I'm a shadow artist." One of them pressed his thumbs to his fingertips and moved his hands up and down independently as if raising and lowering something. "That's right—puppets on rods, that's how I tell stories." He placed one hand to his own chest and the other on his twin's shoulder. Again, she understood his intent as clearly as if he had spoken. "I could—if you want—recite it while you perform. If that's not presumptuous of me."

His eyes widened and without warning he clasped and hugged her. When he let go, she said, "Well. I didn't expect *that.*" He pretended to be shy then, lowering his head. She laughed at his clowning, and he brightened again. His twin shook his head as if disapproving, but glanced her way to see if she was watching. It was all part of their repartee.

"So," she said, "I will go sit over there beside the lights and tell the story as if to the audience behind me, and you'll perform it for them."

They both nodded their accord and shook hands with each other. She walked to the front of the stage, and they strode off into the wings to await her beginning. She sat cross-legged and for a moment gazed up at the roof, which was like an awning overhead. *This is as strange as the parade of monsters*, she thought, *or the Ondiont snake.* The thoughts wanted to drift her into daydream, but she banished them, flexed her spine, and placed her palms on the floor. She inhaled deeply and began.

THE TALE OF THE TWO BROTHERS

There once were two brothers named Baloyd and Suald. They had lived on the span called Kakotara their whole uneventful lives. Both of them had married by arrangement. Their brides had been betrothed to them when they were children. Their father was a respectable weaver, and their mother raised colorful, exotic birds, many of which were purchased for the court of Kakotara. Because of this neither of the brothers worked nor needed to. The two endured not the slightest hardship despite their combined sloth, and often discussed money, but solely as the object of various schemes to avoid employment while they continued to feed from the parental trough.

One night when Baloyd and Suald were wandering the streets of the span in search of a rumored card game, they happened to pass by the entrance to the dragon beam. At the end of the spiraling walkway, the hexagonal bowl hovered in the air on hidden supports. Suald noticed how it glowed in the moonlight and pointed this out to his brother. They stopped and stood there, watching it.

No one else was near. The Dragon Bowl on Kakotara had then been dormant for more years than the two brothers had lived, and no one paid it much attention anymore except during festivals, when unanswered li-bations were poured upon the tiles.

Suald stopped. He said, "Does the *hex* seem brighter than it should?" He called it *hex* because that was the way of that span.

Baloyd, the less thoughtful of the two, had little interest in puzzles. "We should find that game house if we want to gamble," he urged. He walked ahead, hoping his brother would follow. Instead, Suald stepped onto the beam and began strolling out along its curve. Baloyd knew full well that once his brother had fixed upon an idea there was no use argu-ing him off it, so he turned around and followed.

Suald had already completed the first loop of the dragon beam's spi-ral. He came up directly across from Baloyd, nearly close enough that they could have stretched and touched fingertips. He asked casually, "If you could make the *hex* light up anytime you wanted, what would you ask for?"

"It's supposed to be bad manners to make demands of the gods," his brother replied.

"Gulldroppings. This thing hasn't ignited in thirty years. How does anybody know what you can do to the gods, or what they care about? Or if they even exist beyond stories? Has anybody you know of ever tried to get what they want off a *hex*?"

"Probably not." He said nothing further until he'd caught up with Suald, who waited for him at the entrance to the bowl. "I guess I don't need money, I don't need another wife. Wouldn't want to be king—that's too much work. Guess I'd like to be quick. Then I could take anything I needed anytime and get away without having to pay if I didn't want to. You know, dash down to Balrog Harbor and steal a keg right from under the noses of those greedy trolls. Be worth it for all the times they've bled me for money. But hey, we're knights of the *elbow*, let's go find that game—"

"It *is* too bright," Suald said thoughtfully.

Baloyd finally considered the Dragon Bowl at the center of the spiral-ing arm. The tiles were luminescent, and not from reflected moonlight. They glowed still brighter as he looked on.

"I think something's going to happen."

"You'd better say what *you* want, then, since it was your idea," Baloyd goaded.

"Well, I surely don't want speed. Too specific, see. What I want"—and he raised his voice until he was shouting at the sky—"is a way to have whatever I want *later*. That way I don't ask for anything particular now, and I get lots more whenever I want!" He grinned at his brother. "Pretty clever, heh?"

"I think *we're* starting to glow, too."

Suald held his hands up. Sparks danced around his fingertips. His hair stood on end, and sparks whirled around his head. The light came from nowhere and everywhere.

Baloyd began to laugh, his giddiness sharpened by fear. Whatever would happen next, they had chosen to demand, and there was no going back, no reneging. The gods had heard them and would either honor their desires or destroy them. He shouted, "Come on, give me speed!" and his brother responded, "Give me everything I want!"

The light turned thick; the world beyond it vanished. The air pressed them and they moved back to back to withstand the pressure. There was a twistedness to the energy, as if they were about to be wrung from head to foot. The air darkened and squealed mechanically; it stank of rotten eggs, of sulfurous pits. The bowl shook so hard that they both fell. They lay screaming, their bravado forgotten, scared witless now, arms over their heads as certain death mashed them.

Then everything stopped.

Neither brother moved.

The terrible shrieking, as though metal were shredding metal, dwindled like a juggernaut rolling off across the sea. The whoosh of waves against the breakers below reemerged as the predominant—the only—sound.

Baloyd opened his eyes.

The night was dark, but along the horizon a faint strip of dawnlight showed. Hours must have passed, although he had no sense of the lost time. Remnants of sour mist hung in the air, already dissipating in the breeze off the ocean. From a distance footsteps came running, and cries of "It came on!" "I saw it!" and "What'd it leave?" rode the air.

The approach of a crowd galvanized the two young men. They sat up and took stock of their surroundings. They were whole, undamaged. Whatever had happened and whatever had arrived—whether it filled their requirements or not—by right it was theirs. They got up quickly.

The people rushing along the dragon beam drew up. Across the gap sep-
arating them from the platform at the center, they gaped, crestfallen. As a
group they had shared in a hope, a promise, dashed now that others had
gotten there ahead of them. The two brothers crossed to the middle of the
platform.

Four objects lay on the tiles of the bowl: two unsightly red, bulbous-
toed shoes; and a small black metal stylus lying atop a clay tablet.

By instinct the two brothers chose their prizes. Baloyd took the shoes;
Suald collected the stylus and tablet. Then they walked onto the beam
and followed it back to where the others hovered. If the crowd still held a
glimmer of hope that the two might share the treasure, Suald's arrogance
banished it. He forced them back along the path with nothing more than
a cold sneer.

On Brink Lane he turned his back on them as if daring anyone to try
and take him. Baloyd followed, but with frequent glances over his shoulder to make sure no one pursued them. Brink Lane traced the westward
curve of the span, and soon the crowd was out of sight around a bend.
Suald kept walking. He turned up a narrow side street leading back into
the forest of stucco houses and shops, all still dark with sleep. He pushed
open an iron gate and entered a courtyard with a small fountain, bor-
dered on three sides by houses. There he finally stopped. "All right, what
have you got?"

Baloyd held the shoes up by their laces. They had high necks and
spongy red circles at ankle height. The soles were curiously furrowed.

"Well, they're *something*. Why don't you put them on."

There was a great deal Baloyd thought of saying: how his brother always created situations and then left him to resolve them; how, since the
whole idea of challenging the gods had been Suald's idea, he should be
the one to test the Edgeworld gifts—he should be the one to blow up or
ignite or melt. But Baloyd said nothing. A lifetime of habit overruled him.

He sat against the lip of the fountain and put on the shoes. He had to
loosen the laces to get his feet in and afterward left them undone. He'd
never seen laces before; he had no idea what they were for.

Standing, testing, he discovered that the shoes fit him quite well. He
walked around the fountain. Nothing happened. When he'd come full
circle, he pointed at his brother's gifts and said, "What about yours,
then?"

Suald held the stylus and tablet away from his body as if, should they come to life, he might fling them away. For a moment he held them above the fountain, and Baloyd almost snatched them away for fear he was going to drop them into the water.

Suald pushed his thumb into the surface of the tablet. His nail left a gouge in it.

"Why don't you write something instead?" Baloyd suggested.

"I don't see *you* running any races."

"I put the shoes on. I walked around. Nothing happened. They're just shoes."

"Try running."

Baloyd sprinted up and down in place. "They don't work."

"What do you think I should write?"

"Write that you'd like some breakfast. I'm hungry."

"Naturally." He licked the tip of the stylus and inscribed the words A KING'S BREAKFAST. Nothing happened. He frowned. "I don't think this thing works, either. Look, why don't you try naming a destination—somewhere you want to go."

"I don't have anyplace in mind."

"Yes, and no wonder you're not going anywhere. Pick someplace—go to the end of the span. Go to Nourey Gate or something." He stared sternly at the tablet, then wrote above the already inscribed words, GIVE ME.

Baloyd replied, "Fine. Nourey Ga—" He never finished the word—at least not within his brother's hearing.

Suald was reading his own writing when a wind threw him off-balance. He slipped on the cobblestones, caught his foot against something in the dark, and sprawled upon a row of metal dishes. He crushed eggs and pomegranates, figs and relishes, sweet breads and popovers. His elbow flipped a creamer, splattering him with goat's milk.

Covered in the food he'd requested, he started to laugh. He couldn't help himself; it was all too ridiculously glorious.

From one of the buildings bordering the courtyard, someone shouted, "Shut up, yer drunken swine!" which only caused Suald to laugh even harder.

The wind whipped up again. Dust sprayed him. Loose grapes rolled past him.

The wind's screech became a shout—a whoop of unrestrained pleasure—and there stood Baloyd, his hair pushed out behind him like a sheaf of reeds. For an instant he was still, and then he began jumping up and down. "Suald! I did it. I've been to Nourey Gate and back again!"

Suald pushed himself up onto his knees and took stock of the damage to his clothes. "Of course you have," he replied.

"No, really. In seconds. I don't even know what streets I took. They whizzed by so fast, all a blur until I got to the gate. I thought my clothes would catch fire. Then I said, 'I want to go back,' and it started all over again." The shoes practically glowed. He saw the food laid out upon the ground, squatted down, and picked a deviled egg that had survived the maelstrom. He popped it into his mouth whole. "Oh, this is good," he said with a full mouth. "Have you tried one?"

Suald cocked an eyebrow. "*Several*, thanks to you." He wiped the smeared food off his shirt. It should have been a joke—it had been until Baloyd returned, and he couldn't say just why he found his brother's beaming presence so galling. "So you ran the length of Kakotara."

"I did. And you ordered breakfast. We got what we asked for. The gods gave us just what we wanted."

"I shall try to remember to thank them later." He licked jelly from the back of his hand.

"Oh, come on, you can't be angry! Not *now*!"

"I happen to be covered in food."

"Well, then, ask for a bath. Ask for clean clothes. You can, don't you see? You can have *any*thing!"

A shutter banged open above them and a burly fellow in a sleeping gown leaned out and bellowed, "I told you bastards to shut up, and I meant it! If you don't, I'll come down there and hammer you into the stones."

Baloyd leapt back. "Oh, you think so, do you? What will you do if I come up there"—he stood suddenly behind the man; taking him by the shoulders he whispered—"and push you out." The terrified fellow flew from his window and slammed into the stones beside Suald. Baloyd was there just as swiftly.

The man howled in pain. He clutched his head and rolled back and forth. Blood oozed from his nose and mouth.

Baloyd took his brother's arm. "Maybe you should clean up somewhere else," he suggested.

Suald looked at his brother as if seeing him for the first time. "No," he said, and took out the clay tablet. With his thumb he smoothed his previous request.

"That's right, you can fix him, can't you?"

"You're damned right I can." Suald carved letters with the stylus then lowered the tablet and admired his handiwork.

There beside the fountain a huge wharf rat lay trembling and bloody, dying atop a torn nightshirt. Suald grinned.

Baloyd's brow knitted, and he gave his brother a worried glance. "That wasn't what I meant."

"No?" smirked Suald. "Well, it was what *I* meant. What's one rat more or less in the world?"

Somewhere in the darkness above, a woman called out, "Harky? Harky, where've you gone?"

Suald took his brother by the elbow and dragged him out the gate and away.

Thus began the reign of the two brothers on Kakotara. They did not keep their gifts secret for long. Suald performed a few tricks for his wife, Seru, conjuring whatever she named by writing the words on the tablet. She asked for jewels, then necklaces and bracelets. She asked for fantastic, legendary birds that would impress his mother, and they appeared as well. If she didn't like what came, Suald found that he could send the thing away as easily. As their house filled with squawking and cooing, as a rain of droppings began to decorate everything, he made her choose one bird from the batch and then erased all the others as if they'd never existed. She chose a blue-and-violet one that snapped at anyone who passed near it and shrieked for no good reason.

Seru saw the greater possibilities of this magical clay. She demanded a palanquin fitted with gold trimmings and pink silk cushions. Suald exercised his gift again, and the magic spread into the street. Even as he opened the front door to reveal the prize, Suald's neighbors were gathering to behold the resplendent enclosed litter. Four powerful men stood beside it as she had requested. They were barely human, with faces devoid of expression, of curiosity, of thought. They responded only to Suald's commands. The gathering audience regarded him with wonder and fear: Only lord mayors, princes, and kings had palanquins.

He was both annoyed and thrilled by their awe; but soon he was writing one thing after another. Items popped up left and right—here a table, there a suit of clothes, and of course gold. Someone told him he was greater than the *hex* itself, which he liked, and he strutted on that awhile; but he soon grew weary of it all. Every citizen who went off with something told three others, who told others, until the street had become the object of a pilgrimage from all across the span. Petitioners waved their hands, and some waved scraps of fishskin parchment on which they'd written a list of their desires. Most of these requests disgusted Suald in their simplicity, their foolishness; here he was offering them the unimaginable, and they all trembled at the thought of asking for a bag of rice or a small pot to replace one that had broken last month. Only a few people asked wisely—for sustained health, for cures for their afflictions, for wisdom in the future. Suald quickly ceased to follow their requests; his tired hand wrote automatically. Let them waste his gift. He would not offer it again.

While he wrote, he watched Baloyd.

Every now and again during the great wish fulfillment, his younger brother put in brief appearances. He zigged and zagged, zoomed to the top of the highest tower, vanished for ten minutes to return with hot food from a vendor's cart two spans distant. He carried his own wife, Betinela, on a tour of the entire span from end to end, from point to point, wherever she asked to go. He whisked her in to visit Seru, who gave her a handful of the thousand necklaces and jewels that now lay scattered about the house. Baloyd gave barely a glance to the cornucopia flowing from the clay tablet, as if none of it mattered to him. Instead, he ventured into the crowd, befriending children and taking them off for races through the streets. Sometimes they returned almost before they had left, the children not really grasping the speed with which Baloyd could carry them to their own homes around the next corner. Wherever they went, upon returning, the wide-eyed children invariably cried out, "Do it again," or "Go farther!" Baloyd obliged them, every one.

Betinela frowned at her husband's disregard of his brother's treasure. Placating her, Seru remarked, "At least he seems to be having *fun*."

Suald overheard the remark, and it set his mind darkly. He smoothed over the tablet and pocketed it. "That's all for today," he announced. Hundreds of expectant supplicants moaned, cried out that it wasn't fair, insisted he perform at least *their* miracle. The ranks closed around him, and a few faces looked capable of taking the tablet from him. He marked those faces. "Very well," he said, as if giving in to their demands. Then, pulling out the tablet again, he scribbled the words SEND THEM ALL HOME into the clay.

The crowd responded as if he had suddenly vanished. As if some scent rode upon the air, they raised their heads, turned away from Suald, and shuffled off. Suald smirked at his own cleverness: Later he would make them forget that he had this power at all.

He went inside.

Seru pursued him. "Darling, what's wrong, why did you do that?"

He turned on her. "I heard what you told Betinela. You find my brother so amusing—well, go stay with him!"

"What?"

"You find his gift so much fun, while mine is sheer tedium, then take up with him. I'm sure his own wife won't mind another in the house."

She gaped at him until understanding flowed into her expression. "My gods, you're jealous of him. He's enjoying his gift and you can't stand it. You have the whole world in your pocket and it isn't enough for you." Her laugh was a slap in his face.

Suald glared at an unoccupied corner of the room and muttered, "Ridiculous."

"What festers here? If you think they're such a source of entertainment, then why not use the tablet to get your own shoes?"

"Because I want *his.*"

After a moment she shrugged and replied, "Well, then take them. What stops you? You caused fig trees to grow on the main boulevards of all the spans you could think of; how much trouble is it to take two shoes?" She said this as if it were nothing, but she walked quickly away from him to the perch of her blue-and-violet bird, which clacked its beak at her and let loose a piercing screech.

He gripped the tablet in his pocket, finally withdrawing it, staring at it, holding it up as if testing its weight. In his other hand he fingered the tip of the stylus. Askance he saw his wife's lips curl with contempt, but when he looked straight at her, she seemed to be petting the obnoxious bird, not even paying attention to him.

He licked the tip of the stylus while watching her. Her gaze shifted. She followed the arc of the stylus from his side to his mouth and down. She didn't see him at all; only the stylus. Only the tablet. In her focus he read with utter certainty that she would kill him for it—for things she wanted but would never dare ask him to provide. He knew where her tastes ran to the perverse, and where his presence would be unwelcome. She would kill him when he slept, or poison the figs he ate at breakfast so that he would die too quickly to be able to write an antidote. Even if she didn't kill him outright, she would find a way to get her hands upon the tablet. She would write him out of existence the moment he closed his eyes.

He could trust her no longer.

Baloyd arrived late in the afternoon. He was barefoot and carried his magical shoes before him. He seemed confused by his circumstances.

Suald met him at the door.

"I want to . . . to give you these," Baloyd said, and held the red shoes at arm's length. His eyes welled with tears. A kind of bottomless terror gnawed at him, the more terrible for being impossible to understand. But his wife understood.

Betinela had been with him when he suddenly expressed the urge to visit his brother. She'd followed him easily, for he hadn't used the shoes and had lumbered stupidly through the streets as if not quite sure of his location. She knew her husband and all his faults: He was not a man given to acts of unconditional generosity. She glared at Suald as he accepted the shoes.

He smiled as innocently as he knew how.

"And where's Seru?" she asked him.

"Away," he replied quickly.

She looked past him at the bird on its perch, at the jewelry scattered through the room, at everything that denied his statement, finally following his gaze down to a yellowish smear on the floor where he'd crushed a very large cockroach. She chose not to contradict him.

Baloyd wept openly, his brain twisting with frustration.

"Your brother loves you so," said Betinela, "to give up this wondrous gift that had pleased him so much, at the peak of his enjoyment. I never realized he felt so tenderly toward you."

Suald's eyelids half closed. "We've always been closer than people thought." He carried the clumsy-looking shoes outside, where he sat and put them on before she could try and make him give them back. His brother shambled after him as if tied to a line.

The shoes were too big for Suald's feet, but otherwise more comfortable than they looked. It was the first time he'd put them on, and he fumbled with the laces, finally tying them around his ankles to keep them out of the way.

As he started to take out the tablet, Betinela asked, "So where will you go then? You've always been smarter than your brother, Suald, so I assume you'll use the shoes for something greater than entertaining children?"

He looked at her from under his brows, agitated by the accusation that edged her every word. Didn't she appreciate the power he held right here in his hand? No, of course she didn't. None of them did. He could obliterate them and they wouldn't know. He was sick of their small minds, sick of the greedy, petty span of Kakotara.

"I'll tell you, and then I'll bid you both farewell. I'm going to travel the whole length and breadth of Shadowbridge as no one has ever done before. I'll see everything, and when I return I'll be the greatest explorer who ever lived, because I can do it all in the blink of an eye. I'll reign among the gods."

"Fine." She moved aside. Her look mocked him. "Go on then. Travel the whole world."

"I shall—I'll travel the whole world." Upon those words he launched headlong so fast that figs from the trees he'd created rained after him.

The instant he was gone, the spell he'd cast upon his brother broke and the clouds of confusion lifted. Baloyd's eyes widened, first with the shock of recognition, then with the boil of anger. He opened his mouth and shouted at the sky. He flung curses at Suald and plunged back into the deserted house. Sounds of shattering and squawking and screams of rage echoed up and down the street, drawing a crowd. People looked at

Betinela for an explanation. Some asked where Suald was, because they had more things to ask for. She said nothing, but stepped quickly aside as a glass lamp flew through the doorway and struck a man in the back. The crowd scrambled out of the way.

When Baloyd emerged with Seru's blue-and-violet plumed bird dangling from his fist, the crowd scurried farther away, ready to flee. He'd wrung its neck. He dropped the dead bird, turned from them, and shuffled off, barefoot, exhausted, helpless. The neighbors waited until he was gone, then crept into the shambles to sift for treasure.

At home he sat, saying nothing, glowering. His wife chided him. "You could have been a god to those people. If it weren't for your brother, you might have had all the treasures yourself. You could have granted anyone any wish they asked. If he ever comes back . . ." She didn't finish the thought.

The children he'd entertained with rides returned the next morning, but when Baloyd proved unable to perform further feats of speed, they left him. A few of his neighbors came inquiring after Suald, but their inquiries provoked only rage, and they soon stopped coming. Baloyd plunged with suicidal vigor back into his dissolute life—gambling, drinking, and whoring—in a vain attempt to drown out the words his wife had set in motion, that, like a perpetual mechanism, swirled around and around his brain: *I could have been a god. I could have been a god.* He rarely went home, and when he did it was only to pass out until he awoke to go out again. Betinela left him. He had no idea when it happened, whether he'd been home or not, whether weeks had passed without her and he had simply failed to notice.

One hot afternoon while he lay unconscious, shouts from outside woke him. A crowd had gathered before his door. They called his name. As he arose in the shadows he winced and waited for his head to stop pounding. Then, scratching himself, he peered at them from the second-floor window. He supposed he'd done something offensive while drunk— throttled a favorite cat or kicked a child. They might have been there to hang him, although they weren't hammering down the door as he would have expected. They were agitated all right, but not angry. And they weren't going away. He descended the stairs uncertainly and opened the door.

They took hold of him and hauled him through the streets to Brink Lane. He thought of a man he'd pushed out of a window, but that had been so long ago. Maybe Suald's spell had lifted—maybe he wasn't a rat anymore, maybe someone had seen what had happened, maybe he was dreaming, maybe he was mad.

Through the twists and turns of alleys they hauled him. The sun stabbed at his eyes. His head throbbed with each propelled step. He began to think that if they killed him, it could only be a blessing. As they neared the dragon beam, he saw that even more people lined the spiral walkway all the way to the *hex*. Had something else been sent down from the Edgeworld gods—something for him? What if it was an avatar sent to demand back the gifts? What would he say? He didn't know where they were now.

The crowd accompanying him stopped at the edge, but pushed him onto the beam. There was no going back, no escaping. He didn't try.

As he wound the beam, the people ahead moved aside to give him room. He came to the end, and the crowd, almost reverently, parted.

There, in the center of the platform, stood a terrifying scarecrow. Its clothes were rags. Long tangled weeds constituted the hair. It had a face like a desiccated fish—the mouth a wide, howling oval, the dark leathery skin pitted and taut and tanned. Despite its upright position, anyone could see that it wasn't alive. For one thing, it had no eyes in its ragged sockets.

Finally he noticed its feet.

In complete disparity with the rest of the tattered thing, the big, clumsy shoes on its feet were brightly polished and red as blood. Far redder than when he had given them up. He looked at the dried-out and ravaged face again, and finally recognized the features of his brother.

Baloyd knew what had happened. Whenever *he* had chosen a destination, the shoes had not stopped until it had been reached. Suald had chosen the compass of the world: He had run across infinity. He had run himself to death.

His horrifying appearance kept everyone a comfortable distance away from Suald. When Baloyd touched him, the body collapsed like a heap of twigs. He caught it as it fell and laid it down. Then he untied the shoes and took them off his brother's corpse. Bones sprinkled out of them—dust and small bits—all that remained of Suald's feet. He upended the shoes to pour out the rest, then sat and, removing his slippers, put the shoes on again. People stared at him, many with distaste. He didn't care. His brother had stolen the shoes from him, and he wasn't about to let anyone else get the chance. They were his.

He left the slippers there on the *hex*.

The husk of his brother weighed little. Without assistance Baloyd carried the raggedy body along the spiral of the dragon beam, and bits of it crumbled as he walked, sprinkling over the wall and into the sea. The crowd backed away, some with revulsion, others in wonder. With each step the blood hammered in his head. In the pulse his wife's voice chided him over and over and over again: *You could have been a god. You could have been a god.*

When he stepped from the beam onto Brink Lane, something plopped from the pocket of his brother's trousers. The unblemished clay tablet lay at his feet. He turned the corpse to rummage through the other pockets until he found the stylus. It was dark and sharp, ready for use.

He set down Suald, then picked up the clay. In his other hand he held the stylus. What should he write? He could bring Suald back to life, and Seru as well from whatever hell she'd been cast into. With the tablet he might do anything at all.

People dared to come near him. They asked, "What's wrong, Baloyd? Why have you stopped?"

He considered their eager faces. The pathetic, simple fools. "Nothing's wrong," he said. "Everything is very right, and it's going to be better than right." He inscribed the tablet. Then he lowered the stylus.

Halfway.

That was as far as he got before the transformation took place.

A reddish brown dust swirled up from the street, spinning a web around his legs. Reddish brown color spread from his fingertips over his palms and up his arms, too. Like a living sheath the color encased his torso, his neck, his head. In a moment he ceased to be human, or alive.

The people on the street dropped to their knees and bowed down in veneration. They chanted his name, "Ba-*loyd*," each time they bowed. Some of the nearest ones reached out and touched him. Their display brought others who, unmoved by the desire to venerate, came close enough to inspect the rough stone figure that had been Baloyd. Beside him they found his brother's corpse and, lying beside it where it had fallen, the clay tablet. On the tablet they read the words he'd written: MAKE THEM WORSHIP ME LIKE A GOD.

"And so Baloyd was worshipped for many, many years," said Leodora, "until the last of those people who'd been present that day had died. By then, the sandstone form of him had been worn down and scoured by wind and salt. The tablet proved useless to those who'd found it. A few tried writing upon it with sticks and knives to no effect. The stylus had been transformed into stone along with Baloyd.

"Thus we're reminded that the gods are capricious, and that it's unwise ever to make demands of them when instead we should be thankful for what we *do* have."

She faced the twin actors. Throughout the recitation her attention had been focused upon them, upon their movements and gestures—how one jumped behind the other and back again to represent speeding across the span of Kakotara; how one would appear to write on an invisible tablet and the other would become the thing he'd called into being, the birds, the carriers of the conjured palanquin, the fig trees. At the end as she spoke, one of them lay upon the stage with arms bent and fingers curled, as skeletal as he could be, while the other had wrapped his arms about himself and bowed his head, and had slowly sunk down to his knees as his sandstone shape was worn away.

The applause that followed her recitation surprised her, and she jumped away from the edge of the stage even as she peered into the depths of the theater. The two wooden men arose as one and faced the sound. They leaned forward at the waist as if they might stretch themselves toward it.

From out of the dark recesses a figure flowed toward the stage—tall and slender. Drawing nearer the light, it took shape as a woman in a green embroidered brocade nightgown. She was smiling broadly as she approached. "That is the first performance upon that stage in more than a dozen years," she said. "I had given up hoping there would ever be another." She rounded the front of it and came up the steps at the side. "You gave them the story so well, it was as if they *became* your puppets." She drew up before Leodora and added "You are certainly your father's daughter. No one could doubt it."

Leodora blinked up at her. "You knew my father?" she asked.

"He played here. On this very stage, a rare occasion. Because of the size of the theater, we stretched a great screen across the front of it and mounted a lens between that and the screen in his booth so that the shadows were cast in giant proportion—quite the extraordinary contrivance that was, but we drew from four spans for the audience. Can you imagine? Four spans! They traveled that far to see the incomparable Bardsham. They knew he was only here for a short run before sailing off to another spiral, another world. He was covering Shadowbridge then, and every span on every spiral would come to know him by rumor, by legend. That was his goal, you see, which he proclaimed with enormous pride and, well, not a little hubris." Her expression softened as if to say, *It was a forgivable fault,* but Leodora wasn't concerned with her father's ego.

"And my mother?" she asked. "Did you know her, too?"

The woman's express delight buckled. Her gaze clouded, and it was clear she was recalling something troubling. "You could be her sister." She turned sharply to the two players. "Glaise, Bois, go off with you now. It's near morning and will be light soon. Our guests will want their breakfast."

They clapped their hands and bowed, then arm in arm they marched off in matched step.

Watching them depart, she continued, "My husband ran the theater then. It was, well, just as you see it now. A wondrous place. Magic flowed from here and out across those rows, those benches, all the way up into those boxes every single night."

She focused beyond Leodora on nothing that was there, and Leodora knew that she was peering into her past. "Having Bardsham pick our theater for his venue. It was—we thought we had realized our dream."

The melancholy bound up in her words prompted Leodora to ask, "He didn't perform well?"

"Bardsham? Oh, my dear, he was a genius. The shadows came to life. They danced, they strutted, even flew . . . It was so grand, so smooth, so elegant that you forgot there was an agency at work behind them." She stared at Leodora. "Soter wants to convince me you are his equal."

She blushed, suddenly shy. "I don't know. I never saw him perform."

"Of course not. You were a fat little thing when your mother . . . when they left here."

Leodora's eyes went wide. "I was—I was here?"

The woman made a stiff, uncomfortable smile. It was clear that she wasn't certain where the boundaries lay. The more they talked, the more she set sail in uncharted waters. Whether or not Soter had instructed her not to speak of some things, Leodora could tell that she was cracking open a subject that hadn't seen light.

She closed her hand on the woman's wrist and said, "I want to know everything," leaving no room for obfuscation or pretense. She said, "But first tell me who you are."

"Ah, I've been unforgivably obscure. My name is Orinda."

Leodora gaped.

"I was once a player here, much like Bois and Glaise, save that I was never made of wood—although neither were they, once. But if I explain all that to you now, I'll lose the thread of it, and it's so difficult anymore to hold on to such threads. The spirals are unwinding for me, and each turn seems farther than the one preceding it. Mr. Burbage's . . . I'm sure I'm making no sense to you."

Leodora shook her head. "Truly, I lost your thread at your name."

"Orinda." She laughed lightly.

"Yes, I heard that much. There's a puppet of that name in my collection. She comes from a story I know, that Soter taught me."

"Oh. I should like to hear *that* story. I hope she's not a villain. I was a traveling player once, and I've never heard my name in a tale. But as to what I was saying before, the proprietor of the theater, Mr. Burbage, fell in love with me and I with him and I became his wife, and together we ran this—or, to be precise I should say its predecessor—and, oh my, we were in love. I always called him Mr. Burbage because that's what we'd called him when we were all players, not because he wanted formality, and it became more intimate in some way I can't explain, that I did. We were in love, I think, every single day we were together. He took ill right before your father . . ." She looked about herself, at the walls, roof, tapestries, as if to assure herself that they were real. "Right before we fell into ruin."

"Bardsham was connected to that?"

"The members of the high court held us accountable for the blighting of Colemaigne after he left, and they banned all subsequent performances. Of course, we'd suffered as much if not more than any in the blight. The theater was transformed into a ruin, so it almost mattered not at all. There would have been no further performances. No walls, no stage, just rot and crumbling masonry. Nothing held together, nor could we make it hold. Their ban only meant we wouldn't rebuild, but it proved the end of Mr. Burbage. He might have rallied from his illness, but he had no reason to. Oh, if I could only have shown him the state of things now—and Bardsham's daughter here, performing—I'm sure he would have held on. But if it hadn't saved him, I wouldn't have wanted him to suffer interminably, so perhaps it's better. We can't know these things, can we?"

"It makes you wish that the tablet in the story really existed," Leodora replied. "The blighting—how did it happen?"

Orinda made a face that said *It's not important* and replied, "Bardsham had gone. He and his troupe had sailed on . . . It's all long past."

"Yes, but what was the cause, and how did our arrival repair it?"

"You have no recollection, then. You walked into the Dragon Bowl and the gods paid us a visit. The first time in decades. You're the cause, you've freed us from a terrible curse."

The dragon beam—she remembered walking out along it to tease Diverus—and the bowl with enough tiles remaining to suggest a pattern, but nothing beyond that. "I don't understand," she said. "I don't even recall asking anyone to heal your span—I wouldn't have known to, would I?"

Orinda smiled tolerantly, as she might have at a slow child. "It's nothing to do with what you asked, only with the fact that the gods answered when they touched you."

Leodora digested that, then said, "But it doesn't—"

"Oh, my girl, please, no more questions for now. A terrible thing happened in the past and you righted it. You're going to be very popular in Colemaigne, you and your troupe, as I'm certain the ban will be lifted on us now with you here—with you the cause of our healing—and, oh, imagine the hundreds and hundreds who will fill our little theater." She took Leodora by the arm and turned her. "They'll be clamoring at the gates, no doubt, once the sun's up. So you will need to eat, because you might not get another meal today if we're half as busy as I think. Now you should come with me." Orinda led her off the stage.

"There's a ghost in my room," said Leodora.

Orinda stopped. "What?" she asked.

"A ghost. A voice. He spoke to me, but he wasn't there. It's not a very big room, and I reached all the way to the wall and there wasn't anyone there, but I heard him. He knew it was dark outside, and he knew all about the theater."

Orinda clasped both her hands. "Mr. Burbage, when he . . . He wanted to be close to the theater, so at the end he took to sleeping in the balconies of the stage, right across from your room. Do you think it could be Mr. Burbage who spoke to you?"

"He said he was a counselor."

"We'll go to your room and see. If it is my dear one, he will speak to me, surely he will."

They climbed the stairs to her room. It lay dark still, closed off from the light of dawn, but it was possible now to distinguish the bed from the floor, the small armoire from the wall.

"Hello," said Leodora. She knelt on the bed. "Are you still with me?" She half expected silence, but then the same voice as before drawled, "It's not as if I can go off on my own."

"There," she told Orinda. "You hear him?"

"I do. It's not Mr. Burbage, unless his voice has changed."

"Are you Mr. Burbage?" Leodora asked the room.

"That would be impossible," came the reply. It seemed to issue from the bed itself, right beside her. Orinda came up close behind her, and she turned, looked up.

"Why?" asked the proprietress.

"He has passed from this world and into Edgeworld."

"Into it?"

"Why, yes. What else was he to do? But you are not my mistress, and I answer you from courtesy only, as she openly regards you as a friend."

"Oh," said Orinda, stepping back. Leodora pushed her hands through the bedsheets.

"Speak to me now!" she said. "I'm right on top of you, why can't I find you?" She swept her hands through the covers, finding only the pendant with its chain, on which she was kneeling. She lifted it into the air.

"Thus you resolve the matter without resorting to assistance," said the pendant.

"You?" Dangling it by its chain, she clambered off the bed and out the door past her hostess. In the hallway with the light coming through the distant curtains, she could make out the shape of the pendant, a smoothly crafted leonine face with golden eyes. "Speak now," she said. "Tell me who sent you?"

"Sent me?" the lion head asked. "Why, no one sent me, you chose me."

Orinda said, "It's a Brazen Head. Oh, my goodness, I've never seen one before."

"A what?" Leodora asked.

"A Brazen Head. There are so many of them in legends."

"There are legends?"

Before Orinda could respond, the pendant chimed, "Indeed. There's a most famous one in a play. It belonged to a man named Bacon. It only spoke while he slept, and it said 'Time was,' and 'Time is,' and 'Time's past.' No one knows what it meant, but everyone suspects it was important."

"What *did* it mean? What does it mean to say *time is*."

"The nature of Brazen Heads," explained the lion, "is that they speak in riddles or at least in ways that are most obscure. It's not our choice, you understand. It's simply how we're made."

Leodora pursed her lips. "That's like Meersh's argument that he isn't bad, he's simply consigned to try all the bad ideas he comes across."

"I suppose it is, after a fashion," the head agreed.

"I don't believe *him*, either," she told it.

The pendant and she considered each other, scant inches apart. Then the lion's tongue unfurled as it yawned, revealing ivory teeth, and it blinked slowly several times. "Time is that which ends," it said. Then it closed its eyes and fell silent, a piece of jewelry once again.

Leodora sighed. "If this is what I chose to bring back, I'm not hopeful of my acquaintance with the gods."

"Oh, but," Orinda said, "we now know that Mr. Burbage is in Edgeworld. It means a *great* deal to me to know that."

"I suppose it wasn't something we could have learned on our own." She still wasn't sure anything the head uttered could be relied upon. "It seems to have gone to sleep, as if we wore it out." She sniffed the air, alert suddenly to a warm scent.

Orinda nodded. "You smell the breakfast cooking, too, don't you?"

By way of answer, Leodora's stomach gurgled.

"Come along, my dear. After we eat, we can ponder all the questions in the universe without being taken by them, as Mr. Burbage used to say." Orinda clasped her hand and led her toward the stairs.

Leodora pocketed the pendant and let her hostess lead her, but she wasn't giving up on discovering how this span had been blighted. Deep inside she knew that the plague visited upon this place had something to do with her.

Upon another spiral, on the distant span of Vijnagar, something unnatural came flowing along Kalian Esplanade. In the late-night darkness a darker mass moved, topped by five smooth, pale, hairless heads. The mass or its constituents made no sound, yet thrust along the esplanade without benefit of any torchbearer to guide them. Those who plied that trade saw the approaching anomaly and changed course instinctively to avoid it, which abrupt shift caused their clients to take notice of the five heads sailing past, sunken eyes glistening, watchful, like birds of prey. Some people drew up, backed to the seawall, to let the thing by. Bearers and clients were united in their unease, and if anyone spoke, it was to whisper. "Archivists," said some, thinking that the legendary Library had sent its agents to capture some piece of knowledge, a scholarly scroll perhaps. As no one had ever laid eyes upon the rumored archivists, it was a reasonable opinion, though less explicable was why a cluster of library archivists should elicit discomfort if not outright terror, for there were many others brushed against by the flowing mass who instinctively made small gestures to ward off evil before hurrying on their way, all too grateful to be going in the opposite direction.

The place called Lotus Hall, while still open for business, was nearly dormant this late, inhabited by a few regulars who would have sat there no matter what entertainment was proffered. At the moment that entertainment comprised a man spinning four ducks that balanced perfectly poised on the tips of their beaks upon polished clamshells. No one paid him or his trained fowl the slightest attention, although the ducks were working very hard and occasionally let fly a disgruntled *quack*.

The proprietor, Nuberne, was feeling the pinch since the remarkable Jax had gone. The puppeteer had brought in standing-room crowds, the best he'd ever seen. He suspected that his wife, Rolend, had hastened the puppeteer's departure with her unbridled overtures, and things had not been pleasant between them since.

He was standing in his small kitchen off the hall when the sounds of the performance ceased. Even the small, innocuous noises of snoring drunks and cautious conversations stopped. As his head turned, the hair on the back of his neck stiffened and he threw off a shiver in response to the uncanny silence.

The hall, seen through the doorway, became darker than the kitchen, where two low cooking fires tossed trembling shadows as well as heat. Even the wall sconces and the chandelier candles seemed to have guttered and gone out. From the center of this deeper darkness five pale heads gained in size every moment, until he could make out the glassy eyes within the sunken orbits, eager and hungry in their focus upon him. Not until they hovered just beyond the doorway did he make out the folds and darts of their black cloaks. This was the effect they strove for, of course, and though he recognized the manipulation, he could not overcome its dread intent. Later as he clung to his wife's stiff fingers, he would insist it couldn't be real, any of it, because the archivists were a myth. Everyone knew it.

Packed closely together, the five hovered at the doorway as one of them spoke. "You are the proprietor?" The bloodless lips had hardly moved. All eyes still feasted upon him.

Nuberne tried to reply, swallowed, cleared his throat, and managed a raspy, "I am."

"We are interested in a performer who seems not to be performing this night."

He tried to make sense of that. "You're wanting me to hire him?"

The five exchanged looks. "No. What would make you think that?"

"I don't understand then."

At that point his wife, Rolend, approached from wherever she'd been in the depths of the hall. "What's happened here, Nuberne?" she called as she scanned the wide-eyed stragglers, the nonperforming ducks. "Why has the whole place gone—oh!" Finally, she had seen the swarm of figures before the doorway. The five pallid heads turned in unison to regard her.

"Beg—beg pardon," she said. She eased around them and through the doorway, taking a worried step back into the kitchen.

"Quite all right," said one of the five. "We were inquiring after an artist who performs here, by the name of 'Jax.' "

"Jax," repeated Nuberne. "You're mistaken then. He's not performing here anymore. He shoved off awhile ago. But what would the Library want—"

"Yet you have notices pasted up. We saw them all along the esplanade."

Rolend faced him. "Don't you tell them anything, don't you help them."

"Ro, shut up," Nuberne said, more out of fear than anger.

"They don't mean him any good," she argued.

"Ro!" He reached for her even as she stiffened as if poked in the back. She stared at him wide-eyed and managed to utter his name once, faintly, before the color drained from her face and the eyes looking upon Nuberne went blank and flat, the color of her now hardened flesh, the color of the long skeletal hand that was clamped around the back of her neck. The fingers slid away; something glittered in the palm for an instant before it vanished in the black folds behind her. Where the hand brushed her hair, gray grains sprinkled loose. It might have been the hand of any one of them.

Nuberne touched her stone cold wrist and recoiled in horror.

"Quite all right," the one repeated. "We *don't* mean him any good, that is true. It is also none of your concern. You will tell us where he is, this Jax."

Nuberne's face twisted up but he could not stop looking at her, his wife, dead. "I don't know. He moved on," he said.

"The notices s—"

"I *left* 'em up. I was trading on his fame is all! He filled the place, every night, the best storyteller since—"

"Bardsham. Yes, yes, we know."

"Bring her back," he pleaded.

"Ah, I regret, you credit us with too much power," hissed the one. "Where is Jax now? Or wish you to follow her?"

"Jax . . . Jax moved on. To another span, him and his troupe." He was weeping, trembling with shock. His legs could not hold him up and he grabbed for the edge of a table.

"Another span. North or south?"

"I don't know. North, I think. He'd come from the south."

"North it is then. Tell us one more thing. He goes about disguised?"

His hands on the tabletop curled into fists of impotent anger and he lowered his head to them, closed his eyes. "Masked." He choked the word.

"Of course," said the one.

When he raised his head, Nuberne found the doorway empty and everyone in the hall, even the hapless performer and his terrified ducks, staring now at the ossified figure that had been Rolend. He sank down to the floor then, and his wail filled the hall with agony.

THREE

"The girl touched by the gods," proclaimed Orinda. "That is what we'll put on the banner, and surely you'll fill the theater."

Across the long table covered now in emptied bowls and cups, Soter sat with his arms crossed and head bowed as if dozing after the meal. Without moving, he said, "You'll still be wanting to call yourself Jax." Though he didn't raise his head, he opened one eye to watch Leodora's reaction. She straightened as if she'd been jabbed, and her eyes blazed. Before she could respond, he interjected, "I'm not saying you should go masked anymore."

"Then why should I hide my name?"

His gaze rolled to Orinda, and he dipped his chin as if to say *You explain it to her.* Glaise and Bois—their places absent of dishes—looked to their mistress, too.

Then to everyone's surprise Diverus spoke up. "Performance name," he said.

Soter raised his head. "That's so," he agreed, but in a tone conveying his bemusement.

Diverus added, "It's all I have."

Bois responded to his dejection by patting him on the shoulder. Orinda asked, "What do you mean, it's all you have, Diverus?"

He answered, "That's what—my name *is* my performance name. Nobody knew my true name. *I* didn't know it."

Leodora interjected, "You told me Eskie gave you your name long before you'd discovered what your gift was."

"That's so, but it doesn't make it my proper name, it's just what they called me in the paidika when they wanted me to do something, instead of saying *Boy* all the time."

"Ah, performance," Soter replied. "I see what you mean now. Not the same thing as we was thinking, though you somehow arrived at the right word anyway. Sometimes, boy . . . Diverus, you startle me."

If Diverus caught the jibe, he showed no reaction. "I don't mean to," he said.

"Is that what you told your last owner before you ran off—*I don't mean to cause you trouble*?"

"Stop it, Soter," Leodora said.

"You doubted him the same," he protested back.

"I was asking him to clarify, not belittling him."

Soter made no reply, but finally shrugged off the criticism.

Softly, Diverus asked her, "Why don't you ask your new counselor?"

"Ask it what?"

"About the name, what name you should use."

She had laid the polished pendant aside while she ate, for all of them to see, but it hadn't said a word nor even opened its eyes the whole time. Taking hold of the chain, she raised it in front of her, then turned the head so that it faced her. She wanted to ask it about the blight of Colemaigne, not about her name.

Soter pushed back his chair. "That's right. Don't listen to old Soter's advice, but by all means get the contraption's opinion. You *will* let me know what it says, won't you, Lea." He gave a polite nod to Orinda and the wooden men, and then marched off into the depths of the theater.

An uncomfortable silence ensued during which Leodora stared after him, Diverus stared at her, and Orinda looked at everything else.

Then the Brazen Head opened its eyes. "In answer to your principal question," it said, "you *can* only continue to call yourself Jax."

"I didn't ask."

"You didn't *speak* it, which is not the same thing."

"Why must she call herself Jax?" Orinda asked. "She needs the reason."

"It is the name the world knows. In time it will surpass that of Bardsham."

"Please, don't patronize me," Leodora protested.

The lion looked as if it might just close its eyes again out of spite, but then it said, "Didn't Bardsham's name surpass that of Meersh?"

"But Meersh—"

"Meersh, Leodora, is as old as these spans and recognized by all of them." And with that it did close its eyes, a plain and simple pendant once more.

"It sounded a little angry to me," said Diverus.

"Testy," Orinda observed.

Leodora sighed, "Wonderful. One Soter wasn't enough."

For an instant after she said that she saw the face of the other one again— the "Soter" from Edgeworld—before both image and memory collapsed, leaving her with a vague and disconnected sense of there being two realities in attendance, but one invisible and forever out of reach.

Carefully, Orinda told her, "I know you have differences with Soter, and I shouldn't want to wade into the middle of that, but I must concur with him and with your remarkable adviser here. You have created a magical persona in Jax, and it is that which will be whispered and remembered. It also frees you to be yourself when you choose, to leave Jax on the stage, in the booth. In the boxes with the puppets." The two wooden men nodded in agreement.

Leodora nearly confessed to her hostess that there was already someone in the boxes with the puppets—someone who manifested in her dreams to disturbing effect, as if a ghost watched her wherever she went, never revealing himself nor his desires concerning what she did. And yet it seemed this ghost waited for some particular event.

When she glanced down again, the pendant had opened its eyes anew. "Tophet," it said. She had no idea what question she had asked this time, but the lion was already inanimate again.

Despite the quirky nature of her brazen counselor, later that morning Leodora wore the pendant as she and Diverus walked the crooked lanes of Colemaigne. It hung between her breasts, an insentient piece of brass.

Many of the lanes folded back upon themselves, cramped and dark. Already twice she had elected a narrow route out of a piazza only to find that they were returned to the starting point as if by magic. And twice, on the much wider, brighter boulevards decorated with fig trees, the two of them had come upon Bois—or was it Glaise?—pasting up posters announcing the premiere performance tonight of THE GIRL WHO HEALED COLEMAIGNE! This was the title conferred on her by Orinda and Soter after much debate, playing upon the obvious transformation of the span. The posters drew small crowds even as he was hanging them, and she was thankful that her image wasn't on them.

The resurrected buildings lining the boulevard were perfect, glistening edifices, untouched by time, unworn and brightly colored, and the line of them was easily traceable across the span. Only the blighted buildings had been repaired, looking newer now than the rest. The guild of craftsmen Soter had mentioned were indeed wizards if these were what their creations looked like when new. The pigments inside the sugar shells glowed as if with an inner light, an illusion created by the refracting layers of confection. People clustered before new buildings, chattering, admiring. In one courtyard she came upon a flock of children licking the side of a tall house while others scooted up a tree to break off the orange marzipan leaves and drop them to their friends below. It was strange, otherworldly, and perfectly natural. Everywhere stood statues, and all seemed to be the work of the same sculptor, who captured citizens of Colemaigne in lifelike poses. These looked older, too, not part of the regeneration.

"Would they know any stories?" Diverus asked her as they stood watching the children. He had grown tired from all the walking in circles—endlessly it seemed to him. While she had slept and rejuvenated after her encounter with Edgeworld, he had slept fitfully if at all and would on this occasion have preferred to stay behind. He had also begun to worry that they would not be able to find their way back through the maze of alleys and lanes they had traversed. *He* was certainly lost.

"I'm sure they know some," she replied. "But Colemaigne's an ancient span. There has to be someplace where people gather and *tell* their tales. It's been that way on every span, and even on Bouyan, on an island where nothing ever happens. The villagers had a house for storytelling."

"What if it's at the far end, your gathering place?" His tone clearly conveyed his opinion that they should stop looking for now.

"It's possible, I suppose, though I can't believe there's only one such place on a span this long."

"But it was damaged, and performance forbidden for years."

"That's true. Such places may not be easy to find. Maybe I should scale one of the towers. Maybe I could see something from up there."

"You've done that before, then. I remember you saying—" He broke off before he added *right before you were snared by the gods.*

"Before you joined us," she said.

He speculated, "What if the stories here all lie in the upside-down city?" and was surprised when she clutched his arm, bringing him to a stop. "What is it?" he asked, glancing around, expecting there was something to behold.

"You saw that, too?"

He nodded. "When we went to carry you off the dragon beam. There were buildings in the shadows under the span, hanging from the span. I thought it was a reflection until I realized it didn't match the span above at all."

"I remember it—one of the few things I *do* remember. Just for a moment, and then the sky was flashing and I looked up and . . . then I woke up in that room."

"A man came out of one of those houses. He was blue and he was walking upside down. He should have fallen into the sea but he didn't. He came to the edge and he waved to me. And then he was gone." Suddenly he wasn't tired any longer, but strangely roused by the memory.

"How can we get there, do you suppose?"

Diverus thought for a moment. "Well, although it's on the wrong side, there is the opening where the goods from the ship were hauled up. Remember how they were hauled out of sight under the street?"

"Where we climbed the *stairs*," she exclaimed. "We need to go back there, Diverus."

"You think that's a way in?" he asked.

"We have to see. It could be it's the only way in."

Finding their way back to the point of their arrival proved easy. They had only to follow the trail of gleaming resurrected buildings. The line of renewal led back to the square where Leodora and Diverus had arrived. Even that had been transformed. The fountain where Soter had sat had been repointed, the stone animal figures in the center had been polished, their details freshly chiseled. Leodora could count the feathers on the roc, the scales on the dragon. It was a fabulous fountain now, and behind it lay a garden full of blossoms, purple and white. People lazed in the garden, sprawled here and there, some entwined, as if drugged into a stupor. Now and then one person picked a blossom and fed it to his partner, which seemed to be all the energy he could muster before collapsing again with a vague and dreamy smile. The street, which previously had been full of broken and uneven stones, was smooth, the square-hewn blocks so perfectly fitted that they seemed a single surface.

Leodora looked over the wall at the pulley arms jutting from the stone below. One of the platforms on which goods were hauled up from the harbor hung there unattended. The platform had been pulled up—apparently hours before, because there was no ship below now. Baskets and bolts of cloth swung there in the mild breeze.

"Everyone seems to have taken the day off," Diverus said.

"This is the Colemaigne of legend that Soter described, much more so than what we encountered when we arrived."

"Then maybe it's a holy day."

"If it is, we're the cause." She stepped up on the wall.

"Lea," he gasped, "what are you doing?"

"I'm going to jump to that platform, so that I can go into the undercity."

"But if you miss—I can't even bear to look down there!"

"Yes, but I can. I scale bridge towers, remember?"

"You—you shouldn't do this alone. And you've already risked . . . You just recovered from the Dragon Bowl, from Edgeworld. That's enough, isn't it? Besides, there's bound to be a way into there from someplace up here—people aren't spending their whole *lives* down there!"

"Why? They did on Vijnagar, didn't they?"

"Please," he begged.

"I'll be fine, Diverus, I'm not going to miss the platform. There's barely a hand's width between the wall and it. It's hardly a jump at all." With that, as casually as if she were strolling along the boulevard, she stepped off the wall and dropped.

She landed on a bolt of cloth and fell forward onto her hands and knees. The pendant swung and slapped against her, and the platform bounced slightly off the wall but otherwise hung steady.

Where she lay, she was looking directly into an opening, with a pulley arm above her, and the ropes bearing the platform all running to a winch set back far enough to allow for the unloading of the goods. She realized that if she had taken one step to the side before jumping, she would have struck the pulley and possibly missed the platform altogether. Her stomach clenched. She would not point this out to Diverus.

Lifting one of the baskets, she found it to be as heavy as if it were filled with wet sand. She heaved it into the opening and, using its weight as a fulcrum, hauled herself up and in beside it.

The area beneath the span receded into darkness. What light did play through the opening showed nearby containers and amphorae, baskets and crates all neatly stacked. It looked familiar: the cargo from the boat that had brought her here.

"Lea!" called Diverus, and she stuck her head out to show him that she was fine. He laughed in relief.

"I think this might go all the way across the span, Diverus," she called up. "I'm going to follow it. Don't wait for me here, go back to the theater. I'll find my way out."

"But I'm not sure where the theater *is*."

"Just go to the far side of the span and walk down the sea-lane, same as we did before, past the Dragon Bowl. Just don't walk out onto the beam."

Disregarding her levity, he replied, "I'm not happy about this."

"You could come down here with me."

"No," he said, "I couldn't. I can't."

"Well, I can't come back up now that I'm here. So you have to go on top and me underneath."

"You're crazy, Leodora, do you know that?" He shook his head at her and then withdrew.

"All too well," she said to herself.

When he didn't reappear, she ducked back inside, but his final statement stayed with her. He was right, she *had* taken ridiculous risks, although she hadn't seen them as such at the time. She hadn't expected the hexagonal bowl to ignite, to do . . . whatever it had done to her. She glanced down at the pendant, fingering the edges of it. Whatever had been done, she could hardly reverse it now. She was who she was. Jumping down here, though, had been no risk at all, for someone used to scaling bridge towers. Diverus would just have to understand.

She turned her attention to the space ahead.

The underspan had a low ceiling, and while the floor was not a natural formation, it otherwise reminded her eerily of Fishkill Cavern where she'd first met the Coral Man. It was the sound of the place, she realized as she headed deeper in. It was the way her footsteps echoed as in a great cave.

Her eyes grew used to the dimness. There must have been hundreds of containers, perhaps thousands if they continued into the darkness. It was as though ships had been coming here since the beginning of time, their cargo hauled up but never passed along.

She soon came upon the first set of steps leading back to the surface, their zigzag shape like a fracture in the darkness.

She went up them bent low, her hands on the steps above, as if ready to fling herself off at the first sign of trouble from above. Nearing the top, she raised one hand and patted it against the shape of a trapdoor. Her fingers closed around a metal ring dangling from it. As the underspan reminded her of Fishkill Cavern, the trapdoor was all too unpleasantly reminiscent of her boathouse on Bouyan, and an irrational terror seized her that if she lifted that trap, she would be back there with her uncle looming over the opening, waiting for her. For a moment as she crouched in the darkness, she had the wild

notion that she had never left the boathouse and that all the adventure between there and here had been an illusion, and now she must return to the
cold horror, relive it all. This terror so pressed and compacted her that she
flung open the trap in defiance of it.

It wasn't the boathouse, of course. She was in someone's kitchen—there
was a wooden block, and on it knives, pots, and empty red-glass bottles. The
place looked gray and disused, although that might have been a trick of the
light coming through the smudged, distorting glass of the windows. Before
anyone came into view, she lowered the trap and retreated down the steps,
but then sat at the bottom of them until she could see in the darkness again.

The house above might have been one of those that had been blighted
until yesterday. That would explain its sense of emptiness, of stillness. She
didn't know if people had continued to live in the blighted places. Orinda
had continued living in the back of the theater, but did that constitute reliable evidence?

In the murk around her she now could make out jagged edges of more
scattered stairways up to the surface.

She got up and continued walking. She passed a few small barrows and a
larger cart. The cart, half unloaded, had lengths of rope dangling off it, conveying a sense that all work had simply stopped. That seemed to be what had
happened. Perhaps it was because of the rejuvenation of the span, or maybe
this was just a day of rest. She thought of the people lying about among the
flowers above—a day with no obligations, no work to be done. It sounded terribly inviting if utterly alien to her.

She walked deeper into the space and shortly came upon another stairway
to the surface. Beside this one stood one of the stone statues, like those she'd
seen along the refurbished boulevard. Someone had opted not to carry this
one to the surface, although it looked to her perfectly formed. It was the figure of a man. Even in the poor light she could see how well defined were the
folds of his tunic, how the sculptor had dramatically captured every detail of
him. She couldn't imagine why anyone would choose to leave it down here
in the dark.

Off in the distance, someone laughed. She listened, and tried to determine where it had come from, but the sound bounced off a hundred surfaces,
circling her. She guessed at an approximate direction and started walking,
cautiously. She walked past a thick pillar, an unlit lantern hanging from it.

She realized that she was seeing a wan light in the deep distance, one that flickered from behind stacked crates and boxes. She passed by more statuary, figures in crouched poses, looking as if they were in the middle of lifting something, and another pillar hung with another unused lantern, and more small carts. The light from outside, where she'd entered, shrank and shrank until it was like the glow of a distant star. The reflected light ahead looked brighter. She felt her way past amphorae and woven baskets toward a murmur of voices.

Someone cried out, "I serve you with a *writ!*" and she stopped dead. Whatever she expected next, it wasn't the groan of dismay that followed. A woman's voice exclaimed, "That's wonderful. Now I can sue for damages!" Hands clapped. Whoever it was sounded gleefully malicious, but no one else said a thing in reply. Instead there came a clicking sound and the words, "A nine!" and Leodora quite suddenly knew what was going on.

The remaining distance she walked with less concern, then around the stacked boxes that served as a wall enclosing the game. Indeed, it was definitely a game.

Five players—two women and three men—sat in a circle upon wicker chests and boxes. One sat on a leather drum. In the center they'd set up an equally makeshift playing surface—a large flat cloth that was covered in symbols, lines, squares, and two piles of cards. The light came from lanterns hung from the arms of two more statues placed on opposite sides of the game. The players all held cards, and when she appeared they turned as one to see her. At first they gaped, but then they smiled to her. "Fresh meat," said one of the women. She stood. "Find her a seat."

"You composing poetry now, Meg?" asked the skinny man across from her.

"Could if I wanted," she answered, then to Leodora, "Come in, come in. We need another player, you've no idea—someone whose tricks we don't know yet."

"Hang on, now, my dear," said another of the men. "She could be here for supplies. You here for supplies, girl?"

"No," replied Leodora.

"Lost, then?"

"Not exactly. That is, I know how I got here."

The second woman laughed, revealing a mouthful of crooked teeth. "If you know that, then you're ahead of most of us. Come and sit." She tugged at the wide wicker case she perched on, dragging it to the side to give Leodora a place to perch beside her. "Tight quarters but still room enough, heh?"

Leodora circled them and sat on the end of the case. "I'm Garna," said the woman. "That's Meg, then Pelorie, Hamen, and Chork."

"Leodora."

"Now, there's a name. Brave name," said Chork.

"How would you know that?" asked Hamen. He had a flushed, dissolute face, but friendly. "You don't even go up to the surface anymore."

Chork was wall-eyed and she shifted her gaze from one eye to the other, trying to determine which to look at. He said meanwhile, "Never mind how—I just know it from the sound. So tell us, do you know how to play?"

She looked at the cloth, the four dice, the game pieces, which looked to be whatever had been lying about—a cork, two pebbles, a striated shell, and a heavy ring set with a green stone. "This is what I think it is?"

"It is if what you're thinking is Lawyers' Poker. We don't have a judge. You need a minimum of six to play with a judge. So we been taking turns as needed. It's not the same, though, is it?"

Leodora didn't want to disappoint them. "I can try," she said. She had never played the game and knew of it only as referenced in one of the stories of Meersh.

"Well, then, toss in your cards," instructed Pelorie. "We'll deal a new game." He raked the cards into a heap and began to shuffle them.

Off in the distance someone called, "Coo-ee! Lignor Alley!"

"Damn," said Hamen. He got up, groaning, stretching his stocky frame. "I'll be right back then." He lifted the lantern behind him from the statue's arm and walked off. His voice echoed back: "What's it want?"

"Lingonberry wine!" came the reply.

Chork scratched his ear. "I'm sure there's some left that *we* haven't drunk." The others chuckled.

"Maybe one or two bottles were overlooked," added Meg.

As if in response, Pelorie set down the cards, lifted a bottle, uncorked it, and drank. He passed it on to Garna, but placed the cork on the board. "This'll serve as your piece, Leodora."

She nodded.

He said, "So, what is it you're doing down here, then? Nobody ever comes down here."

"I saw it when we arrived. We came on a ship and they had mostly cargo, so when we climbed up I saw the goods hauled in."

"That was us all right," agreed Garna. She handed her the bottle. "But how'd you figure to come visiting? Lots of people go up them steps—or used to. They don't usually come swinging in here on a rope."

"I'm a storyteller. I thought—"

"Oh, what kinds of stories?" Meg asked.

"Shadowplays."

"A puppeteer?"

She nodded.

"You'll want to take that drink *today*," urged Chork.

Leodora took a pull from the bottle. The liquor was sharp and sweet at the same time, and her eyes teared.

"Lemons," said Meg, as if answering a question, and Leodora nodded vigorously. She passed the bottle to Chork, who leaned forward to take it.

"You came here to perform," he said, "only to find out they's banned all such here for years and years now. That's a shame."

"No. I'm performing. Tonight."

"Naw! Where? Not on *this* span!"

"At the theater?" she offered.

"What theater would dare?"

She didn't recall that anyone had named it in her presence. All she could say was, "Mr. Burbage's?"

"The Terrestre. That old ruin? You can play there all you like, but all you're going to have for an audience is a lot of rubble and some rats. And even so they'll arrest you for it, see if they don't."

"He's right," Garna agreed. "The ban's a very serious thing."

"Not anymore, apparently," called Hamen. He walked up with his lantern and handed a sheet of yellow parchment to Meg. "Proprietress at Lignor give me this just now. Someone's passing 'em out up there."

Leodora knew what it was without reading it.

"THE GIRL WHO SAVED COLEMAIGNE?" Meg recited. The group looked from her to Leodora, who tried to smile at the same time as she would happily have climbed inside the wicker container on which she sat.

"Oy, but this calls her Jax. THE REDOUBTABLE JAX. Not Leodora."

She started to explain but Hamen replied first. "Stage name, like." She met his amused gaze and bobbed her head.

"That's fine and all, but how'd she save Colemaigne? Did it need saving? We didn't hear anything about it."

"We wouldn't, now, would we?" Pelorie answered. "Anybody been up there so far today? I bet Hamen's come the closest with that paper."

"What day *is* it?"

"Who knows?"

"Celebration day, by the looks. So how did you save us, exactly?"

Leodora wrapped her arms about herself. "I don't really know, exactly. All I did was walk out on the dragon beam."

"What? That thing hasn't fallen off yet?"

"Garna, hush," Hamen said. "Go on."

"That's all—all I know. I seem to have gone to Edgeworld, but I've no memory of it. When I woke up, the span had been put right. The theater—"

"Terrestre."

"—the Terrestre's whole again, like it's brand new. The blighted buildings, they're fixed up. Repaired. I saw them on my way here. Children were licking them."

"I used to do that," said Chork, "when I was tiny."

"Well, tie me to the gods' gofe," Pelorie said in wonder. Then he glanced over his shoulder. "Hang on, though. How come they didn't change?"

The players eyed the statues suspiciously.

"Why didn't you change *them* back?" Garna asked her.

"I didn't—I don't know what that means," she said, and then all at once she did. "Those were people?"

"Once," Pelorie replied.

Chork focused one eye on her. "When the blight swept through, they were standing in its path. Down here."

"That one's me dad," Meg said, pointing to the one on which Hamen had hung his lantern.

"I'm sorry."

"Long time ago, that. I'm used to him this way now."

Garna asked again, "Why didn't they change back? The buildings but not the people—what's the point of that?"

"I don't know." She fingered the pendant nervously. "What is the point?"

The pendant opened its eyes. Meg gasped and Pelorie fell off his seat.

"The point," said the pendant, "is that a building can go forward in an inert state but life cannot. Once stopped it stays stopped."

"Time is that which ends," Leodora recited.

The pendant said, "Ah-ha," then closed its eyes and was silent again.

"What the mummichog was that?" Pelorie climbed back onto his seat.

"Orinda calls it a Brazen Head."

"Who? The Orinda that lives in the Terrestre?"

Meg and Hamen exchanged glances. "I'm thinking we might want to go up on the surface tonight," she said.

"Take in a play maybe, like?" Hamen looked at Leodora. "What do you think of that?"

"You live down here all the time?" she asked.

He shrugged. "It's akin to being a miner. We have our shifts, live mostly in the dark. We go home, some of us do."

Distantly someone called, "Coo-ee, Arbady Lane!"

Meg got up. "Hold my place," she said, as though someone new might sweep in and take it. She walked off into the darkness.

"Does that happen all the time?" asked Leodora.

Pelorie replied, "Nah. Most like in the morning. Sometimes we'll go a whole shift without a call. Not often, mind you, but it's happened." He took another drink from the circulating bottle, then asked, "So what are you doing down here, 'redoubtable'? You only said that you weren't lost."

"I'm looking for stories."

"The kind you can play out with your shadows?"

She nodded. "I like to hear how stories are told. Every span's a little different. Your characters might have a different name than elsewhere, or the tale reach a different outcome. Maybe they don't cut off their toes to make the magic slippers fit."

"I know that story!" Chork proclaimed.

"Of course you do," she went on, "and I like to hear how you learned it, what names everyone in it has, how it's changed, how it's become part of this span and not of any other. Then when I perform, I'll get it right for here. I mean, I could tell them in a general way and everyone would be pleased, but I would really rather tell them in the way they belong here."

"Never realized it was so complicated," said Garna.

"I'd a'thought you just told 'em," Chork added, then loosely waved his hand. "Of course, it's been so long since there was a story here, we can't remember. But it's what I'd do."

"And that's why *you* unload ships and *she* performs stories," Garna told him.

"Well, thankee for nothing," Chork replied.

"I don't want to cause a squabble," Leodora said.

"Oh, you're not causing anything. He's like that all the time."

Pelorie added, "To everybody."

Chork looked at the two of them and started to laugh.

"I know a story," Pelorie offered. "Fella off a boat told me it last week. You want to hear?"

"All right."

"But then you have to be our judge, just so we can play a real hand of Lawyers' Poker. That's my price."

"That seems fair."

"Well, good, then." He leaned back against the statue behind him and closed his eyes.

Leodora quietly asked Garna, "What's he doing?"

"Waiting for Meg."

"Oh."

"Meantime, I'll show you the rules of the game so you'll know how to play it." Garna reached across the cloth and grabbed the deck of cards.

By the time Meg returned, they'd gone through half the deck, and Leodora had seen enough to understand and act her part. She urged them to play first and tell the story after, and that's what they did.

The game—or so Meg claimed—went much faster than usual now that they had a real judge. They shouted at one another, bickered, threatened. As a group they cheered when she threw one of the dice, picked a card from the judge's pile, and handed down a sentence upon Chork that took him out of the game until Garna handed him a card that claimed he had tunneled from jail and into a brothel. "At least," he said, "I'll be happy in my retirement."

"Too bad the whores can't say the same," answered Garna.

In the end the play all came down to a lawsuit between Garna and Hamen. They argued their positions and then the judge had to rule. Leodora threw the dice and read the first card, which was called the amicus curiae. It meant she had to consult with the players who'd been kicked out of the game and get their answers. They talked and then outshouted each other, but without any agreed position. Chork and Meg wanted Garna to lose, while Pelorie opposed Hamen on the argument that someone simply should. She threw the dice again, and the card that came up was called bona vacantia, and stated that the properties owned by the remaining parties had to be divided equally between them. As she ruled, Garna stood up, outraged, bellowing furiously, and Leodora considered diving for safety under the cloth, at which point Garna, unable to maintain her façade of fury any longer, collapsed in laughter. Pelorie decreed, "Thus we know that law laughs in your face while it picks your pocket."

"Just like real life then, is it?" said Meg.

"But now," Hamen said, "our judge has earned her reward. Eh, Pelorie?"

Pelorie patted the cards into a neat stack. He drew the top one and held it up. "Ad arbitrium," he read. "At your will, Leodora."

"You still talking lawyerish, then?" Chork said.

"All right, fold up the game cloth," Garna directed. "I want to hear this story, too."

They passed the bottle around another time. It finished empty, and Pelorie set it aside. "Well, then," he said, "I got this off a navigator. He carried it here from another spiral, so it's not one of ours nor known hereabouts."

"Fresh, then, is it," said Chork.

They all settled back comfortably. Pelorie stood and leaned back beside the statue.

THE NAVIGATOR'S TALE

"There was a girl," said Pelorie, "who lived on an island. It was one of those backwater places where the vermes breed in the salty shallows and one day is like any other. Almost nobody ever escapes from islands like that. This girl, though, she had the desire, you know, the dream. She wanted to leave the island and see the world." He gestured at Leodora.

She said, "That's a real dream, all right."

"Oh, yes. But the villagers, now, they would have none of it. 'You're of us, you stay with us!' is what they said to her. They gave her tasks to wear her down and wear her out, forced her to do the work of three, and fed her just enough to keep her alive. She was a slave, a prisoner, and her own family sided against her. That life was good enough for them, it should have been good enough for her. The village tried to break her will. That's what they intended. It was a fishing village, so life was hard anyway, but it could always be made harder. The family, they treated her like a slave for her pride. No matter what they did, though, she clung to her dream of escape.

"These folk had trained generations of kraken—trained the tentacled beasts to carry the fishermen about upon their backs. Only the men were allowed to ride them. This idea became the law of the gods, and violation of it brought dire consequences."

By now Leodora had become uneasy with the story, but she didn't interrupt.

"One day while the men were off fishing, the girl escaped from her captors. On foot she traveled perhaps halfway around the island before she gave up. Continuing would only take her all the way around to where she'd started. Soon she saw that there was no escape, no friend willing to defy the whole village and sail her away—any such a friend would have had to stay away ever after, too. She came to realize that her life was doomed, her fate inescapable. She could only circle the island and come back to where she'd begun. And then they would treat her even worse than before.

"She turned and started back.

"It was then that she encountered a mystical kraken. It surfaced out of nowhere, stuck its head up out of the water and called to her. Called her name.

"It told her it had heard her anguish and had come to take her far away. All she had to do for this to happen was climb upon its back.

"You can imagine that she didn't hesitate a single moment. She threw off her clothes and waded out to the beast, which lifted her in its tentacles and settled her upon its back, to ride as the fishermen did. The beast carried her out into the deep, but soon she realized that it wasn't going where she wanted at all—it was headed straight for where the village men fished. She cried out for it to stop but it didn't seem to understand. She beat upon it, but it didn't flinch nor change its course. It was a kraken and this was what it did. The beast swam right through the fishing grounds, letting all the men see her, naked upon its back. They gave chase, driving her and the kraken back toward shore, toward the village. There was a spit of land there that projected like a finger into the sea, and the women—who by now had discovered her escape—came out and saw her. They shouted at her, called her a witch: the witch that conjured monsters.

"Seeing her displaying herself so wantonly, the women picked up stones and hurled them at her. They pelted her, pelted the kraken. The women shrieked at her like a flock of birds. And finally one stone struck the beast a mortal blow. Ribbons of black ink billowed out of it, turning the sea to darkness. It floundered and started to sink. Rolling its great eye toward her, it said, 'Forgive me, forgive me, I've failed you.'

"In some other story, the beast might have transformed into her lover, or into an enchanted prince, or someone else special. But in this story, it was as it appeared, and it died. Then the girl was struck in the head and slid into the water beside it."

Leodora could not conceal her horror at the specifics of the story. "Did . . . did the navigator tell you what became of her?"

"Oh, yes. The villagers drowned her in that black water, tore her body to pieces, and fed her to the fish, to the barbed and poisonous vermes. In one sense you could say the beast had not lied, for it did take her away from there. She *did* find escape."

Meg, watching Leodora's reaction, remarked, "It's not a very pleasant tale."

"That's true, I suppose," Pelorie agreed. "This fellow, though, he swore it really happened on an island not three spirals from here. He'd got it off some crippled-up fishmonger who came from that island and had seen it all happen. He claimed he wanted folks to know what fate awaits you when you aren't satisfied with what you have."

"More like it's a tale to keep you from ever hoping for anything," said Garna. "It'd be like telling me I'm never leaving *this* place."

"But you aren't leaving, are you?" said Chork.

"Not the point of it. If I wished to, I could, anytime, same as you or them. I choose not to, but it's what I choose. Now, women stoning their own child— that's just cruel for no good reason. That's a place where the rules have defeated the common sense of folks."

"If they ever had any," said Meg.

"Rules is like tradition," argued Chork. "You do what your family's done for every generation since the world began. You don't have no more choice tharr that girl. None of us does. What would we do different, anyhow. What would you know how to do?"

A long silence followed his question.

"It was just a story," Pelorie apologized. "For Leodora, is all."

She made herself smile, and thanked him for telling it. She didn't try to explain that his tale was strewn with real elements of her and her mother's lives, mixed together by a demented fishmonger who couldn't tell them apart anymore. The story was out on its own now, a version of her released by her uncle or whomever, and whether or not it was an utter lie seemed of less importance than the conclusions being drawn from it, conclusions that said life was defeat, hopeless and pointless. The thing she knew absolutely was that she would never perform it anywhere.

"As Garna chooses," she said, "so must I, and I have to choose to go back up now. Thank you, Pelorie, for a tale. I've a performance to prepare for, and I hope you'll all attend. Do you know if there's an entrance to the Terrestre?"

The others glanced at Hamen, and she followed their gaze.

"Not in it, but next to it," he said. "I'll take you." He stood, a little unsteady on his feet.

"Oh, be careful with him, Leodora," said Meg. "He's drunk enough I'm not sure where he'll lead you."

He waved off the criticism. "I could find my way through the underworld in the dark."

"Blindfolded," added Chork.

"We could test him," Pelorie suggested.

"Test your own selves, spit-frogs," he answered. "Come on, Leodora. *I'll* get you back safely."

She started to follow him, but then remembered the reason she had come down here in the first place, before the game and players had distracted her. "I've a question before I go. Can any of you tell me, is there an entrance from this level to the inverted city?"

"To what?" asked Garna.

"I don't really know its name, or if it has one. I saw it from Colemaigne's dragon beam. The houses pointed toward the water, and I think it must have been below this."

All of them gaped at her. Chork leaned toward her and quietly said, "You actually *saw* it? You didn't just hear of it? Have the notion of it planted in your head by somebody?"

"No, I saw it. And—"

"She *saw* the Pons Asinorum," Meg said in wonder as she eyed the other players. "When is the last time anyone ever saw it?"

Pelorie replied, "Drunks in the blighted lanes say they see it all the time. Drag themselves to a rail to spew up, and there'll be someone looking up at 'em as if the water had moved up close and they were seeing themselves, but it's not themselves nor like themselves, it's someone dark and shadowy, blue or black with fire for eyes. And who believes what a drunk sees?"

"Then is there anyone whose opinion is trusted?"

Pelorie shook his head. "Been twenty years or more, I think."

"Longer than the blighting itself even."

Pelorie reconsidered Leodora. "You saw it, though, you swear."

"She's been noticed by the gods. 'The girl who saved Colemaigne,' isn't it?"

"Don't know as I'd much like to be noticed. Nobody who is ever seems to come to a good end."

"Capricious, that's what everyone calls them—*the capricious gods.*"

"Me, I think we've been blessed by your visit," Hamen told her.

"But then again, you only been here two days," Chork added.

"I hope—" Garna began, but hesitated.

"You hope what?" asked Leodora.

"I hope they take only a passing interest, those gods." She gave Leodora a worried smile.

Hamen said, "Enough of this jabber. Come on, I'll lead you back to the theater." He lifted a light from a stone figure and walked past Leodora. She acknowledged the group with one final nod, then set off after him.

Meg stood watching until the darkness had swallowed the lantern light. Then she said, "I think we'd best see this performance tonight."

"Because there might not be another?" mused Chork.

"Exactly."

Hamen led her past dozens and dozens of small stairways, past embedded foundations of whole buildings that evoked a walk through a maze, past kegs and barrels, crates and clay jars and cloth sacks, and past dusty, stony upright corpses. In one place they passed an overturned boat that was a little too reminiscent of her uncle's ruined esquif, and she made haste to close the distance to walk beside Hamen, secure in the lantern's pool of light.

"I'm going to dally once I've taken you up," he said to her. "I want to see your performance. The others, too, they'll most likely come along once they talk themselves into it. The idea that something might happen and they'd miss it will play on 'em till they have to see, too."

She nodded but said nothing.

"Pelorie's tale—I saw how you reacted. That was all about you, wasn't it?"

She eyed him askance. "It seemed to be," she admitted. "Everything he said, I kept thinking—hoping—the next wouldn't be more of it, more of me, and then it was. And where it wasn't, it was as if someone had replaced the missing stones in the mosaic with a different color of stone, was all. But the picture—"

"You'll not be performing it, then."

"Not ever, I think."

"Makes you wonder a bit. I mean, how many of the stories you tell do you suppose used to be about somebody—somebody real, once upon a time. And then the story took over—some of the stones, like you say, got replaced with different ones, made-up ones—and the real person and their story went different ways altogether. Separate ways, like. I mean, do any of us ever perform our own stories," he asked, "save for the one time?"

She shook her head, both in answer and in surprise at the depth of his comments and question. "I don't know," she said.

"No, nor does anyone, I expect. You can't know your story when you're part of it. And until you die, you're always in the middle of it, aren't you."

"I never looked at it that way, Hamen."

"Well." He gazed down, as if embarrassed by his own sudden metaphysical opinions. "Besides, what you want to know about is the Pons Asinorum."

"I do."

"Well, then, I hope somebody above can help you, because I can't. I've never seen it, nor really believed in it, nor have the others. Just stories to us." He chuckled then. "All just stories."

When they'd walked a little farther, he spoke up again. "I was thinking, you know, I said that the group of us all live in the dark here, and, well, so do you, don't you? I mean, with your puppets and all, you're in the dark, you know, a lot. People don't see you, just see what you offer 'em."

"That's so," she agreed.

"Yeah, well. Same with us."

"You seem to think a great deal, Hamen."

"Don't know about *a great deal*. No more nor you, I expect. But if the Pons Asinorum exists, I think it'd be good if you found it."

"Why?"

"Can't say, quite. I'd have to think about it some." Then he grinned to himself, and she laughed.

"One more thing—what are vermes?" she asked. "Some kind of fish?"

"A terrible fish. Can climb up on land and pull down an ox, tear it to shreds. That'd be one of those stones of another color in your mosaic you were talkin' about."

"It would, yes," she replied, and wondered where that element had been added to the story. What isle or span did the notion of vermes hail from?

Before long they approached a great curving wall of stone. "The Terrestre," Hamen pointed out. "That's its foundation. The prima pietra's around here somewhere, got Burbage's name etched on't."

Around the far side of the wall they came to another flight of steps, and Hamen delivered her to the surface. The steps led to a narrow gated portico across the alley from the rear of the theater. It smelled of a rusty wetness. She unlatched the metal gate and stepped out. Overhead, the sky was going dark, with the first stars twinkling.

Hamen followed her into the theater. Diverus, seated at the long table where they'd eaten earlier, leapt up at her appearance. "Lea!" he cried, which brought Soter and the others. By then Diverus had wrapped his arms around her with such obvious relief that she blushed.

Soter pulled Diverus back and said to her sternly, "You age me every single day, child, you don't know how much."

So nonplussed was she by their reaction that she didn't try to explain. Instead she turned and introduced Hamen. Orinda said, "I believe I recognize you, good sir."

"And you, madam," he replied. "You're of my district. It's my services you call on from time to time when you want something brought up from the cellar, you know?"

Her expression brightened. "*Coo-ee?* That's you? You will stay and sup with us then, before the theater opens for business?"

"I should be most happy to attend your company. Thank you."

"It's nothing," she said. "You've returned to us our savior, it's the least we can do."

Leodora blushed again at being called their savior. As the others turned about, she grabbed Glaise by the sleeve. "I've had an idea for the performance tonight," she told him. "I want to know what you and Bois think of it, because it involves you both."

Bois came over, and the three of them walked off toward the stage, leaving Hamen in the company of the other three.

The kitsune watched as the long-snouted tanuki took a black stone between his middle and index fingers and snapped it onto the gō board. "Atari," said the tanuki, and its black eyes gazed meaningfully at the cadaverous figure on the opposite side of the gō ban. Two others, nearly identical to the seated player, stood motionlessly behind him as they had throughout the game. Torches burned on either side of them. They stood as still as moonlight.

The player of white stones pursed his thin lips and then raised his hands in a gesture of capitulation. The tanuki nodded respectfully that his opponent had recognized defeat. His whiskers twitched.

The seated figure arose, tall and gaunt. One of its companions said with dismay, "You lost."

The white stone player ignored the observation, but turned to the kitsune and said, "Now I've played your game and it's time you told me about these storytellers."

"You lost?" the second figure repeated.

The player turned coldly about. "Yes. I lost. The stars still burn in the sky, last I checked."

The kitsune looked overhead. "They do," he agreed. "As to the storytellers, what can I say? They came, they watched a game unfold, we told them a story—a very good one I might add—and then they joined us for the parade. Would you like to join us for the parade?"

The bald player's lips drew back over his long teeth. His sunken eyes smoldered, as if he thought he was being toyed with. "What I want to know—was one of them called Bardsham?"

"Well," said the kitsune. "What would your Bardsham look like? I have never seen him, and I had always fancied that he died long ago, for surely he hasn't performed anywhere I've heard of, and our kind do hear things."

"Unusual things," the tanuki chimed in. "It's past sunset," he told the fox.

"Yes, I know," replied the kitsune. "Gentlemen, you've indulged us, and we appreciate it, but we know nothing of whether your Bardsham dwelled among the storytellers. But then we only encountered two of the troupe, and as I understand these things, most troupes of players contain four or more. How many were in your Bardsham's troupe?"

"Three," the player stated.

"Four," his companion corrected. Their eyes locked. "There was the dwarf. Grumyfin or some such name."

"Four, then," said the player to the kitsune. "It doesn't matter. Whoever they are, we must find them all. It's most urgent that we do."

The kitsune adjusted his kimono. "I am sorry, but there you have it. We met two, and who can say if they were, either of them, the one you seek. And anyway they haven't come again."

"I dislike being taken advantage of," the player said, and his words dripped with threat.

"We did not swear to have your answers, only to have *some* answers, of which none seems to belong to you."

"You—"

"We. Must be leaving now," explained the kitsune. "The parade does not wait. If you care to return to the park tomorrow, I'm certain you can learn more, though not more certain of its benefit."

The player stared at his hands, flexed his fingers. One palm glistened as if coated with blue glass. Suddenly he reached for the fox's arm. His hand closed upon empty air. The kitsune had vanished and only the tanuki remained, with bared fangs and bristling fur. "Unusual," he snarled. "Not alive, and not dead enough." The player lunged at him, but the tanuki flipped the *gō ban* into the air, and the stones covering its surface peppered the trio, forcing them to stumble back. When they lowered their arms, the tanuki still stood there, observing them. "*Most* unusual," he said. Where the white and black *gō ishi* had struck their faces, the flesh was pocked and gray. "You're not at all nice. We shall not help you further." Then, like the kitsune, he vanished. It was as if the wall drank him up. The torches guttered and went out, leaving the trio of agents in darkness lit only by the stars and the twin moons.

"I hate conversing with the supernatural," complained the player.

"You lost the game, Scratta."

"If you remind me of that once more, I'll strip the rest of the glamour from you and you can remain fixed right here for pigeons to spatter. Now." He paused to regain his composure. "We will return to the ship. Possibly the others had better luck."

"If not, what then?"

"Tomorrow night we'll hunt the venues, find out where they performed. They had to have performed *somewhere*."

"Why not simply go north to the next span? We're close behind them now."

"I see," he said, and then asked the third one, "Is that what you want to do, too?"

The third glanced nervously between his two companions. Prudently he ventured, "They must have moved on, so why continue looking here? It would *seem* reasonable."

"Fine. Then that is what we shall do. If you're right," said Scratta to the second, "we save time. If you're wrong . . . well, every ship needs an anchor." He turned and strode off.

The others followed. "You can't intimidate the supernatural," said one.

The other replied, "We should know, and better than any."

"So then, when we catch up to this troupe, what if the teller, this performer, *is* the supposed-to-be-dead Bardsham?"

"Then he's doomed."

"And what if he's not Bardsham?"

"Then he's doomed."

"Oh, good. I like simplicity."

"Indeed. Complications are for stories."

The Terrestre was only half filled, but the audience included the governor of the span, who wanted to see for himself what creature had coerced the gods into healing Colemaigne.

Soter complained about the way the stage was set. He had put the puppeteer's booth front and center, but while he ate and chatted with Hamen, Leodora and the two woodmen had moved it to one side, leaving most of the stage open. He was further dismayed when she told him that she didn't want him narrating the first story as he often did. She would do it herself.

He replied, "Merely because you're revealing that you're a girl, now you want to change the process? Will you be performing the introduction as you manage the puppets, too?"

She told him, "I won't *be* managing puppets for this performance."

Diverus joined her in the booth. She explained to him what she was going to do, and his ritual began. He sat on the floor and spread his instruments in a circle around him. There were new ones she hadn't seen before: Orinda had shown him the Terrestre's instrument collection, and he had selected various items, including a snaky horn that seemed more designed for processionals than accompaniment. Now he closed his eyes and lowered his head. His hands reached out and took hold of one of these novel instruments from the Terrestre, a theorbo. It looked like a lute but with an extended neck and second pegbox. He lay it across his lap and then reached again, adding three small percussion instruments to his choices. One was a clapper. The other two, she couldn't fathom. Then he sighed and leaned back. His eyes fluttered open and he stared, bemused by what he'd picked, despite which confusion he told her, "I'm ready."

Orinda strode out from the curtains and welcomed the crowd. Most of them knew her. Some, like the governor, had known her husband. They applauded her, and cheered her announcement that theater was coming back to Colemaigne. She gestured to the governor in his box, and the audience stood to give him an ovation for dismissing the ban. He bowed, then gestured broadly for all of them to sit, so that the performance might begin.

It had seemed only fitting to Leodora that the first story recited should be "The Tale of the Two Brothers." Bois and Glaise strode out upon the boards, took their bows, and then, as she recited from within the booth, pantomimed the tale as they had done with her earlier. Accompanied by Diverus's score, their movements seemed more fluid and precise. The graceful music carried them along, and punctuated each step deeper into cruelty and greed.

Soter stood beside Hamen in one of the stage balconies. He was edgy and complained unhappily about this unprecedented change in how they did things, until Orinda entered the balcony. She moved between the two men and said, "Your Jax does us great honor by letting them perform the first story. They've waited so long. Mr. Burbage would be elated." He knew from her tone that she believed he'd had a hand in the decision and he did not attempt to dissuade her, but allowed her to kiss him on the cheek.

When she leaned over the rail to watch, Hamen edged close beside him again and said, "Don't worry it, your secret's safe with me." He winked.

Soter replied, "Why am I not comforted, knowing that?" If Hamen heard him, he gave no indication.

The recitation of "The Two Brothers" ended. The two figures, wrapped about each other, seemed to have melted together into the great worn sandstone lump that Baloyd had become. They held their positions as Leodora emerged from the booth. For effect she wore her trademark mask, black silk stitched with a diamond pattern, covering the top of her head to just above the tip of her nose. But now her thick red braid swung behind her, and the loose-sleeved red bodice she wore removed all doubt as to her sex.

The audience uttered not a sound, as though uncertain if the play was finished, or what their role was supposed to be in response.

Then the governor stood and began to clap enthusiastically, and like a lead bird drawing its flock into the air, his applause brought the rest of the audience to its feet. The din of approval surged until the half-empty theater shook with clapping and calls of "Jax!" Leodora swept off the black mask as she bowed. The footlights flashed over her copper hair. As had happened on Hyakiyako, the audience shouted louder. Those nearest the front of the stage reached toward her, tried to touch her feet. She knelt and squeezed their hands, gestured Bois and Glaise up beside her, and although they were known to everyone in the pit, the hands reached for them as well. They met her gaze, eyes full of wonder, but no more than her own. The charge from this audience crackled through her, made her heart pound, her brain spark. She arose, took one more bow, and then retreated behind the booth again. Diverus stared at her as if in wonder, and she said, "Oh, Diverus, come out," and took him by the hand. At the last moment, she seized upon an idea and drew her domino mask over his head, tying it quickly behind him. He carried the theorbo in one hand, following along as if in a daze. She told him to bow and remove his mask, too, and he did as she ordered, if uncertainly.

The noise must have spread through the streets and alleys, because more people were pushing through the doors, as if they'd been waiting for the signal the applause represented. They entered and marched up the aisles. Even when the ovation died down, more people continued to enter.

Bois and Glaise ran to the side of the stage and began dragging the sections of the booth out into the center. First came the giant screen and, behind it, the tall lens that would enlarge her puppets so that even those at the back could see. Once that was set up, Diverus hauled his instruments behind it and then helped Leodora move the cases from the booth, which the two wooden men would carry. The poles and screens weighed next to nothing. Meanwhile the audience milled about, chattering, imbibing.

From the balcony, Hamen spotted his comrades seated together in one of the front rows. He thanked Orinda for her kindnesses, and she invited him to sample them another night. Soter scowled at the exchange. Hamen saw the look and winked at him again, then walked down into the theater as Leodora came up the stairs and joined them in the box. Though she'd only known him briefly, Soter noticed that she watched Hamen's departure sadly.

She said, "They're setting up the lens you described—the same one Bard-sham used."

"Glaise found it," said Orinda. "I'd hoped he would."

"And what other surprises are in store," Soter asked sharply. "Will we be setting someone on *fire* perhaps?"

"Why are you so contrary?" Orinda asked.

Soter glanced between them, and then insisted, "I'm not contrary. We do things a certain way. Suddenly you're taking charge and changing the performance without even asking if I think it's a good idea."

"Afraid you're obsolete and we don't need you anymore?" Leodora asked.

"To tell you the truth, yes."

Leodora closed her eyes and shook her head. "Oh, Soter. How can you believe that?"

"Not *believe*," he said, "it's not that obvious and clear. But you certainly don't need me to teach you anything anymore, and now you don't need me even to narrate the occasional tales that have always been mine rather than yours to recite."

"*One* story, Soter."

"Not for long. Jax is Leodora now. Your voice could be the one that tells *all* the tales and they'll listen in rapture. There's no longer a reason to divide the task with me. You are the consummate storyteller, how can anybody deny it? You could narrate and perform and never so much as open your eyes. In any case, my fear is *my* burden, not yours, and I will settle with it on my own terms. Now, what do we do next?"

"Another story. I was thinking it's about time we do a Meersh play."

"I think if you perform any of Meersh now, you'll have a riot on your hands. They might pull the walls down, this crowd. It's filling up out there like a tower in a flood."

"If they tear it down, I'll simply walk the dragon beam again," she replied.

"Don't even joke about that."

Orinda had been peering around the balcony curtain. She stepped back again. "It looks as if the whole span has come out."

"What *are* you charging them?" Soter asked.

"A penny."

"But how can you expect to pay us from that?"

"She doesn't," Leodora said. "We're taking a smaller cut, too."

Before he could object, Orinda explained, "It's the first chance they've had to see puppets in more years than some of them have been alive—you said it yourself, this crowd is dazzled. Look at all the children out there. I can't greedily squeeze their families. You want them to return again and again, yes? To tell everyone, here and on other spans. We want other theaters to reopen, to compete with us, which will make the quality of the performances that much better. And if none of that should come to pass, then let them have this event to remember." She parted the curtain again. "Oh, I hope Mr. Burbage can see this where he's gone. It's what he always loved, the sound, the energy."

Soter found himself strung between wanting to complain about the misappropriation of still more of his power and wanting to give Orinda the impression that he was in complete accord with her. The result was that he said nothing.

Diverus entered the balcony. "What are we going to do next?" he asked. "The theater's mayhem." Leodora told him about Meersh, and he smiled. "Well, *I* want to see one even if nobody else does. You and Soter have gone on and on about Meersh stories ever since you found me."

"They'll certainly have their money's worth," said Soter, without any vitriol. "But I'm narrating this."

Leodora laughed. "Of course you are."

"Good. I'm glad you're listening."

Out of the corner of his eye, he saw Orinda cover her mouth so as not to laugh, too.

"Now," said Soter. "Which tale of Meersh do you propose we tell them?"

"I don't want to do one of the long ones. So I was thinking of 'Meersh and the Sun God' or 'How Meersh Tried to Become Immortal,'" she replied.

"'Sun God.'" He stared at her critically. "You wouldn't be," he asked, "proposing this tale because of your horrid Coral Man that we should have dumped overboard before we got here."

He watched her dwell a moment upon the implications before she shook her head. "There's no ulterior motive, Soter," she assured him. "Now, Diverus needs to pick out his instruments. We've kept them waiting as long as we can." The two of them left the balcony, Diverus glancing back as always, as if trying to comprehend the meaning of everything around him after the fact. Soter took a step after them, but Orinda touched his shoulder. He turned.

"She loves you, you old fool," Orinda told him. "You both fight jealously for every knuckle's distance of territory, but do you suppose she learned that on her own?"

"I—"

"Shush!" She put her fingers to his lips. "I'll not listen to your explanation. It's not for me anyway to know it. Tell the walls if you're looking to persuade something. Not me." She slid her hand to his shoulder blade then and impelled him to leave.

Below, in the booth once more, Leodora selected her puppets while Diverus chose his instruments—the theorbo again, and a duduk. She had the feeling the theorbo, with its more resonant bass strings, was going to become a permanent addition to his repertoire.

Once he had his choices she perched upon her seat, raised her hand to the lantern, and slid a blue filter in front of the side facing the screen. Then, slowly, she raised the black curtain and the theater was bathed in a blue glow. The hidden lens in front of the booth redoubled the strength of the light, and even over the top of the booth she could see the glow, like the most intense moonlight striking sapphire.

The audience shrieked with joy. Some whistled or yelled, but their noise soon fell to a murmur and then the silence of anticipation.

From the case beside her, Leodora lifted out the figure of Meersh. Her hands nearly trembled upon the rods controlling him. Here was the figure Soter had once used to represent her father, the puppet most closely tied to him, the one who like Bardsham had acted on impulse and stolen a million hearts as he did.

She raised him to the screen. They all knew that profile, even if they'd never seen him before—the beaky nose, the wicked smile that knew your secrets, the wide and mischievous eyes: the consummate trickster.

Applause and more shouts greeted his appearance.

Soter, standing on the far side of the booth, just beside the larger screen, began an introductory speech. "You know this story already, many of you, because once upon a time the immortal Bardsham told every tale of Meersh the Bedeviler, and told them so well that we have them still. Here, tonight, the old Bedeviler returns to us, now in the hands of the formidable Jax." Some of them repeated the name. Someone shouted it.

Soter continued: "As you know, Meersh had *many* adventures, and not all of them turned out for the best. Meersh, helpless in the face of his own desires, paid a price for his every pleasure."

THE TALE OF MEERSH AND THE SUN GOD

Back in the early times, when only a single strand of spans graced Shadowbridge, Meersh the Bedeviler took a wife named Akonadi and settled upon Taprobane. Akonadi was a remarkable huntress who could stand in a boat, throw her spear, and skewer a whole school of fish at once. Meersh had married her out of lust, as he did everything, but especially because she kept him well fed. The old saying goes, "When you want to eat, marry a huntress." And when you want trouble, marry Meersh.

Now, even in the earliest times, Meersh had difficulty staying in one place for very long. This is why he's known far and wide across Shadowbridge. And even though she looked after him so well, did our Akonadi, he could not resist his peripatetic urges. Thus he went traveling while she remained on Taprobane, hunting and keeping house.

Meersh stayed away a long time, and Akonadi pined for him. She prayed to Edgeworld that he be returned safely to her, for even when they were furious with Meersh, women loved him, and Akonadi loved him the deepest of all, for most of his follies were still to come. Nevertheless, after many months had passed, she began to pray that *somebody* be delivered to her, whether it was Meersh or not. If any gods were paying her the slightest attention, they offered her no sign.

One day while she was fishing, she sailed farther out than ever before and came to an unfamiliar shoreline, an island she'd never visited. Its shore was rocky, precipitous, and hazardous. Before the sheer cliff face, many stones jutted out of the sea like teeth or tines. One in particular had been worn by the waves into a familiar shape. Upright in the shallows, it looked like Meersh himself. The play of shadow and light chiseled the stone into his recognizable visage, an illusion to be sure, but illusion, she

decided, was better than nothing, and she took the rope from her spear
and tied it around the shapely pillar. She tugged on the rope and, mighty
warrior that she was, dislodged the stone. It tilted farther and farther until
it wrenched loose. The rope pulled but she held it and, with the figure in
tow behind her, steered a course for home. The wonder is that the weight
of the stone didn't pull her boat under, but by now you might have
guessed that there was something unnatural in it all.

She tied up her boat at the base of her span, and then hauled in the
stone figure. As it bobbed to the surface and rolled, Akonadi saw that the
swirling waters around the island had endowed the figure with another
prominent feature of her husband's, and she was careful not to damage
this as she dragged the stone up the many steps to her house. Neighbors
saw her and clambered down the steps to help her with it. If they thought
anything odd about the stone, they said nothing. They helped her carry it
through her house and into her garden, where she stood it upright and let
it dry in the sun. In the daylight in her garden, the stone looked less like
Meersh, save for that smooth phallus that the water had shaped and polished, an object of ceaseless arousal. That was *very* like him.

That night, every time she walked past the garden, she found herself
glancing at the stone figure. The twin moons cast their light so that once
again the facets of it resembled her husband.

Finally, Akonadi's longing broke free, flooding her thoughts, drown-
ing her senses in need. She rushed to the stone, embraced it, kissed its
cold hard lips, its face. She hiked up her skirt, wrapped her legs around it,
and slowly, steadily, with immense pleasure, impaled herself upon its
most prominent feature. She rode the stone figure for hours. Conscious-
ness fell away and wonderful sensation consumed her. When at last she
stepped into the dirt again, her legs would barely hold her up. It was as if
her spirit had flown to some other place and returned. She stumbled off
to bed, leaving the stone figure glistening in the moonlight. The essence
of Akonadi was absorbed into it, permeated it, ran like divine blood
through it.

Sated, Akonadi slept soundly. In the morning when she awoke, she
was astonished to find that the gray stone figure lay beside her in her bed.

She sat up and scrabbled back the way a crab scurries across a beach.
The stone rolled over. Its features were more distinct than before, the face

real. A piece of the stone figure seemed to tear loose from the body. It stretched toward her—an arm. Fingers uncurled, invited her. Tentatively, she gave it her hand, and the stone man drew her to him, lifting her up on top of him. She impaled herself once more and began again the previous night's lascivious ritual. How long it went on, Akonadi didn't know or care. She succumbed to sensation, lost all thought, all awareness, and only later came to her senses lying beside the stone, now warmed like flesh by the sunlight, and she drifted away to sleep.

For weeks after that Akonadi and the stone man lived in bliss. Each day it seemed he was more alive. He attended to her every need, obeyed her every request, strong but always looking to her satisfaction. The only desire he did not satisfy was her eagerness for conversation. His mouth remained no more than an imperfection in the stone. He said nothing.

Some time later, word arrived from the neighboring span of Valdemir that a great convocation was going to take place to elect sun and moon gods. The span of Valdemir, then newly formed, did not have any, and in those early times Edgeworld was not so cleft from us as it is now—a span could elect its own gods.

The news meant little to Akonadi, but it traveled along the spiral and reached Meersh wherever he was, and he came running home, for the idea had come to him in a besotted epiphany that he might be able to have himself elected a god.

Entering the house at night, he discovered the great stone pillar lying in his place and feigned outrage. "I'm gone a few months and this is how you replace me?"

Akonadi answered, "Husband, you've been gone a year and more."

He brushed aside her defense. "All the same, you replaced me! And with a brute. I'm not at all pleased."

"You weren't at all *here*," she countered, growing angry. "For all I knew, you had found someone else and weren't coming back."

Meersh's penis stood up and said to him, "She's right, you know, and hardly far off the mark. Best you'd be contrite."

Meersh, who had in fact dallied with too many to count, changed tack. "Well, I'm back for now so we must all get along, mustn't we? What is this hard fellow's name?"

"I don't know. He never speaks." She refrained from telling him how the stone man had come to life, but Penis whispered, "Look at the size of *that!*" Meersh knew what Penis was looking at.

"You probably just don't know how to talk to him," he said. "I have traveled so widely that I know how to speak to anybody. If you'd but asked I would have shown you."

She marveled at his ability to deny his absence while proclaiming his skill, and only shook her head at the hopelessness of arguing with one for whom reality had no permanent shape.

Meersh unloaded his pack. As always it was full of games, and he drew these out and set them aside—boards and playing pieces, markers of various sorts. From the bottom of it he produced three multicolored, polished pebbles no bigger than his thumb. He held one to his ear and nodded to himself. He pressed that pebble to the stone figure's face where its mouth should have béen. Around the pebble a gap formed, spreading to either side of it. Abruptly, the stone man gave a sucking sound, drawing his first breath, the pebble disappeared into the gap, and Meersh snatched his fingers back before they vanished, too. "There, it's really very simple," he said.

"It's really very simple," parroted the rock man. His voice creaked and clacked—the sound of stone grinding on stone.

Then Meersh took the two remaining stones and pressed them with his thumbs into the hollows where the Stone Man's eyes might have been. When he drew his thumbs away, the stones remained, like bright irises embedded in the deep sockets. The pebbles shifted as the stone figure looked from Meersh to Akonadi.

To her, Meersh said, "I know where you found *him*. There's enchantment in those isles. I've seen it before." He addressed the Stone Man then. "Hereafter, you can speak, and I'm going to make use of your new-found talent."

"What do you mean, husband?" Akonadi asked.

"On Valdemir they need a sun god, and I need someone who will nominate me. It's never a good idea to nominate yourself. It looks suspicious." He patted the Stone Man's shoulder.

"And why should he do that for you?" she asked.

"Because he's in my debt. I've given him a voice and much improved his eyesight. Once I'm sun god, who knows what I might do for him? And for you, as well, wife. I'm sure I'll be a benign sun god." And he wandered off, contemplating how he would transform Taprobane once he had become a god, and how he would sleep when he wanted to and eat what he wanted to, and no one could gainsay him.

The Stone Man waited until Meersh was out of earshot, then said, "I will do this for him because I am in his debt, but I can tell you, no good will come of it."

"None ever does," she said, and was about to turn away when he touched her, a delicate touch for one so huge and seemingly brutish.

He whispered her name then, and the sound came from deep within him. It was thick with all that he felt, that until then he had not been able to express. All he said was "Akonadi," but the syllables thrummed with the desire all women want to hear when their lover speaks their name, and she embraced him and remained there.

The Stone Man learned his lines. He knew what Meersh wanted and didn't care. To him such cupidity meant nothing.

At the palace of Valdemir there were hundreds of petitioners on hand in the great hall. Most stood in a circle around the few seats, which had been taken early; and most stood with their backs to the center, as if they were interested in the architecture of the palace. It was impressive: Glass panels decorated the walls and ceiling of the hall. The eastern side, lined with slender columns, became an open balcony overlooking the ocean.

Beyond the crowd something sparkled brightly, and Meersh, magpie-like, was drawn to it. He cozened his way through the crowd. He misdirected some, and wheedled others, slipping through the gaps that appeared as people turned, until finally he could see it.

There in the center hung the robe of the sun god. It so dazzled Meersh's eyes that they teared immediately. Penis complained, "That's so bright it could blind a one-eyed mouse!"

Others beside him shielded their faces from its glare. Thus he understood why almost everyone had turned their backs to the center. Far easier to look upon was the robe of the moon, hanging like an afterimage beside it. Meersh saw those robes and knew he had to wear one of them.

Behind him, the Stone Man followed without a word. For his imposing figure the crowd parted immediately. He stood behind Meersh and with his pebble eyes looked upon the robe as if it gave off no light at all. Penis was laughing gleefully at the prospect of becoming a godhead, until the Stone Man's pebble eyes fixed upon him, and then, unnerved, Penis shrank away.

The governor of Valdemir entered with a small retinue. He surveyed the crowd carefully as he strode before them to a marble rostrum. The chatter grew as he stepped up, and he waved his arms, calling out, "Friends. Neighbors. Please!" The conversations quieted. "I'm glad you have all come." He glanced at an adviser, who nodded solemnly. "It's as Edgeworld predicted—so large a body, a group, and somewhere in the midst of you our sun god. It comes to me now—"

Before he could finish, the Stone Man had stepped forward and said, "I would like to nominate my good friend, Meersh, who is certainly worthy of the title." His voice, raised to a bellow, rumbled about the room. "He is widely traveled across these many spirals. He is widely known."

"That's a true statement," someone interjected. "Widely known, and as widely *sought*!"

The crowd roared. Penis scolded Meersh, "You should have let me write this."

Unfazed, the Stone Man continued, "Of all those here, he has seen the sun from more places, more mornings of the world."

"And more often hanging from a windowsill!" called another member of the crowd. The laughter that followed drowned out everything the Stone Man tried to say. He was treated to slaps on the back, and even the governor and his staff joined in the merriment. Meersh clucked his tongue at outraged Penis. *He* had anticipated it all. In fact it was as he'd intended.

With the Stone Man drawing all attention, Meersh walked straight to the sun god's robe. No one could look at it and none paid him the least mind as he shamelessly snatched the robe and placed it upon his shoulders. He strutted about, enjoying the sense of self-importance it conveyed. Let them laugh, he didn't care. He was going to be divine.

Nobody realized what he had done immediately . . . until he burst into flames. "Aah!" he shouted, and ran in a circle. The nearest of the crowd lurched back from him. "Aah!" he shrieked, and then charged straight at the balcony. "Aah!" he screamed as he flung off the robe and leapt over the railing. "Aahhhhh!" The cry descended through octaves as he plunged from sight and into the sea.

Here Leodora turned the lamp from bright day to cool blue evening and eased the glittering glass-encrusted robe from the screen. She rested while the audience laughed and shouted and applauded. For many it was the first interlude they'd ever seen and they fell silent at the blue glow, where an experienced audience would have known to stretch their legs, to stroll about. The silence told her that they expected her to continue.

She worked quickly to make the changes in the puppet of Meersh, prepared her new props, then craned her neck and gave Diverus a nod.

A note of music took to the air behind her. She lifted Meersh to the bottom of the screen and let him show up just slightly, had him rise and fall, rise and fall, as if floating upon waves. Watching the screen from outside, Soter cleared his throat and continued the tale.

Many hours later, Meersh drew himself out of the ocean. His body was blackly charred; his hair stuck out like burned twigs. Most of his clothing had disintegrated. He had little hope of recouping his loss and would have been better served by slinking away, but Meersh never chose what would best serve him, only what appealed to his appetites.

He climbed the steps up the span to the balcony. His penis, burned as badly as the rest of him, muttered, "You should have asked me, I'd have *told* you not to touch that robe."

Meersh's doubtful response was drowned beneath a great cheer from overhead. A light pulsed from within the palace, its beams shooting out between the rails like a mist, spurring him to climb faster.

At the top he stepped through the rail to discover there in the hall a huge figure wrapped in the robe of the sun god, the robe that should have been his. The incandescence of it had flowed into the figure, whose shaved head glowed now like copper rather than stone. It was only when the figure turned to face him, and he saw the bright pebble eyes, that he recognized what had happened.

"Ah, friend Meersh," the Stone Man said, his cheeks burnished and smooth. The crowd around him began to laugh at the burned, wild visage

Meersh presented, but the Stone Man ignored their caterwauling as he came forward. "You survived, and that's good. I was going to come resurrect you if you hadn't, for you do fall under the aegis of the Sun, whether you know it or not."

"I what?"

"I have to look out for you . . . or, rather, *we* do." He turned and gestured back to the robe of the Moon, and who should be wearing it but Akonadi.

"What is this?" asked Meersh, although he'd already gleaned the answer.

"Oh, dear," said Penis. "I could have told you this was bound to happen while you gallivanted about on the other spans. But would you listen?"

"You?" Meersh snarled at it. "You're the one led me all about from one debauch to the next."

"Akonadi has consented to be the Moon," said the sun god. "I could think of no huntress as skilled."

"I . . . how could you? You'd take my *wife*?"

"I'm surprised you remember that she is for all the attention you've paid her."

Meersh glanced about, taking the time to work himself into a state of outrage. He would gain from these events yet. "So *that's* how it is. Well, if you're taking Akonadi with you, then I should be recompensed. It's only fair."

The sun god considered him a moment. "All right. Anything you like that I may give you."

"One thing," Meersh said, and he reached into the glowing robe, grabbing hold of the smooth copper phallus on the front of the sun god. "I'll have this."

The sun god didn't even flinch. His pebble eyes bored into Meersh, who sensed that they saw all of his plan, and every bit of his scheming soul. "As you wish," said the god.

"Wait!" cried Penis, the very last sound he made before he was encased. Meersh stared at himself, erect and polished. "Now we're even."

The sun god chuckled. "Very well, Meersh."

Meersh slapped his new member. "*This* one will do as I say and not taunt me." The Sun, the governor, and the crowd roared with laughter and taunts of "a suit of armor for his little knight."

The Sun and Moon stepped hand in hand to the balcony, then opened wide their arms and blended with the evening. The shimmer of their robes hung afterward in the sky as a swath of stars.

Meersh went home. He left behind him a trail of charred bits. He was only mildly dejected by the loss of Akonadi. He had wanted her as he wanted everything he saw, and the wanting had more sway than the having. His spirits were further buoyed by the wine he'd stolen from the banquet in the sun god's honor. On the way across the spans he strutted proudly to show off his phallus. "Hard as a rock and twice as shiny!" he proclaimed to any women foolish enough to venture near.

Later, seated on his bed, he admired it between drinks of wine. "Now," he said to himself, "at least I won't have to put up with the taunts of that evil Penis anymore!" He blew out the candle and settled back to sleep.

A moment after that the candle rekindled as if by magic. The top of the copper sheath rose up like a tiny helmet. Penis peeked around cautiously and, finding Meersh deep in slumber, slipped free of him and scurried off, tittering, in search of more trouble.

". . . in search of more trouble," Soter solemnly finished. Leodora turned the lamp to the solid side and the great, lensed screen went dark.

The house had fallen completely silent once more, but this time it lasted for only a moment.

The applause exploded, almost solid in its force. The stage and booth poles shook, jolting Diverus from his trance. He dropped the chimes he'd played and hunched against the rear corner.

As Soter had often described it—as it had happened so often for Bardsham—the audience began to chant not the puppeteer's name, nor even Meersh's, but rather: "Pe-nis! Pe-nis!" Even though Soter had recounted it to her dozens of times, Leodora found herself howling with joy at the daft sound of it. She stood to take her bow again, but found that she couldn't move. A ghost hovered in the booth beside her, hearing the same cacophony from the audience; his hand rested with hers around the rods that controlled the puppet of Meersh. She could not see him clearly but only in the periphery, at the very edge of the visible, where she could just assemble an impression of his sparkling eyes, bright with pleasure, expressing such pride that her breath caught and the heat foretelling tears burned her cheeks. He had stood there—in the very spot—basked in this very afterglow of the performance. She retained no memory of his face, knowing it only from Soter's descriptions, yet she'd no doubt who was smiling upon her.

She managed to whisper: "Father."

A hand touched her opposite shoulder. She turned to find Diverus there, and in that instant the sound of the crowd, which had submerged below the strangeness, came roaring over her again.

The ghost of Bardsham was gone.

"Diverus," she said.

He took a step back. "The audience. Soter."

The words meant nothing. She couldn't focus on that. She turned to the open undaya case into which she placed each puppet after its use, grabbed the ribbons at both ends of the top boxes, and lifted them away.

"Lea, what is the matter?" Diverus asked.

"Him. You saw him. You must have." She handed the boxes to him, stacking them on his arms.

"Saw who?"

She tugged up the false bottom, holding her breath in anticipation . . . but his question penetrated. "You didn't see?"

Diverus studied her face, back and forth from eye to eye. Then he peered past her, into the box, and her own gaze traveled after his, into the recess where the powdery gray Coral Man lay, silent, calcified. Lifeless.

"I thought—" She broke off. Now the tears came and she couldn't explain why or what had happened. She wrapped her arms around Diverus, buried her face against his neck. His hands pressed tight to her back to hold her. He asked for no explanation. He let her weep.

The crowd thundered so loudly that the theater shook with their calls for "Jax!"

When Soter stuck his head in and saw them, he yelled, "Are you two insane— get out here!"

Diverus looked across at him, a face Soter had never seen before, one that was cold and protective and challenging. He understood then the nature of the embrace, if not its cause. Then he realized the Coral Man had been exposed and he reeled back. Whatever had happened, he could not venture in to find out its nature. He fled into the protective confines of his role, in which he had only to face the far less intimidating ire of an audience about to be disappointed in its demands. He waved his hands and hoped he could control them.

II
PONS ASINORUM

ONE

Diverus awoke far too early. The theater and its environs lay so dark and silent
that the only thing he could hear, lying in the small room, was the distant
chatter of morning birds in the fig trees along the boulevard. He rose onto his
knees, pushed the unlatched shutters apart, and leaned out the window for a
better look.

The boulevard lay off to the right, around the curve of the theater's white
stucco wall and just out of sight. His view was of the smooth wall of a neighboring building, purplish in the predawn light, with a single, dark window directly across from his own, its pane made of round colored quarrels of yellow
and red. He wondered if the quarrels would taste sweet if licked.

It had been three days since Jax's premiere performance on Colemaigne,
and it seemed to him that life had become a perpetual bustle ever since that
name had roared up into the sky. That first evening had provided a modicum
of what once had been a nightly occurrence here. Word had spread quickly,
and ever since there had been a line outside the entrance to the theater.

Sometimes it wound past the fig trees and as far along the boulevard as anyone could see; and as a result, Orinda had insisted they perform both mati-
nees and evening shows the next day and the next. Although Leodora had
complied, even repeating the same tales at each performance—which he'd
never seen her do before—it was clear to Diverus that she was reluctant to remain in the booth once she'd set down the last puppets. For her the space was
haunted. She said nothing, but she didn't have to. He knew her routine too
well, and knew when she'd deviated from it.

Now at each performance audiences flooded the theater, clogged the
aisles—and praise the gods there'd not been a fire or some other incident, because no one would have reached the exit alive.

The first night had been the maddest celebration he'd ever witnessed, far
more frenetic and dizzy than anything that had ever happened in the paidika.
Upon emerging from the booth, Leodora was immediately surrounded by a
crowd that rushed the stage to get near her, to touch her, to shout her name.
They sang toasts to Meersh and his penis, to Jax and her skills, and it had gone
on almost until the sun came up. Leodora had finally thrown off the effects
of whatever had happened to her in the booth and joined in the celebration,
drinking and cheering with the crowd. Soter, well lubricated much earlier,
even went so far as to embrace Diverus, calling him "my dear boy!" as if he
were some long-lost nephew. That familiarity evaporated the following day as
if it had never been, but the next audience was already hammering at the
doors for the upcoming performance and there was no time for reflection.
For the matinee they had to stretch awnings over the stage from the highest
projecting balcony, out past the thatch, to keep the sun from ruining the
shadows, and then they unleashed Jax on another penny-paying crowd.
Orinda might have been charging nearly nothing in those first days, but even
so they were making more money with each performance than they had on
Vijnagar or Hyakiyako.

It seemed to him that they'd been doing nothing but preparing for or re-
covering from performances, and if anything the crowds were getting larger.

Diverus ought to have been asleep; nor did he particularly want to be
awake, but now that he was, he couldn't help but brood over what had happened that first night in the booth, what was haunting his only friend. What
had Leodora seen? She would not say, but he knew, or thought he knew. The
Coral Man, who haunted her dreams, had appeared to her, beside her. She'd

called the apparition "Father" and then she had done the thing that truly terrified him. She had begun to cry. In an instant she had transformed from the enigma he all but worshipped into a child, a simple girl devastated by loss and loneliness, and while he had no words to explain himself, his heart ached with love for her the more because of it. His goddess was human, and she had turned to him for comfort. Even Soter, the cursed old bastard—even he had seen that. But the question—the real question—was what had *she* seen and what did it signify? The phantom hadn't reappeared since, but that proved nothing, did it? Standing behind her the first night, he hadn't detected any apparition in the booth. The statue in the bottom of the puppet case was just rock. Soter was terrified of it. She was haunted by it. Yet Diverus, who'd slept in the booth on top of the very case, had experienced nothing. His dreams . . . his dreams contained apparitions of another nature altogether.

Diverus drew back from the window and sat cross-legged on his bed.

The sphinx came to him in his dreams. Most of the time he didn't recollect the dream itself, but awoke with the image of her lingering in his mind, receding even as he recognized the desolate surroundings of his waking life and knew that she had come again. A few times it had been one of Bogrevil's milk-eyed afrits instead, descending from the cracked ceiling of the paidika to suck the life from him. But those dreams he remembered vividly. Those dreams jolted him awake. They weren't real. The afrits weren't real, but recalled.

He folded his arms and considered. Supposing that the sphinx *was* his mother, transformed or reborn in another world he could only access through dream—was it possible that the Coral Man was Leodora's father, also transformed, and that Bardsham also visited her in her dreams? It was as reasonable a speculation as any, although it didn't explain why the same ghost would terrorize Soter. Why should Soter fear Bardsham?

The old man thought Diverus hardly more than an idiot, and that was fine by him. He'd learned to play that role in the paidika. Soter had no idea that he was listening and watching, nor that he'd overheard enough drunken rants and whispered gibbering to know that Bardsham's ghost or something very like it was stalking Soter from span to span now. It had put him to flight twice. How long, Diverus wondered, would they stay here before the specter beset Soter again? It would be more difficult to convince Leodora to leave the Terrestre. The span of Colemaigne treated her like a treasure returned. Remembering the ovations, Diverus smiled, but as quickly frowned and shook his head.

Already his mind had wandered off the topic, which was whether or not the ghost of Bardsham traveled with them, and whether or not it emerged from that piece of cold chalky coral. He knew, as with everything else, that no one was going to enlighten him on the matter. Nobody had yet informed him what the Coral Man was doing in the box in the first place. If he wanted to know, he must find out himself. The notion of ghosts didn't frighten him. Compared with afrits, a human phantom was positively welcome.

He rose up, dressed, and then crept from his chamber and along the darkened hall.

The middle balcony had its own stairs to the back of the stage, something he had learned the second day, and he slid around the rear curtain, through the small doorway to the side, and down the darkened stairwell. It had a fusty smell to it. Cautiously, although he knew nobody was about, he eased open the door in the back wall of the stage and stepped out. Closing it again, he walked quickly, head down as if that would help obscure him, into the puppet booth.

The cases were as Leodora had left them, open upon their respective collapsible biers, the case on the left draped with the discarded puppets she'd used in last night's performance, with more piled inside. She wasn't lingering long enough anymore even to put them all away.

At the top of the pile was the hook-nosed figure of Meersh. Diverus took hold of Meersh's rods and lifted the puppet from the box. Then, clutching the two main rods in one hand, he raised the one that pushed Penis up from the body of the puppet. Penis was still sheathed in the yellow-dyed skin she placed on it to signify the transformation courtesy of the sun god. The larger body of the puppet was draped in a translucent gray membrane to reflect that it had been scorched. He thought of Meersh launching himself over the balcony and into the sea, and for an instant relived the memory of his mother's corpse sliding down the chute, down past the foul layers of habitation beneath Vijnagar and into the dark swirling waters around the piers. Such a small splash, instantly erased and untraceable. From that height, the water flow had created the illusion that it was the bridge that moved upon the water.

He set the puppet down and stepped away from the box.

The confined booth was stuffy. Behind the undaya cases, his instruments—shawm, theorbo, sarangi, piba—lay strewn around the pillow on which he sat as he played. He glanced up at the thatched roof far overhead, at the striped awning still unfurled against midday sunlight, at the wan light bleeding in. He let his eyelids lower halfway and tried to listen, to sense with his body what might hover around him, but apprehended no presence other than his own in there. No Coral Man, no Bardsham's ghost. He didn't want to deny Leodora what she'd seen, but he couldn't make it manifest for him. Why couldn't he experience what she had? That would unite them further, wouldn't it?

Stepping back beside his instruments, he reviewed how she had turned to him, her eyes welling with tears, her hair swinging like a great skein of rope behind her as she reached out for him, and he opened his arms to her, embraced her. Once more he smelled her as she pressed against him, and this time he let it stir him, and closed his eyes and fell into the memory and the sweet smell and the slick, sweaty feel of her. Gods, he loved the smell of her. For how long, he couldn't say, but eventually he became aware that he was standing with his arms curved, his hands pressed against a back that wasn't there, and he lowered his arms and sighed long and heavily.

He trudged to the rear of the booth and pushed his hands through the gap in the curtains beside the corner pole, emerging on stage. One of the wooden men, standing at center stage, jumped with mute surprise at the sight of him.

"Sorry, I didn't mean to startle you," Diverus said, and the wooden man pantomimed fluttering his hand as if to express that his heart was racing. Did they have hearts now that they were wood? He didn't know. Bois or Glaise—Diverus couldn't tell them apart, though Leodora seemed able to. Then the other one entered from the back of the stage and came up beside his partner. They shook hands as if they'd been formally introduced by someone, then both faced Diverus expectantly.

He thought it strange that he could understand them so well.

"Do you believe in ghosts?" he asked.

They looked at each other, then back at him. In unison, they gravely nodded.

"Have you ever seen one in this theater? I mean, a real one, not part of some play."

One of them shook his head immediately. The other gazed toward the ceiling while tapping one finger against his chin before he, too, shook his head. He then spread his hands in query.

"Leodora thinks she saw one in the booth, the first night we performed." One of them pointed at the puppet booth. "Yes, in there. I just wondered if the theater was known to be haunted. Orinda, the way she speaks of her husband, I thought maybe . . ."

Again they shook their heads, with obvious sadness this time.

"Well, there's my answer, then. Good morning, gentlemen." They bowed and he started to leave, but stopped after a few steps.

"I know. I've one other question. Are you acquainted with an upside-down span?"

This time they nodded in the affirmative.

"Is there a way there? Can you take me?"

They gestured back and forth at each other then, finally reaching some agreement, stepped up beside him, each with an arm slung over his shoulders, and impelled him to come along with them. They climbed down off the stage and walked up the center aisle of the theater, then down the ramp to the main doors, which were barred. One touched a finger to his lips and the other charily lifted the bar and opened one of the doors.

Outside, a few dozen people sat or lay dozing in the dark street. Diverus and the woodmen stepped quietly among them. Posters pasted on the wall, already ragged and torn, proclaimed JAX! in great squid-ink-black letters. Diverus supposed that was all anyone needed to say now. Her name had become a promise of a cornucopia of delights.

From the small street the trio strode up the boulevard only a few blocks before turning and entering a street Diverus hadn't been on before. It made a wide curve, and he supposed it must direct them around the far side of the theater and back toward the sea-lane that ran past the Dragon Bowl.

In the distance ahead, above the rooftops, the top of the bridge tower across the southern end of Colemaigne was cast golden by the early sunlight, its pennants flying languidly, dotting a parapet above an arcaded passageway that ran like the top of a wall the full width of the span.

The curving street did at last empty into the lane that ran along the sea edge of the span. This was the opposite end from where they'd arrived, though, with the Dragon Bowl a distant feature back the other way, a cup riding on the horizon.

The whole of the lane glistened in the light of dawn, the surfaces of the buildings reflecting like polished glass. The tower leg ahead was cylindrical, rising into a fluted turret on that end of the tower face. Unlike the few bridge towers he had encountered so far, the wall of this one appeared to be fully habitable across its length. Three rows of round windows lined it, interrupted in the middle by the archway of a great gate. Some of the windows were bright from lights flickering in the chambers within; the rounded bulwarks of attached and window-lined bastions jutted from it at regular intervals — perhaps ten of them across the breadth of Colemaigne.

The tower leg sank out of sight below the railing. Diverus, wedged between his guides, couldn't lean over the edge to see what lay below. He was being guided toward a small portcullis in the leg.

Along the front of the tower wall ran a wide avenue, still in deep shadow. Beneath the lowest tier of windows in the tower stood carts and makeshift stalls. The street itself was littered with confetti and streamers as if a parade had passed by earlier. Neither of the woodmen seemed to take any notice. They crossed it briskly.

The portcullis turned out to house a gate that opened on well-oiled hinges. Inside the tower leg, dank and dark, stairs spiraled down along a central shaft, and Diverus followed his companions in their descent beneath the surface of Colemaigne.

The pillar did not offer any windows or landings along the way. The light, what there was of it, came up the open shaft from the water far below, while the way to the top, so far as he could tell from leaning his head back, receded into darkness. There must have been doors to the various levels of habitation, but those likewise all must have been closed.

The trio spiraled to the bottom. There the exit was barred with another iron gate, and this one seemed to be locked, reminding Diverus all too uncomfortably of the paidika. While the woodmen fiddled with the latch, he circled the open well to the water in the middle. If the tower leg extended all the way to the seabed below, as it surely must, then there had to be holes or cracks in the stone, letting in the dark water.

Finally, the gate creaked open, and he looked up to see one of the woodmen lifting the lock aside. He followed them out onto a wide shelf that girdled the columnar leg. One peered over the edge. The other struck a pose and indicated that Diverus should look above.

He turned as the two of them glanced at each other with obvious consternation.

Overhead was a huge transverse arch, its ribs chalky with calciferous stalactites. It curved to the center of the span, where more support pillars jutted down. Beyond them another arch reached to the far side. Even at its lowest point the ceiling was high enough for small sailing vessels to pass, but it was nowhere near the height of the span, and there was no undercity there, no levels of desperate, squalid habitation as he had known beneath Vijnagar. The thicker structure didn't allow for them. Diverus said, "There's nothing at all."

The woodmen circled the tower leg, scanning the arch. They completed their circuit, then dejectedly came over to him and patted his shoulders.

"So," he said, "there *was* an inverted span up there once?"

In unison the two shrugged.

"You never actually saw it yourselves, did you?"

One shook his head. The other pressed fingers to thumbs repeatedly.

"Talk. You heard people talk of it."

The nearest woodman touched one finger to his nose and smiled, opening his hands as if to say they'd meant no harm. For all they knew, after all, it might have been here.

Diverus started to say that he had actually seen the place, then decided against it. What could they possibly add to what he already knew? He'd asked them if they had heard of it, and they had. There was nothing more they could tell him.

Disheartened, the two woodmen plodded back to the gate. Diverus ushered them along and then closed the gate after them, choosing to remain behind by himself. They reached through the bars for him, but he said, "No, I'll be fine. You tell them at the Terrestre where I am. I'll be along in a while."

He watched them climb out of sight, unable to explain to them why he felt compelled to linger when there was nothing to see. He couldn't have explained it to himself.

He sat on the shadowed side of the ledge, removed his sandals, and dangled his feet into the water, sloshing them back and forth and peering into the ripples. Sunlight reflected in the depths below him revealed the moss on the bridge support, thick tendrils of it waving lazily back and forth in green-gold depths full of darting fish. He tried to imagine a fathomless world where the light never reached. A kingdom in the depths. He'd conjured it once with childish ignorance, a place for his discarded mother to be reborn; but he wondered now what sort of creature *could* thrive in such darkness. Not someone he knew—not someone close. Rather, someone transformed beyond his knowing.

The undulating light upon the water and the tendrils of moss below proved hypnotic in combination, and his eyelids lowered. The tiny fish suddenly zipped away in all directions, and ripples hinted at a coalescing shape in the depths below. The light grazed the side of something pale that slipped into the shadows again. It should have jolted him alert but instead his eyes grew heavier, his head lolled, and he folded onto his side, dozing but also aware, as though in some lucid dream-state, of a shape sliding out of the water beside him. He heard small splashes, followed by a wet and supple emergence. Try as he might, he could not open his eyes, although—as if his eyelids had turned to glass—he saw at the rim of his vision a shape of milky skin, of round moon-like eyes. In his dream he instinctively recoiled from the horror that had once sucked in his thoughts, his memories, and would have absorbed his life, given more time. The afrit. He remembered Bogrevil, or was it Eskie, explaining that the creatures dwelling in the giant hookahs were water demons, repelled by light, forever rapacious, seeking an easy sup, so of course they would hang about piers in the hope of finding the occasional dozing watchman . . . or a fool musician who'd already been sampled and had about him the scent, the taste, of one already opened to them. It explained to him why he'd stayed behind: He'd been under the influence of the creature even before he saw it. Easy prey. And now he could not fend it off, the remnants of his conscious self urging his entranced body to resist but held motionless. He thought how Leodora didn't know where he was. No one knew, nor could help.

The pale shape edged close. It touched his cheek with gelid fingers, then crawled upon him. He strained and strained and in the end managed to open his eyes, or at least his dream-self did. He was staring into a face that was no afrit after all, but something entirely unfamiliar. The skin was bone white, and the eyes as fully black as marbles. Hair that wasn't hair hung about its face in wet, knotted strands of green and brown, parted about shell-like ears, and dripped upon him. Long sharp fingers tenderly combed his cheeks but could have flayed them. Soft slits in her throat waved open and closed. He felt her breasts pressing into him.

She smiled, her thin lips drawing back from a row of short bony fish teeth.

"Sing for me," he heard her say, and the music emerged out of him as it had out of the multicolored cat. Thus in an instant he remembered: the gods, an open pavilion with fountains and pools like no place he'd ever seen because it was no place he'd ever seen, it was Edgeworld, and beside one pool lay a cat that he'd been drawn to, that he'd touched and stroked, and which had stood up and produced the purest, most exquisite sound; then someone had proclaimed, "The choice is made," though he didn't understand what that meant at all, but the cat had licked him, opened its jaws wide as if yawning, except that the mouth had grown and grown until it surrounded him or he fell into it, tumbled down into darkness, into deeper depths of memory than he'd ever known before.

The light above receded. Somewhere below lay her home, his mother, and she, with the unraveling winding sheet waving above her like a ribbon, would come looking for him, would rise up to take him and never have him return to that living world of spans and bridges, spirals and magic and the confusion of what they all expected of him, whom the gods had shaped and fed to a cat. Farewell to them, farewell to the music. Farewell to Leodora. He whispered her name and it rippled through the waters. From high above came a distant reply. He cast his eyes toward the surface and through the green he saw her—pale skin and hair ablaze, Leodora in the beams of sunlight above, and he knew he didn't want to leave her. Not yet, not before she understood what she meant to him. Why couldn't she recognize that? It wasn't so much.

Far below lay the kingdom of the afterlife and if he turned back now, he would never arrive. Choose, demanded the situation, like the voice in Edgeworld. "Choose," said the apparition of his mother far below in her streaming pall.

Why was it either one or the other? He objected to the options even as he sensed that he was on Colemaigne, embraced by a dream that even now was withdrawing—never his mother at all. That was a layer of meaning pulled out of him, not one imposed by the creature. She wasn't stealing his soul; instead she was sharing, stirring his memories into her own. She had his and he had hers now, hints of it anyway, like flecks of sunlight scattered across the water's surface.

The image of Leodora blurred into striations, into colors woven through the green and the gold beams of light, with dark darting fish playing around her, all glittering, and then his real eyelids, which had been closed all along, parted, and the glittering light became the fierce brightness of the sun blazing upon his face. He was lying on the pier, on his back, and the sun had toured the sky until it was warming him where he slept. He could think Leodora's name but not make his lips obey enough to say it. He told his body to sit up and it refused. The most he accomplished was to turn his head enough to see the stones beside him. She was not there, the sea creature, but the puddle of water and the strands of seaweed assured him that she'd been no dream.

With enormous effort, he finally rolled over, dragging his legs out of the water. For how long she had embraced him he couldn't be sure, but the sun had moved up to midmorning position, so an hour or more at least. "Why," he protested to no one, "does it have to be *me* they come for?"

After a while he was able to get up unsteadily.

The puddle of water became a wide wet stripe leading to the gate into the bridge support, which now hung open. She had not gone back into the water.

He picked up his sandals as he tottered beside the trail. It narrowed and then, as he entered, the stripe separated into wet uneven ovals. He closed the gate behind him. Wet footprints with discernible toes climbed the stairs ahead of him, but shrank as they ascended until they were just smudges, vanishing altogether by the time he'd made it halfway up the spiral. Her feet had dried. He gave up, and had to sit and rest then.

The climb the rest of the way back to the surface seemed to take all morning.

The name of the street that ran along the tower was now visible, sunlight splashing across the carved plaque and the nearly redundant designation of TOWERSIDE THOROUGHFARE:

People moved about up and down its length. None of them appeared to be either a sea creature or naked. More likely she, whatever she was, had climbed to one of the levels above. He wondered how long she could endure out of the water, if she transformed utterly, becoming a land creature when it suited her, and if she did, then how many others of her kind had he met and never known? How many might have passed through the paidika? He shook his head, dismissing the matter. There was no way he could resolve it.

Music echoed off the buildings, tugging at him. He smelled food cooking and instinctively followed the scent. Though he might have been disoriented and uncertain from his encounter, he was ravenously hungry.

Shortly he came to a stand selling sweet buns, and he bought three. He'd eaten the first one by the time he paid. The others he ate as he continued walking. They were filled with some kind of fruit in a thick paste. He'd never tasted its like, and he determined to go back and buy more of them for everyone in the theater—but not until he'd taken in the scope of what had assembled on the thoroughfare while he slept.

He could only call it a fair, but it must have come together haphazardly. Citizens stood in clusters in front of various booths, most of which were nothing more than a few poles with a simple curtain across the front if they were closed, swept aside if they were doing business.

In short order he saw a jeweler—a horned faun—selling bracelets and necklaces, many of which dangled from its leathery wrists; a chandler peddling bulbous orange candles—according to a sign, these would replenish by day to be burned again by night; a huge, ogreish seller of knives and next to him a duo performing sword swallowing to the delight of a small crowd. Farther on, a woman with vestigial wings was juggling painted balls while balancing barefoot on a rope a few feet off the ground. These performers must have gathered as word got out that the ban had been lifted. Had they been waiting in their houses for a dozen years, practicing in secret, or were they newly arrived off the neighboring span of Sacbé, which after all lay just on the far side of the great tower gateway?

The central gateway was framed by figures carved in high relief, one male and one female. Seeing them, he stopped, turned, and approached. On the left was a winged male figure with arms pointing skyward above it, in the act of bursting from the pedestal base. It was an exciting, active figure, but he paid it hardly any mind after the first glance, because of the effigy to the right of the archway. It was a female figure with long unjointed arms that ended in sharp sinuous fingers. A wild halo of seaweed hair on which small shells and starfish balanced surrounded her face, which was not entirely human. The eyes, wide and as perfectly round as her breasts, were like the eyes of an afrit, blank and terrible, although he knew they were black. Her mouth smiled in fierce and irrefutable invitation. *Sing for me!* Her command echoed in his mind. The lower half of her body, emerging from the elaborate plinth as out of a fountain, appeared to metamorphose from flesh to scales. Her sex—the lowest part of her showing above the lip of the plinth—was masked by a ribbed shell. He raised his eyes to the circular windows dotting the whole length of the wall and wondered if such creatures lived behind each.

As he stood gawking, a stilt walker abruptly materialized out of the dark gateway before him, wearing loose bright blue-and-green skirts almost to the ground, scarves and clinking bracelets seemingly awhirl. Affixed to the walker's head was a grotesque and oversized laughing mask. Long, thickly woven strands of dark hair surrounded that face of japery. Then, in an impressive feat as he walked past, the walker somehow doubled over on the stilts and reached down to hand Diverus a coin. It was copper and bore a face like that of the stilt walker's mask on one side. He flipped it over, and a similarly distorted face snarled at him from the other side. Glancing up again, he watched the stilt walker pivot on one leg and then seemingly—at least from Diverus's perspective—continue along while walking backward, with the cruel face from the back of the coin now facing forward.

He watched transfixed as the giant figure strode nimbly around every impediment; meanwhile the laughing face jeered back at him like a taunt, a clown's jape. Encountering a group of people, the walker bent over again, parallel to the ground, and flung out more coins, then righted up, pivoted, placing the snarling face in the back once more, and strode on. Diverus could no longer be certain which was front and which back.

He pocketed the curious coin but chose not to follow. He'd been teased and tricked enough for one morning.

Later then, as he waited in line to purchase more of the sweet pastries for everyone in the theater, he gasped with the sudden realization that for the first time in his life he was alone and free in the world. He was with no one and no one knew where he was. He could have turned right then and run through that broad gate and into worlds unknown, or gone up inside that tower wall and hunted for the merwoman who'd beguiled him. And knowing that he could, he knew he never would. He never would abandon Leodora, the more so because she had handed him this gift of freedom. The merwoman had shown him he could embrace a death that he'd yearned toward secretly since the moment his mother had sunk from view in the underworld of Vijnagar—whether she'd intended to or not, the creature had proffered that choice. If he had accepted it . . . *She could have taken my life,* he thought. *If I'd agreed, she could have taken it easily.*

The desire to follow his mother into oblivion, which had been his unacknowledged companion since before he'd left the squalid undercity of Vijnagar, he now acknowledged and rejected. A threshold had been crossed, one he hadn't known he had to cross. He was Diverus now, free and complete and self-aware. Because of her, his human goddess.

"Diverus, you terrify me!"

"I didn't mean to. They were supposed to tell you where I was. Bois and Glaise." Diverus had given out the treats he'd brought back. Soter had glowered at him, but Soter always glowered. Sober, he seemed to have no other expression these days. But it was Leodora who chided him.

They'd gone into the booth, and she was setting up for the next performance. She chided him because his absence meant she couldn't be in the booth. She could no longer endure the space by herself. Alone.

He answered her charge by pointing out, "You go off all the time. You mount the span towers and overlook the bridge. You told me so. You hunt up stories. Why shouldn't I be free to go off, too, if I want? I mean, I could have run off and not come back. I'm free to do that now." He spoke the words of defiance as if surprised by them.

She set down the rod puppet of the fisherman, Chilingana, a figure from the second story she would perform today. "You know, you're absolutely right. Don't listen to me. I was worried, but Bois did explain they'd left you down at the waterside. It just, when you didn't come back . . . well, I don't know what I thought. That maybe you'd found the inverted span, that something had come out of the water and swallowed you, that you'd decided not to come back at all. All of those things, I guess. And how could I sit in here without you? If you'd never come back, we'd never have known what happened." She drew a breath, dismissing her careworn expression. "All the same, you're right. I suppose I cause Soter such terror every time I go off."

"So now you appreciate how Soter feels?" he teased.

"Let's not presume too much. I still mean to climb towers if I'm so inclined."

"This one will prove a strange journey. It's inhabited. It's like a great wide palace dividing the two spans."

She was intrigued. "Did you have any luck finding it, the Pons Asinorum?"

"The what?"

"That's what it's called, according to the porters down below—the inverted span is known as Pons Asinorum. The Fool's Bridge. Did you see it again?"

"No." He sighed, then muttered, "Fool's Bridge, that's what it is all right. Bois and Glaise told me they knew where it was, but it turned out what they really meant was that they'd *heard* about it being there, or heard of it being seen from there. Or something. But there's not even space for an underspan down there—no one's living there like on Vijnagar. It was just arches to let boats pass through. I don't see how the Pons . . ."

"Asinorum."

"I don't see how it could ever have appeared there. Besides, we saw it in the middle of the span, you and I, where the Dragon Bowl hangs."

"I think it doesn't appear in just one place," she answered. "It seems to come and go."

"Come and go," he repeated as if that had some other meaning. Then he brightened. "You probably will want to see the street fair. Where I purchased the buns, there's a fair, with all kinds of performers. Fortune-telling and sword swallowing and the like. A lot of them are different, not exactly human. It must be a good place to find more stories, with all those creatures."

"We should go this afternoon. You can take me there."

"I would like to, Leodora," he said, and tensed up. She heard the peculiar notes in his words, too, and stared at him curiously. He blushed under her scrutiny, and abruptly concentrated on arranging his instruments in order, an act that both of them knew to be superfluous: When she told him what story she was performing, he would grab the appropriate instrument regardless of what lay nearest.

She gently placed her hand on his shoulder. He turned to her much too fast. His features were twisted in misery. Before she could ask what was wrong, he took her face in his hands and kissed her. His lips crushed hers, his whole body trembling behind the kiss as if even the energy he needed to stand up was pouring from his lips. Then he let go, wrenching himself away as if to escape some intense force—let go and dove out of the booth, kicking the theorbo, which spun like a compass needle, coming to rest with the neck aimed at her.

She brought her fingers to her lips, and stared at the blackness of the booth. "Oh, gods," she whispered but couldn't move.

They didn't go to the fair. When the sun dipped below the theater's walls, Orinda let in the sizable crowd for the early performance. It was the last show in which she would charge a mere penny, and word had spread.

Until the time of the performance, Diverus could not be found anywhere. Soter strode about behind the stage, loudly complaining that he'd never trusted "the thankless boy" and that they should be glad he'd run off. Leodora was too lost in her own distress to object, leaving Soter to enumerate Diverus's various offenses: laziness, disrespect, thievery, and, worst of all, bad musicianship. Orinda, at the gate with Bois collecting the entrance fees, heard none of it, and Glaise—who could say nothing in anyone's defense anyway—ignored him.

Then Orinda returned and it was time to begin, and Leodora, ignoring the shouts and cheers, sullenly walked into the empty booth, while Soter continued quietly to denigrate the absent Diverus until Orinda said, "Hush!" with sufficient authority to shut him up.

It was at that point that Hamen and Meg appeared in the wings. They dragged between them a barely conscious and groaning Diverus. Dark purple stained his shirtfront.

Soter took one look at him and pronounced, "By the gods, the rascal's *drunk.*"

Orinda remarked, "Of course *you'd* recognize that." Soter twitched at her tone and held his tongue. To the two porters, she said, "Here, set him down."

"Very sorry about this, madam," replied Hamen, "but we didn't discover him until Melangia Street wanted lingonberry wine, and there he was, having hacked open a cask and drunk most of it hisself."

"What he isn't wearing, that is," Meg added. "Good thing Hamen recognized him. Most thieves get tossed off the span, we catch 'em, and I doubt too many survive the plummet."

"We'll pay for the wine, of course," Orinda said, and she offered them a handful of coins.

"We'll give it to Chork. It's his territory."

"We're about to begin a performance. Would you both care to stay?" she asked.

"Looks like you've got a full house already," Hamen said.

"We do, but I have a private box that can't be entered save from the back, and you're welcome to that. It gives a very good view of the screen."

They accepted her invitation with the rationalization that no one would miss them for an hour or two; but before Orinda led them away, she turned to Soter and said, "Get him to the booth so we can start."

"He can't play like this."

"Not from back here, no."

Soter snorted contempt, but withered under her steady gaze and dragged Diverus onto the stage. The crowd thought this was part of the show and hooted at them. Diverus stumbled free of him and lurched off to career in a circle until Soter could catch hold of him again, by which point the crowd was roaring. Soter cursed as he shoved Diverus through the opening, and Leodora, where she sat between the puppet cases, swiveled around. She watched Soter deposit his besotted burden with obvious contempt. Diverus collapsed in a heap amid his instruments.

"He's in his cups," Soter carped, "*and* at the start of a performance, too."

"So then, he's adopted you as a role model."

"You sound just like Orinda," Soter answered. "Does everyone hold so low an opinion of me?"

"Just the ones who know you." She said it almost as an afterthought, because her attention was on Diverus. She knelt beside him and helped him sit up. His head drooped, but he looked up at her with bleary eyes. She said his name. He focused on her briefly, then let his eyes roll and closed the eyelids.

"Lemme go," he slurred. "Just lemme go."

"I can't. You have to play now, you have to accompany me."

He shook his head.

"Lea, he can't—"

"Would you please shut up and get out of here? Go announce us. Do your job instead of weighing in on everyone else's!" She stared daggers at him until he left. Then she ministered to Diverus as best she could. She cupped his cheek, then picked out the shawm and placed it in his lap. "Here, I think you should use this."

"No, I . . ." He shook his head again. "I can't anymore. She tore it out of me, wanted my song."

"Who did?"

"The wraith. Water-wraith."

"What water-wraith?"

He tried to answer. She watched his mouth working to shape words. Finally he lowered his head in defeat. Only a few hours ago he'd been teasing her, asserting his newfound independence. Now he couldn't even explain what had happened to him.

From outside came Soter's call to order: "Hear-ye all! Welcome to the

Terrestre, returned like your span itself from the ash pit of the gods!" The crowd cheered.

Leodora left Diverus and returned to her seat before the screen. The puppets for the first tale were laid out there—the thief, the vizier, the princess, the emperor, and the dragons.

Overhead, dusk was coloring, darkening the sky. She lifted the flap on the screen, to which she'd already pinned the frame of a palace; she reached up with her other hand to turn the lantern on her cue. Peripherally she looked at Diverus, hunched over, motionless.

Soter finished his introduction, asking them to enjoy to the fullest the artfulness of Jax. Applause and whistling followed, the crowd rowdy and eager. She turned the lantern slowly to light the screen in the blue of evening.

From behind her, the eerie tenor of the shawm rose, tremulous, out of the booth, snaking up and around the theater like a lasso looped about them, drawing them tightly into its spell. As the last note of the introduction faded away, there wasn't a sound from the audience.

Leodora relaxed, let go of the lantern, and began the tale of the Druid's Egg.

TWO

The Druid's Egg was followed by the tale of "How Chilingana Brought Death into the World," although here in Colemaigne his name was Sparrowgrass and he shared certain ignoble traits with Meersh, and sometimes even replaced Meersh in stories. All of this Leodora had learned from Orinda.

At the end of the performance she stepped past Diverus and went out to take her bows. He, still in his trance, set down the wooden fish drum he'd played at the end in imitation of the rattling of Death's bones, and then lay upon his side between the santur and the drums. When she returned, she found him softly snoring, which struck her both as amusing and oddly endearing, reminding her of the gulf of unvoiced emotion between them. She didn't disturb him. The puppets lay strewn about, but there would be a second performance tonight and she would put things in order later. She had a few hours now, and at the moment what she wanted most was to speak to the one entity that must tell her what she wished to know. She left Diverus asleep on the floor.

She went to her tiny room and scooped up the Brazen Head.

Before she could ask it anything, Bois was at her door and gesturing furiously. Someone, it seemed, had come calling for her specifically. When she asked who, he made as if to stroke a huge plume coming off the top of his head, which she finally translated as someone of importance, at least in their own opinion, and from that arrived at the identity of the visitor: the governor of Colemaigne. She was wanted downstairs.

"All right," she said, "but in a minute."

Bois nodded and went off, his task complete.

When he'd gone, she dashed up the hall and through one of the balcony doorways, making sure no one saw her.

At the bottom of the ramp, before parting the curtains, she crouched low and waddled onto the balcony. It lay in shadow, the only light coming from the sconces around the theater below.

Sitting cross-legged on the floor, she held the pendant up by its chain. Its eyes were already open, staring back at her.

"You heard my question already, did you?"

"A shout can wake even the dead," the lion replied.

"Don't misdirect me with one of your riddles. Tell me true. How do I find Pons Asinorum?"

"Symmetry is the answer," it replied as though that explained everything.

"How so?"

"Looks to and fro, inside and outside, true and false. At once forward, at once backward."

"What looks to and fro?"

"Why, what you seek. That was your request."

"Why is it you can never just say *Go see Vorparal the Vintner and he'll have your answer*? Why is every answer a challenge?"

The lion yawned.

"Don't you dare go to sleep on me, you. I picked you and you *have* to counsel me."

"Just so. Then be warned that the thing that unites also divides."

"No clearer, beast."

"You stand on but one side of a reflection, yet exist on both sides together."

"That's no answer, either."

"Perhaps, but it frames the most important question." Then, infuriatingly, the lion waited for her prompt.

She withheld it as long as she could, but clearly the lion could outwait her. With a loud sigh, she said, "All right, what would the most important question *be*, then?"

Smiling, the lion answered: "From the other side, can you see yourself before your reflection? From the other side, does the mother see the daughter?"

"I don't understand. Do you mean does my reflection see me? Or something else entirely? Who's the mother?"

"It's a question of time. Time—"

"—is that which ends," she interjected angrily. "Yes, I know!"

The lion's brow lowered. "Not what I was going to say at all." His eyes closed, and he was inanimate once again.

"What were you going to say? Tell me!"

She shook the chain, but the lion didn't wake. She had a petulant urge to fling it at the wall, to smash it. But destroying it was hardly the way to get what she wanted. It would gain her nothing.

"I'm sorry," she told it. "I didn't mean to be impolite. Really." But of course she had; she'd responded as she would have with Soter. Unlike him, the pendant didn't have to abide her rudeness.

She understood that it had told her the truth in its fashion, and that she had to decipher what it had said. The head would argue, of course, that it wasn't being perversely elusive, it had to answer that way, just as she was compelled to prove her cleverness.

When she'd coaxed and cajoled further to no avail, she gave up and put the pendant back around her neck. Maybe it would wake again before she took it off for the next performance. For now the governor of Colemaigne awaited an audience with the redoubtable Jax and had been kept waiting long enough.

The huge table at the rear of the theater lay buried beneath silver trays, copper tureens, bottles, earthenware mugs, wicker platters, and assorted cutlery, all lit by a circle of tall candles and outside that circle another formed of servants. It was obvious the governor had brought his celebration with him. He sat at the far end of the feast. When Leodora entered the room, he looked to Orinda and asked, "Is it she?" and Orinda replied, "Yes," and he rose, beaming, as if Leodora in her gray tunic were royalty herself. He wore a powdered wig cascading in ringlets, and an embroidered salmon-colored coat with silver buttons down the front.

"I marvel," he said, "I marvel. The hands that work the rods."

Leodora flushed and lowered her eyes, embarrassed and thrilled, but he wasn't having any of her modesty. He came around the table and extended both his hands to take hers. His fingers flashed with a dozen rings. She obediently held hers out to him. He cupped them on his palms and then busied himself studying them; brushed his hands across her palms, felt her wrists, peered at her short nails. "Clearly, the hands of a young woman, so you are no ancient, accomplished crone in disguise. I can feel the strength here in the wrists, but truly the calluses at your fingertips offer the only definite clue to your craft."

Orinda, looking amused, explained, "M'lord is a student of hands."

"Palmistry, is it?" Soter guessed.

"Not at all," replied the governor, keeping Leodora's hands clasped in his. "Palmistry is absurd, mere physiognomy focused upon the hands. The idea that how you are shaped reveals your deep nature is ridiculous. Should we say that if you'd been born without hands you cannot live because you lack a lifeline or heartline to chart? Of course not.

"No, this is the art of observation. I look, I touch, I discover. It tells me what you do but it cannot tell me how well you do it, do you see? Your skill, that is not apparent beyond a certain equipoise, a balance to both hands. No, to know your skill I would have to see the performances themselves, which as it happens I've done now thrice. Your gifts, m'lady, are extraordinary and were I not chaste in my vows I would certainly chase you."

"Thank you," she said uncertainly.

He released her hands to roll up the sleeve of his coat so that he could reach across the mounds of food for a pastry that had caught his eye. "The burning question addressed to both of us is always, *How is it done?* Your craft looks like magic to we who lack the talent, exactly as my conjecture from observation looks like magic to those who don't notice how it's brought off." He waved his treat in the air. "Of course no one sees the hours of practice, trial, and error that go into the final performance, hey? They see only the culmination. The rest can but be inferred . . . can be nothing else, just as all of our citizens hear my judgments but cannot discern to what extent I have anguished over them, weighed discourse and debate to arrive at my answer."

Behind him Orinda was covering a smile. His servants were looking mildly embarrassed, too. Leodora intuited that, whatever the topic, he invariably brought the focus back to himself. She took a seat.

"The interdict on performance must have been a terrible burden, then," she said.

"Ah, before my time, that, and enacted by a body of jurists in any case. Mind you, I was on hand to witness the blighting itself."

"You saw it?"

His eyes looked inward for a moment, and he shuddered at the memory. "I was standing in the doorway of my house, no farther from Tophet than you are from the end of the room right now. I remember him huge and bright."

Tophet—it was a word the pendant had spoken. So it was a name. "Who was he?"

"A fiend. Tophet the Destroyer, the god who drinks life. He came from the other side of the world—at least that's what my father said. From a part of Shadowbridge where death reigns. He has drained the life from whole chains of spans, drunk their lives."

"Bright," she repeated. The image of him conjured by the governor was nothing like bright.

"Oh, yes," said the governor. "So bright that you couldn't look at his face, couldn't make out his features at all, as if his face was a great shining mask of metal lit by the sun. And the blight, now, that unfolded in front of me. It literally spread along the street right before my doorway. The stones crumbling, the figs on the trees shriveling up, the people . . ." He closed his eyes. "Had I stepped out into the street for a better look, I would have been turned to stone along with them. That is how those distant spans died. He simply willed it and it was so."

Leodora thought of Meg, pointing to the statue behind her: *That's me dad.* She imagined him, below the street, oblivious to the events above, to the decay sweeping inexorably toward him. Did he realize at the last moment? She doubted it. His petrified pose was of someone reaching to take hold of something. Life had changed that fast. It did, after all, didn't it? Outside of stories. Stories always painted the bigger pictures, showed you the terrible transformation approaching so that you, watching, listening, knew what was coming. It was more compelling that way, more horrible, really. People in the audience had been known to stand up and cry out warnings to characters— to the little thief in the Griffin's Egg tale, to the vagabond who spent the night with the woman known as the Fatal Bride. They knew what the characters, embedded in the story like insects in amber, could not perceive.

She realized that she had been sitting in silence too long. She said to the governor, "It must have been very hard for you, then, to *reverse* the ban."

"Indeed. The memory of that day haunts me still. But Tophet never returned. Neither he nor any of his ghoulish Agents has been seen since that day. Nor is the cause of his wrath present among us any longer."

It took her a moment to realize that he was referring to her father.

"Still, yes, difficult," he said. "I had to wrestle with the question of what was best for us all. All of Colemaigne. I decided that we'd hidden in the grayness of fear long enough." He beamed at her again. "And now that I've witnessed your art, I know I chose right. So please, no more darkening the night with reflections of the Destroyer. Come, sit, and tell me how many stories you know. That is the *real* secret *every*one wants to hear."

For the second show Leodora and Glaise propped Diverus into a sitting position, handed him the shawm, and hoped for the best. He moaned and complained in a sloomy way, but was too slurry-witted to do more. With his head down, his eyes closed, he muttered her name, but she had already taken her position beneath the lantern and Soter was already making introductions to the audience, and she didn't hear him. He barely heard himself. He sagged in defeat, his bones seemingly going soft. He had time for one final coherent thought—*This is how Soter goes through life*—before the tale was announced: "The Dream of Fortune." Immediately his comprehension of his surroundings evaporated. Then the spirit invaded him. He acquiesced—not that he could have fought against it, which would have been like fighting against an undertow. He let it have his arms to raise, his lips to shape around the reed. It was as if he were observing himself from outside his own body, as though the source of his skill wanted nothing to do with him in his disgraceful, besotted state.

Then he blinked and the sensation of separateness collapsed. He became bound to the song, living but a fraction of a second ahead of it, his fingers guided to the holes of the shawm as if born to it, flowing eerie trills to shiver the bones. Music filled his mind to the exclusion of everything else. He became forged of music.

When it ended, the tale, he collapsed in a gray slumber, insensate, out of which he arose only when the succeeding tale was announced. His conscious self didn't even hear his name, but his body took over, reached for the hourglass drum, which he could flex with his knees as he played.

Somewhere in the middle of that tale he began to sober up. An edge of self-awareness flowed through the movements as he drummed, as he picked up a guiro and scraped a stick along it to imitate the clacking of bones. *I am Diverus*, he repeated in his head. *I am Diverus, and Leodora—* He couldn't finish, wasn't even sure what it was he had intended to say. No, he wasn't all that sober after all. Besides, he had no idea what she thought of him now, and it didn't matter, not really. When he'd slept some, he would leave. If he was lucky, he would wake up in the middle of the night and nobody would miss him until he had gone far enough that he could begin as someone else, someone with no past, no name. He yearned to be the idiot that the gods had unmade, the simple creature that only felt things in a dumb way and didn't have to think them.

When the performance ended he sank down again, aware as at a distance of applause, of cheers and shouts. They were happening somewhere else to someone else. He drifted into unconsciousness beneath the roar of waves pouring over him. *Back into the water*, came the thought. Let it pull him under for good and let sea creatures feast on him, turn him into a new coral man.

He considered it a fitting end, imagining himself as the creature in the case, down below the puppets, and like the case his mind grew dark and silent.

It was while Bois and Glaise were carrying Diverus up the steps to his room that the copper coin fell from his pocket, bounced on the step, and came to rest on Leodora's bare foot.

In the light of the lamp she carried, she couldn't tell what it was, just something shiny. "Wait a moment," she called to the woodmen. She bent down and picked up the coin. Holding it up to the light, she muttered to them, "Go ahead, sorry, it fell from his clothes." The distorted face on the coin seemed to be leering at her. She was certain she'd never seen it before.

Up the stairs then while she held the coin between thumb and forefinger, she'd almost caught up with Bois and Glaise when idly she turned the coin to see the other side, the second face.

She stopped.

The two woodmen reached the hallway, where they waited for Leodora to catch up to them with the light. When she didn't arrive, they turned, but Leodora barely noticed them. She was hearing the lion as clearly as if it had just then awakened, saying to her: *At once forward, at once backward.* She flipped the coin over and over. "To and fro," she whispered.

When she looked up, Bois and Glaise at each end of the drooping body of Diverus faced each other like mirror images, almost identical in stance, in shape. But, she thought, nothing like the coin. It couldn't be that obvious and simple—the coin wasn't pointing the way to them. In any case, they had tried to show Diverus the Pons Asinorum and failed. They wanted to help but had admitted that they didn't know how. They knew only the stories that everyone else had heard. Yet viewed another way, perhaps they hadn't failed at all—not at their true task, which had been hidden even from them.

She sprang up the steps and then led the way to Diverus's room. The two men placed him upon his pallet. Leodora held up the lamp and showed them the coin. "Have you ever seen this?" she asked. They shook their heads with looks of apology. "It's all right, don't apologize. Now you go on, I'll attend to him."

Bois crossed his arms over his chest and looked farcically affectionate.

"You're wrong," she insisted. "It's nothing like that."

Glaise rolled his eyes as if to say he didn't believe her, either, and followed Bois out.

"I'm simply going to wait here," she said to no one.

She stood over him, the lamp held waist-high. Her hand holding the coin shadowed his face, and she lowered it. He winced as if the brighter light penetrated his sleep, but she didn't move to shield him again. His black hair was tousled and matted, his face shiny with sweat. Drink made him look feverish. Shortly, he began to snore.

She knelt to brush back his hair, and her hand touched his cheek. He needed to shave soon, or else grow out the hair on his jaw and chin. He couldn't remain in this median state between boy and man anymore. The paidika had cultivated the child in him, but that life was behind him forever. No one owned him any longer. His shirt, unlaced, showed his naked breastbone, the hollow of his belly almost to his navel, the rhythm of his breathing.

He was, she thought, very like the puppet of the little thief who stole the Druid's Egg and defeated the wizard. And won the princess.

A sharpness cut within her, and her nostrils flared. She knew what that tender sensation meant. Her heart suddenly had an edge. Each beat tore it loose. Each scored her. She put her hand to her throat. It slid down and grasped the pendant. Where was the counseling for this?

She could not remain here beside him or the pain would swell until it drove her to action. Looking at him in that moment, all she wanted was to lie beside him, with him.

She got up and backed away from her desire.

At the doorway, she pressed to the wall. Would there ever be a time when they could express such feelings, either of them? What sort of troupe would they be, then? She didn't know, only knew that now wasn't that time. Both of them were confused. Confusion had driven Diverus to drink. If only he had said . . . but the kiss had said it, hadn't it? He'd lost his words but had still expressed what he felt.

Realizing that, she suddenly understood him better. He was afraid of rejection, afraid that his were the *only* feelings in play, and so to avoid that pain he'd drowned his sensibility with drink. "Oh, Diverus," she whispered. He didn't stir. She fled the room.

In the hall she stood against the wall awhile, eyes closed, hand over the sleeping pendant. In all the time she had lived on Bouyan, she'd never felt anything like this for Tastion, although he'd wanted her to, and maybe he had felt thus himself.

Finally she slid down into a sitting position with her heels tucked close. The lamp rattled against the floor as she set it down, and she stared at it as if unable to recall what it was doing there. What she was doing there.

She must have dozed, because she came awake at the sound of a floorboard creaking in front of her, opened her eyes to see two legs that sprang past even as she raised her head. It was Diverus running.

"Wait!" she called and hobbled after him. Her left leg had fallen asleep and she pounded on her thigh to make the blood surge as she half stumbled down the stairs behind him. "Diverus!" she yelled, fearing as she did that she would awaken the whole of the Terrestre and the street outside as well; but when he threw open the door, she saw that it was not so dark, but the gray of early dawn. Diverus stopped abruptly in the doorway. She caught up and saw why.

Soter, wearing a green shawl, stood outside, blocking his way.

Diverus retreated inside, his head down, as if sure it had been a trap they'd planned for him. Soter, at his heels, looked at the two of them and asked, "What are you playing at, hey?"

Glum Diverus didn't answer. Leodora said, "What are *you* doing awake this early? I thought after all the celebrating you did last night, you'd be sleeping forever."

Soter didn't want to change the subject but felt compelled to defend himself. "In the first place, for all the celebrating, I in fact did very little. The governor talked incessantly and on every imaginable topic, and damned if he didn't repeatedly ensnare Orinda with his prattle. It was all I could do to keep him from running his hands under her clothes right in front of us. Other than that, you wouldn't notice, but I sleep very little these nights. Very little. Seems to be my nature, unlike *some* drunken louts." He stared accusingly at Diverus. "And now before you elude me altogether, I will ask once more. What are you two about?"

"We're off to look at something with two heads," she told him, and Diverus glanced at her from under his brows, an uncertain look that she attended with her own. The silent exchange did not go unnoticed by Soter.

"Listen to me, Leodora. You won't like what I'm going to say, but then you never do. Do not tangle yourself up with this boy, do you understand? No good ever comes of these affairs."

"Like Leandra and Bardsham?" she said.

"Exactly like—" He clamped his lips so tightly that the color drained from them. "That's not at all what I meant."

"Of course not, seeing as I'm the *no good* that came of that particular affair."

"I'm trying to warn you about something."

"Then you've done your job. I'm warned. Just as I have been by everything you've taught me. And one day, you are going to stop giving me warnings and tell me the truth about what lies behind them. Clearly that's not today." She pushed herself around both of them. "We'll be back later. Come on, Diverus." At least the boy had the decency to avert his eyes from Soter as he made his more tentative exit behind her.

Soter didn't watch them go. He didn't have to. He already knew what was developing between them, even if they still didn't admit to it. From the moment the gods had deposited her in that Dragon Bowl, Diverus all but mooned over her, and her quick defense now only proved to Soter that there was partiality on her side of it as well. It was their secret that wasn't a secret to anyone with eyes. He suspected that even Orinda had worked out why Diverus had been brought home drunk.

Fine, then, let them have their secret for the moment. Let them gambol about Colemaigne, collecting stories and kissing in alleys while he worried for their safety. He hadn't told them the truth, either, about why he wasn't besotted, why he hardly slept; but to explain his fear to them he would have had to tell them everything, including more about that *no good* union of Bardsham and her mother. There was no piece of it he could tell and not be forced into revealing all. That was Leodora, cut from the same cloth as her mother—not about to let anything go without an answer.

What they were up to could keep for now. He would find a way to address the problem of Diverus later—hire someone to get rid of him if no other methods worked. More pressing now was the very real need to come up with an excuse for leaving Colemaigne before history repeated itself, which it would surely do if, as Orinda and the governor claimed, they were drawing an audience now from four spans in either direction. Word was spreading here faster than it had on the other spans, faster even than it had in Bardsham's time. Soon her name would stretch the length of this spiral, and only the gods knew how far that was, how many spans. Sooner or later, word would reach the one person who mustn't hear of her. He feared that had already happened, and that death was on its way even now. *You'll be found,* the Coral Man had told him in his dream on Hyakiyako as a tentacle gripped his arm, and he suspected that statement would come back to haunt him wherever they went, no matter how many times he put them in a boat and sailed to another strand of spans, until he'd sailed them around the world and back again. It wouldn't matter. It was Fate the Coral Man had warned of. Inescapable Fate.

He looked at the fading mark on his wrist, the round red suction scar that told him it had been no dream, no illusion. It was a reminder ensuring that he didn't change his mind.

Soter hardly dared drink more than a cup anymore, certain that if he did that damned coral monster would return to gloat as it twisted his entrails with terror. If it was Bardsham's shade, then that shade was far crueler than its corporeal self had ever been. He mustn't lose control, because if he did that Destroyer would strike again. Destroyer—it certainly suited. Soter's whole life and livelihood had been destroyed.

He glanced out the door. "If he finds you, you'll wish those fishing folk in Tenikemac had drowned you," he said to the long-gone Leodora. "And so will I."

From there, Soter wandered through the darkened theater like a lost man, along the halls and then out onto the stage, where he strode boldy into the booth. He lifted the puppets out of one undaya case, pulled up the false bottom, and stood the case on end. Then he dragged Leodora's stool before it and sat down.

"Go on, then," he told the Coral Man. "Come out, emerge, manifest right here. Stride out of your box and scare me. Threaten me with doom." The figure did nothing, lifeless, all but faceless. Soter finally let go of his lingering terror. "No, I thought not, not when I'm watching, you can't. You know you can't scare me now, not compared with the fate that looms out there across the water. Why, you bastard? Why did she have to inherit your skill? Why could she not have been clumsy and stupid? Want me to admit that I thought I could minimize the attention she would get? Fine, I admit it. And it's not even enough that she's skillful, she has to be the favorite of the gods. Does *nobody* want her to live a long life? They'll come, you fool, the same as they did for you and that red-haired witch of yours. And this time, he'll obliterate this span, turn it into one of his sterile palaces, and she'll end up joining her mother in whatever abyss she's been consigned to. So come on, burst into being again and terrorize me, if you've anything left at all."

The Coral Man didn't move. It was as lifeless as rock, and nothing took shape in the darkness of the booth. Soter got up. "I'll go and sleep now, I think. Come and invade there, if you like, show up when I'm helpless to resist you. I'm tired of the burden of guilt. I'm tired of being responsible for your absence, and for the witch, too. It was *me* you should have confided in. Who'd been with you longer? Who *cared* for you? If you'd just given her up . . ."

There was no more to say. He could not make history revise itself. And anyway, the coral figure wasn't going to do anything, was it? He'd jettisoned Leandra's ghost on Bouyan, and now he would deny this one, too, its assaults upon him. The threats it had leveled in the past would not have a hold any longer. It was a piece of detritus, a shape fashioned by dead sea creatures. If anything of Bardsham lingered beneath that crusted surface, it didn't matter.

Bardsham wasn't the danger to him. Bardsham had done his damage already, long ago, to himself, to them all.

"And you stop haunting your daughter at night, too," he added. "It's enough that you inveigled your way into her life just so you could travel the spans one more time on her back. Leave the living alone, you chalky wretch. You hear me? Leave us alone!"

The figure stood as if at attention as Soter exited the booth. He glanced at it once more, then drew the cloth closed and stormed into the wings.

<hr>

THREE

At first Diverus walked slightly ahead, and neither of them spoke nor knew if the other's thoughts tracked anywhere near his or her own.

He strode from narrow lane to narrower alley, his movements sharp, turns brusque, as if daring her to keep up, as if angrily urging her to go her own way, to let him be. It soon became obvious to them both that he would not break into a run and try to get away, nor would she fall back or fail to match his every turn; and so he slowed enough to let her catch up. Yet even when she drew beside him, he continued to walk along as if unaware of her presence until, peripherally, he saw her reach toward him—he thought—to stop him. Instead, she held between her thumb and forefinger a copper coin identical to the one he had . . . or was it his? Now he turned to face her.

"You dropped this," she said.

He stared at her, anger beneath the gaze. "You stole it while I slept?"

"No," she replied firmly, "it fell from your trousers as Glaise and Bois carried you to your room last night. I wasn't about to return it to your pants myself while you were asleep."

As he reached for it, she closed her other hand over his. He gave an instinctive twitch in response to her touch, but took hold of the coin, and she opened her fingers beneath his and thereby pressed his hand between her two. He didn't try to pull away. In truth, he didn't want to. He came to a stop with her.

"Where did you get it?" she asked.

"The fair. The street fair I started to tell you about, where I thought you'd find more stories. Leodora, I—"

"Shh," she hushed him. "Don't speak it. I know what's there between us, the same as you do, but if we say it, either of us, then it becomes something we have to confront and act upon, and I don't know, Diverus, I don't know if I'm ready to compound the journey I'm already on with that one as well. I don't want to risk it."

He swallowed.

"It isn't because it's you, it isn't that you're unworthy or anything else that Soter might intimate. It's because I'm not certain of me."

"And if you were certain?"

"Then . . . we would have to see," she answered.

They stood a long while, gazing into each other's eyes, joined by their hands wrapped around the coin, in an alley lined with empty urns, debris, and rotting vegetables. She could not tell him that her fear arose more than anything from the Brazen Head's warning, *The thing that unites also divides*; that to speak aloud what was between them would set in motion some unpredictable destructive force that might sever them forever, an idea she could not bear. So in superstitious fashion she protected herself and him by not voicing anything.

Finally, she slid her hands away, and he lowered his. He said, softly, "I'll show you where I got it." They struck out then side by side.

The fair was assembling when they arrived, but they smelled it before they'd even reached Towerside Thoroughfare. Once again someone was cooking the sweet buns that Diverus had purchased, and because it was impossible to pass by the booth and not want one, they bought their breakfast before moving on.

As Diverus had described, the bridge tower was itself an inhabited structure with rows of windows, ledges, and small balconies across the breadth of the span. At the enormous gateway in its middle he drew up. "This is where he came from, the stilt walker who gave me the coin. Out of there." He pointed into the dark tunnel between the two statues.

"Then I suppose it's where we're going," she replied.

They walked beneath the gate, Diverus keeping his eye on the huge relief figure of the water creature that seemed to be undulating up the side of the tower. As they crossed into shadow, the spiked bottom of the barbican was just visible in its niche overhead. The tunnel floor was wet as well as dark. The grooves between the paving stones glistened with puddled water, the surface sloping on either side of the middle to a wide channel at the edges that appeared half filled with brackish standing water. The smell clogging the air beneath the arched ceiling suggested that sewage from the tower must drain somewhere close by—perhaps behind the various square grilles set in the wall at street level.

Past a pile of what appeared to be panels, poles, and uprights from dismantled stalls, two small fires clouded the air with a greasy haze. Dry sea grass lay in loose patches on the ground as if someone bedded for the night here in the tunnel, but they had gone now. Jars and boxes were piled up against the tunnel sides. Diverus drew Leodora's attention to a huge figure leaning against one such pile of red earthenware shards. "There," he said, "that's the one gave me the coin."

They walked up to the cowled stilt figure, which appeared to be napping against the wall. The hood was pulled so low that the grotesque masks matching the coin faces could not be seen beneath it. In all likelihood the walker had removed them to nap, but if so, its face in the depths of the cowl wasn't visible, either.

"Hello?" Leodora said. "Can you help us?" The figure remained utterly still. She extended her hand to Diverus for the coin. He flipped it to her. As it reached the apex of its arc, a gloved hand shot out from the loose folds of cloth and caught the coin. The stilt figure shifted away from the wall and hauled itself upright, so tall that its head appeared to brush the tunnel roof. The scarves draping it danced as in a breeze, as if to bewitch.

The stilt walker lifted the coin close to the cowl. "One of mine," it said, the voice sonorous but rough, reminding Leodora of the voice of Shumyzin and Diverus of the groan of the paidika gate on Vijnagar. "What is it I can do for you? Is it a story you're looking for?"

How did it know that about her? "I'm looking for the Pons Asinorum. I think you might be able to help me."

"No secrets from the storyteller. She wants to know it all." When the walker laughed, she was surprised the stones didn't shake apart. The black gloved hand emerged from the layers of cloth again, and the angular figure bent over her. It held something. She reached up to accept it. "I hope," said the stilt figure, "you are as fearless as you seem."

She felt a cold thing placed in her palm, and brought it down to eye level. It was a dark stone phial about the length of her smallest finger, but thicker around with two tiny pierced flanges through which a cord ran. The phial might have been malachite; she couldn't be certain in that uneven glow. One end of it was corked. Beneath it in her palm lay the copper coin.

"One drop upon a dark reflection," said the figure. "No more. And take care that you hold your destination in mind."

"A dark reflection?"

"No more," repeated the figure, and it canted over to the side and returned to leaning against the wall.

"Wait a moment," she said. "That's no better than my fool of a counselor. I don't know what you mean—whose dark reflection?"

Diverus took hold of some of the walker's blue-and-green skirt material and tugged.

"Hey!" came a cry from farther along the tunnel. "Stop that!"

They turned from the stilt figure. A tall, lithe woman dressed in a dark leotard was approaching them. She balanced something on the top of her head, which proved to be a mask. Another mask dangled from the strap in her hand. Diverus recognized the stilt figure's laughing face. "You won't get an answer out of him," the woman told them, "not without *me* in there."

"What do you mean?" Leodora asked.

"I mean, without me he doesn't walk, much less talk," said the woman. She was a head taller than Leodora. Cropped blond hair framed her face. She had a broad smile and a gap between her front teeth. "Clererca," she said. "A big puppet is all I am, really." She gestured to the stilt figure. "It's not going to do anything for you unless I'm in there among those scarves."

"But—"

"Say, *you* look familiar," she said to Diverus, then squinted more carefully at Leodora. "By the doors of Janus, you're the puppeteer. I saw your first night's show. The very first performance of Jax."

"That's her," Diverus answered.

She clutched Leodora's hand. "You don't know how grateful I am—we all are—for what you've done. Any of us who wanted to perform—we've been exiled to Sacbé for years. You've made it possible for us to have lives again in Colemaigne, to have a livelihood."

Leodora blushed. "Clererca," she said.

"That's right."

"Forgive me, but you say this figure is just your giant puppet."

"In a sense."

"He's not alive."

"Good grief, no. Not until I get inside him. Here, I'll show you." She ran around behind the figure and climbed the stacked pottery shards. "I have to set him down carefully, where there's a ladder or something I can use." She pulled up the back of the loose costume. "Has to be high enough to let me stand, you see." The figure shivered as Clererca slithered through the back of the costume, her head finally poking out beneath the dark cowl. She pushed the cowl back and drew the scowling mask down over her face. The other she hung on the back of her head. Then with both hands she pushed off hard from the wall and came upright. "There we are." She waved her hands, which were separate from and much shorter than the dangling arms of the figure. She shoved her hands down into the sleeves, and a moment later the stilt figure's arms waved about in front of it. Each hand held a coin. The figure seemed to bow and extend its arm to Leodora. The fingers parted and a copper coin dropped into her palm.

"What's he called?" Leodora asked.

"Cardeo, because he lives on the threshold of things."

"He certainly does that."

The figure of Cardeo spun about on one leg and now presented the laughing face.

"How do you walk backward that way?" asked Diverus.

"Practice," she answered. "A lot of practice. I'm sure the great Jax knows what I mean." Cardeo strode off in the direction of Towerside. "You be sure to find me when you come out into the thoroughfare. Let me introduce you," she called back. "They'll *all* want to meet the girl who healed Colemaigne."

Diverus walked up beside Leodora. "I don't understand. She wasn't in the puppet. She . . . how did it talk to us? How did it *move*?"

"Edgeworld," Leodora said.

The word set alight his memory—the memory pulled free by the wraith. "I remember now. Something happened, I didn't tell you, I didn't get to—but I remember."

"Remember what, Diverus?"

"Fountains jetting out of all kinds of colorful pools. And rainbows rippling on the surfaces of them as if oil had been poured upon the waters." His eyes closed. "The pavement was smooth beneath my feet, too, and the light, the sky, it was molten gold." He looked at her.

"Where was this?" she asked.

"In Edgeworld. I can remember Edgeworld now."

The incredulity on her face caused him to grab her hand and drag her out from beneath the arch. In the street there he turned her and pointed at the sea creature statue carved on the wall above. "One of those came out of the water. Bois and Glaise led me down to it, trying to show me the upside-down place. And they didn't, it wasn't there, but I stayed behind. And that came out of the water . . . It *did* something to me, and all of a sudden I could remember being in Edgeworld. Everything was so queer there. Golden. And this woman spoke to me, guided me about, told me to choose my prize. I can see her hands, long, purple nails curving from her fingers. Her face was hidden, hidden under a mask, or it *was* a mask with nothing under it. I'm not sure."

She searched through her own memory for something that matched his descriptions, but nothing did, not even a hint. She gently shook her head, recalling nothing.

Insistently he went on, "There was a cat. A huge cat. It perched on the edge of one of the pools. It had fur so long that it looked like quills, and all different colors flowed across it, the same as the pool. I remember that I went to it. The mask woman said *Choose*, and I chose it."

"And when you stroked it, the air filled with music," said Leodora in awe.

"That's right, that's why I went to it. People were stroking it and the music drew me. You saw it, too."

She squinted, staring hard into memory. "I can—I can almost see it, where I was. Not bright like yours. It was dark. Different. I can't—it won't let me see it. But I remember that cat, and someone stroked it and music came out of its mouth, and then they all tried to sing, to harmonize with it. I can almost see them, but they're gray like shadows. And there's someone talking to me."

"Telling you to choose."

"Yes." Her eyelids fluttered. "Oh, it's just right *there*," she said, frustration in her voice. "I can almost reach out and clutch it."

"It was a woman. She told you to pick."

"No, a man. A man spoke to me."

"She was, that is—the mask she wore was my mother's face."

"Like someone you knew," she agreed. "I think they trick us that way. The gods can look like anyone they want. They can be anything." She looked at the green-and-black phial in her palm. "We think we're acting upon our own whims and choices, but we're not. We're guided, ushered through the unseen pattern, some labyrinth or maze—like the world has all its spirals, we've each got our own." She pondered. "Our memories of Edgeworld could be called dark reflections, but you can't pour a potion on a memory. That can't be what it means."

He apprehended where her thoughts had led her, and he looked around as if expecting the answer to present itself. From the booth at the mouth of the tunnel, a large man in a sleeveless tunic emerged, carrying a bucket. He walked to where the gutter began and tipped the bucket, pouring gray and soapy water into it.

"The water," said Diverus, and he left Leodora and went back into the tunnel. Up the street the stilt walker was gesturing in her direction, but she turned to follow Diverus.

He stood at the side, overlooking the drainage channel there. The water, with bits of debris floating in it, looked black and greasy. When she came up beside him and peered down into it, she could make out both their faces, like flowing apparitions. "Can there be a darker reflection than this?" he asked.

"Water in shadows."

"Or at night," he added.

"Should we wait for night?"

"I don't know. If it was night, would we see our reflections in the water?"

"Not without a torch or a lamp. So then, maybe this is what it meant?" She smiled at him. "Only one way to find out, I suppose." She made to pull the cork from the phial.

"Only a drop, Cardeo said," he reminded her.

"I know." She tilted the phial ever so slightly. A thick drop of glowing blue liquid formed on the lip of it. The drop clung tenaciously as she held the container outstretched over the water.

"Jax!" called a voice, and she glanced up to see the stilt walker approaching along the thoroughfare and surrounded by dozens of people.

Diverus watched the blue drop let loose of the phial and start to fall. He recalled the other thing the figure had warned. "Leodora," he asked, drawing her attention back to the business at hand. "Where are we going?"

"Pons Asinorum," she answered as the drop hit the smooth surface in the drain.

"Jax," Clererca called, but her voice wavered strangely, as if the tunnel was distorting it. Diverus's hand found hers and gripped her tight as the blackness in the water turned bright and spread with impossible speed between the paving stones, then across them from every direction, congealing into a great oval, like a mirror. From the opposite side of the oval, oriented upside down to them, two faces looked back—ebony dark and with burning red eyes. Leodora thought of the Brazen Head's riddles, of reflections and of which side one stood upon, and she said, "I want to be on the other side." Still holding his hand, she placed one foot into the reflection. Diverus yelped as her weight fell through the reflection and tugged him in after her.

They stumbled as if they'd been running. She fell to her knees but stood up again immediately, compelled by fear. She faced a cherubic little man and a tall woman. Their eyes blazed like flames, and their skin was a dull blue. Their hair was black, shot through with oily blue streaks like reflections upon the wings of a raven. Their ears curved to points at the top, and their noses were long and sharp. The man babbled something that sounded like "Kadnari muus kelado pwee."

She shook her head that she didn't understand and happened to look up, which must have been down, for there far above/beneath her was a surface of luridly bronzed water. Vertigo rushed over her and she clawed at the air, certain she was about to fall away. Diverus tugged free of her hand and dropped to hands and knees on the metallic street above/below. She knew she must fall. No one could be upside down like this and not fall.

And then the world wheeled about her, the water was flowing overhead, spreading into a burnished liquid sky, and Diverus was kneeling by her feet.

On every span she'd entered there had been a moment of disorientation, of a membrane pierced, where everything was alien and incomprehensible; and invariably that moment yielded to sudden acclimation, to the strange made normal as the newly penetrated world enfolded and welcomed her. This was more expansive a transition than any other in that the world itself turned to give her balance.

The round-faced man grinned. "By your expression I see you've adjusted. That's capital. And your friend—I can't tell you how rare it is to have two travelers at once."

"Or really any travelers at all," the woman added.

"*And* of their own volition."

"Hush!"

"Where *have* we come?" Leodora asked, looking beyond the couple at the intensely colored buildings, which bore striking resemblance to those of Colemaigne.

"Where, she asks," he said to the woman, who laughed mellifluently and answered, "Nowhere and everywhere. Where you are depends on where you've been. We are the Pons Asinorum you sought because that's the name Colemaigne maintains in its thoughts. But we are known far and wide, as Nazar, as Breasail, as Yggdrasil and TirNaNog and a thousand more besides."

"How can that be?"

"We're the world of the timeless, of desire and elusion."

"It looks very much like Colemaigne. The buildings, I mean."

"Yes, but that's also because of how you arrived. Enter from, say, Palipon, and we are an island world full of cells, although ours are open, the inverse of a prison."

Leodora pondered that. Diverus shook his head in incomprehension. "What's Palipon?" he asked.

"Would it help," asked the woman, "if I told you that your upright world is connected everywhere below the surface by us, through us?"

"Connected to what?" said Leodora.

"To everything else, everywhere." Both of them grinned, and while their demeanor was outwardly gracious and jolly, beneath it lurked the slightest hint of something not quite as generous, as if some darker truth was not being shared.

"But you are our guests," said the man, "and you must stay. Feast, relax, and please yourselves in our company. Everyone will want to meet you, storyteller."

Her hosts turned. Leodora glanced again at Diverus. With his head, he gestured at her hand. She surreptitiously showed him the corked phial still clutched there and then slipped it into her tunic.

"I don't know if we should," she said. "We have a performance—"

The woman turned back to her. "Oh, but you cannot *refuse*. You're questing for stories and we have them, the oldest, the most arcane, the least retold, the original, the consigned to oblivion."

Over his shoulder, the man said, "We connect everything. We *are* story." He looked back. "It's why we've become your preoccupation. The omphalos of your obsession."

"What you *need*," the woman emphasized as she followed the man.

"What I need," Leodora repeated. Her voice seemed to come from someone else's mouth.

Diverus urgently said her name, but it barely penetrated. They, these people, had the world's stories. Many times over the years on Bouyan she had expressed a desire to Soter to travel to the mythical Library of Shadowbridge, there to retrieve all the stories that had ever been; but now she needn't bother. She could learn every one of them here.

Diverus clutched her arm. She stared at his hand and blinked away her disorientation.

"Diverus," she said. "Surely we can stay a few hours, hear a few stories before we have to go back. It's only morning, after all."

"I don't trust them," he said, but smiled pleasantly when the woman looked back. "I don't trust *here*. What sort of world can transmute the way they claim?"

She peered once more at the oceanic sky. "One that isn't real," she replied, "but let's find out more first, before we decide. Please? If they have all the stories . . ."

He could not deny her that possibility. He knew how much that mattered, but mistrusted the place all the more that they knew what to say to ensnare her.

Shortly they left the broad bright street of orange, red, and yellow houses for narrower crooked lanes of more subdued and empurpled tones. The street surface remained oddly metallic, with a sheen running through bands of color as if from various alloyed minerals. People greeted them as they passed, and then fell in after them. Glancing back, they found the way clogged with dozens and dozens of inhabitants.

"Does it ever rain?" asked Diverus, watching the liquid sky.

"Of course," the man remarked. "It falls up from the ground most nights."

They arrived before a decrepit hovel. The stone walls were cracked, the thatchwork bald in places. Sitting on a stool before the hut was a small fellow with hair and beard of silver. He had a table before him and, on it, a copper pot that he held inverted over some kind of spindle allowing him to rotate the pot, as he tapped at it with a tiny hammer. At their approach, he set the hammer down.

They drew up before him. "My lord," said the man to the tinker.

"Yes, Archimago?" the old fellow replied.

"Our guests." He gestured to Leodora and Diverus.

The tinker, hunched with age, stood stiffly, then shuffled forward with his hand out. "My lady," he said to Leodora. "An honor to meet you. And you, sir." Diverus gave an irresolute bow.

To Archimago the tinker said, "There's going to be a feast, then, isn't there?"

"Well, of course, of course."

"Ah, and what's it to be?"

"Boar," replied the woman.

"Oh. Lovely. Brought back from—"

"Yes. From a hunt."

"Brodamante, you fill me with rapture," he told her, and she made a deep and formal bow, her red eyes focused on Diverus as if she was demonstrating to him that *this* was how one bowed.

She straightened, then asked Leodora, "Is there anything you would like to ask of our king?"

Leodora's brow knitted. "Do you mean him?"

"Indeed."

"Oh. Well. How did . . . how did—"

"How did you come to be king?" Diverus asked.

The tinker pressed his hands together. "That is a story. It was time for a new king and as I am sure you know, the old king sends out an army of advisers to find a successor. They have so many questions to ask, a list of them, and they go absolutely everywhere asking them. And it's finally a matter of who gives the best answers.

"Well, I was here, right here at this table in fact, and was mending Miggins's kettle, which had a hole in it because he had gone and cut himself and they'd needed a pot to catch the blood in, and wouldn't you know they picked one that reacted badly to his blood, and it cracked open and so he bled all over the floor anyhow, and now his kettle was in need of mending to boot. And so while I'm staring at it, up comes this fellow in green pantaloons and waistcoat, and he says to me, 'What do you know?' And I tell him, 'I don't know anything at all for certain. Not a thing.' And it just happens that was the best answer anyone gave them, and they proclaimed me king. That very same morning. I wasn't even allowed to finish fixing Miggins's kettle."

"That's mad," Diverus responded.

" 'Tis," agreed Brodamante. "But it makes him the *best* king. As he knows nothing, he can but listen and decide, unprejudiced by strongly held opinions."

"But what if his advisers lie to him?" asked Leodora.

The blue people looked puzzled. "Why would they do such a thing?" Brodamante said.

"Greed?" she suggested.

"What an uncommon idea."

"Yes, unlikely," Archimago concurred thoughtfully. "We would have to cut off their heads. For a time anyway."

The old king shook his own head heavily. "Oh, I would hope never to have to decide such a matter as that. Life and death, what business is that of kings? No, no. I have my pots to fix. Much more important. You can't have a feast without pots. Can't eat without them."

"I suppose not," Leodora agreed.

"Of course not." And he settled back on the stump beside his table again. "I'll have to get this one repaired then."

Archimago's eyes shifted from the king to the guests. He pressed his hands together and said, "There, now you've met the king, we ought to . . ." He stopped as he turned about and found the lane choked with citizens as far as they could see. "Oh, dear. Should have known. We'll never get through there again."

Leodora looked back the way they'd come, and just for an instant way off in the background beyond the long and tightly packed crowd, she thought she saw a parade go marching by. She couldn't be certain—not at that distance—but she thought it looked like the parade of monsters from Hyakiyako.

Archimago, apparently seeing no distant parade, said, "They'll be wedged in for hours while they try to turn about and go home. Here, you two, follow me this way instead."

He led them past the old king, who was so intent upon his pot repair that he didn't seem to notice. Archimago opened a low door into the hovel. They had to crouch to enter. Straightening up on the far side, they found themselves in a large blue-tiled room as big as a palace, complete with a great sunken pool in the middle of it. Squares of lapis formed a band around the lip of the pool. To their left and past the pool, three rows of blue stone columns, nine columns in all, polished and smooth, held up a ceiling that was easily two stories above them. Beyond the columns lay an open courtyard where a fire was burning in a pit. The columns obscured most of it, but the smell coming from there made them salivate. To the right stood four more columns flanking an entryway.

Leodora turned just as Brodamante closed the small door, the interior side of which was bronze with decorations and shapes hammered into it. It had a large middle panel containing a cross-legged figure with long, thorny horns growing from its head.

Diverus commented, "This can't be the inside of his hut."

"Who claimed it was?" asked Archimago. "You are correct, not the inside of the hut but it *is* where we're feasting over that boar they're roasting right now. It will take the rest of the citizenry quite a while to get here from where we left them, as they can't take this shortcut. It's not allowed them."

"What is a boar?" asked Leodora.

"A very tasty meat, which comes from much farther away than you have. Brodamante hunted it herself." He strode over to the pool. "I think you should have a soak before the festivities. We would be most disrespectful hosts if we didn't allow you that."

"How," asked Diverus, "can you have a king that knows nothing?"

Brodamante replied, "Because he has the great wisdom to recognize that he does know nothing, and so, knowing nothing, he listens carefully to all persuasions before ever rendering a judgment. 'Tis the wisdom of innocence."

"I still don't see how, if he's that innocent, there's anything to stop someone trying to bribe or otherwise persuade his decision in their favor."

Brodamante and Archimago traded horrified glances. He said, "You have the most barbaric ideas I think we've ever heard, young man. Where do you come from? I want to stay away from there."

"Are such acts common in Colemaigne?" asked Brodamante.

"We wouldn't know. We're travelers."

"Well of course," Archimago said, as if that settled things, but he shivered as though at the horror of the notion of cheating, and the blue-black hair seemed to curl upon his brow as if alive. "Now, please, we have attendants who will assist you, and you must avail yourselves of our every service while you are guests here."

"Yes," said Leodora, "and we do appreciate this, but we also have a performance later this day—"

"Oh, but we won't keep you all *that* long. In fact all of Epama Epam will turn out for your performance . . . once you've bathed."

Leodora was certain the name of Epama Epam hadn't been among those Brodamante had named earlier, and she wondered if that was a different span or still another name for this place that was no place and every place at the same time. She had no chance to ponder it, however, as a cluster of four more of the blue, red-eyed creatures came running from behind the columns. The four wore diaphanous skirts that glittered with stars of gold, and all were naked from the waist up—two males and two females. Each had four arms.

"We leave you in most capable hands," said Archimago, and he laughed as if at a joke. Then he and Brodamante walked into the forest of columns from which the servants had come.

Leodora's attendants took her by the hands and shoulders and directed her to the opposite side of the pool. Then they disrobed her. She tried to stop them, but it was futile. One set of hands removed her belt while another unwrapped her tunic, fingers tugging on its hidden ties as if intimately familiar with it. The second attendant knelt and removed her boots and trousers while the first folded up the tunic and set it aside. When they turned away, she looped the phial around her neck again. In short order she stood naked save for it and the pendant. When one blue hand reached for the Brazen Head, she slapped it aside, and neither attendant tried again.

Her attendants led her to the water. There were semicircular steps below her, three of them. She put one foot in, discovering that the water was warm and also somehow oily, buoyant. She drew her foot out, and threads of blue ran between her toes. On each side of her the four-armed female attendants smiled warmly, but their eyes were fierce, eager, urgent. They moved onto the first step with her and gently compelled her deeper, down the next step, the hems of their skirts now immersed.

Across the pool Diverus was likewise naked and no less uncomfortable. He and his two attendants all but mirrored every move. On the second step, he stared back at her with wide eyes, his body lean and, she saw, aroused. The look in his eyes was of hunger, yearning, and fear, as though the emotions he felt shocked him. Those beside him looked at her with hunger alone. They were waiting for something to happen, and all that expectation focused on her. She puzzled as to why.

The Brazen Head spoke up suddenly, the voice such a shock that she nearly stumbled and fell in. "The waters of desire!" it proclaimed. "Of eternity, if you desire that, though I could not recommend it."

"I didn't ask."

"You did, but you didn't notice. It is no normal pool they wish you to enter."

The women beside her hissed and said, "Shush!" to the lion.

She stood in the pool to her thighs now, on the third step, and the attendants beside her, their skirts darkening from white to blue. "What if I go in?"

"Then what you desire will consume you. It is the opinion of those around you that you most desire your companion as he does you. Most travelers here arrive alone and are persuaded to stay, by a maiden or a gallant, by beauty or by indulgence upon which they are fixed. But you have brought your own."

"And the traveler swims in the pool," she said, "to what end?"

Behind her the girls urged, "Go on. You must. Don't listen to that."

"Bliss," the lion replied, "at a price."

"Go," said the attendants. "Swim."

Even as she hesitated, Diverus stepped into the water.

"Your friend is in. You must join him," urged the attendants.

"Why must I?"

Diverus swam into the center of the pool. His head went under, and when it came up it was blue, stained somehow by the water. He treaded water as if lost and unsure where to go, turning in a circle until he spied her. Then he swam straight to her. She held her place on the final step even though she was revealed, naked before him. He drew up below the step. His eyes burned into her. "Oh, Lea, I love you," he said.

"Go to him. Take him," the girls urged. "He wants you. You're his desire, all he can see. You feel the same, you know you do."

The tug of that desire almost drew her off the edge of the step but, tottering, she pulled away from it and fell back, with a splash, onto the second step. The two attendants stood over her. "You can't, you mustn't! He wants you. You want him."

She looked at Diverus, at the passion in his gaze. For her and nothing else. It was love without conditions or limits, and to resist it cut her like a searing blade. All the desire that had twisted inside him and driven him to flee from her, all that he'd held in check, denied, or confessed to himself alone— all of that blazed in his eyes. If she entered the pool with him it would bind them both. With all the passion of a thousand lovers from all the stories she knew, they would be the kitsune and the emperor, Akonadi and the Stone Man, the thief and the princess—the love that lived in dreams, in all of the stories. She would have all of that and more, an eternity of it, and she had only to surrender, let the color of bliss inundate her. Diverus already bathed in it, and she wanted that no less than he.

She could not bear the look in his eyes. It brought tears to her own. She closed them and answered through clenched teeth, "My greatest desire is not to remain here forever!"

The women gasped. "No one refuses," they cried. "No one can."

"*Enough!*"

The word echoed through the hall, off the columns and balconies. Even the water seemed to shiver. The hands let go of her. Leodora opened her eyes.

A figure emerged from the entryway and strode to the head of the pool. Light thrown off the pool danced across his fine red robe, so that it shimmered as if knit of liquid. His features, also subject to the rippling, were so transformed that she didn't immediately recognize him. Even without the reflected light he had changed completely. His hair had twisted into small spires like points on a crown, like the tips of his ears. His pale gray beard now hung in a row of skinny stalactites, which were mirrored in the smaller spikes that jutted up from his brows. No longer a ragged, simple tinker, he looked like a sea god, majestic, decisive, and terrible.

The attendants, both hers and those of Diverus, retreated from the pool as the king stepped to the head of it. "It's rare we have guests," he said. "But far, far rarer is the one who has the will to rove free among us. We know your traveling name and your profession, but tell me, lady, who *are* you?"

"My name is Leodora. My mother was Leandra. My father gave himself the name of Bardsham."

The king's eyes lowered and he smiled. "We know that name."

"So you knew me only as Jax."

"Just so."

"How? Was my coming foretold?"

"Not foretold. Inevitable." He swept his arm across the pool. The long sleeve of his robe seemed to flutter like a sail after the arm. "You may bathe now in comfort and contentment. No magic of ours will be thrust upon your will in there. It is become a pool of healing."

She glanced at Diverus, still moon-eyed below her. "What of my friend?"

"Your . . . lover is released as well, although the water has rather swiftly drawn his desire to the surface." He stepped out upon the water and walked to stand over Diverus. "He is susceptible. Has he perhaps encountered spirits of the water before now?"

"Afrits," she said. "On another span on another spiral."

"Oh, more recently than that, I think." He knelt upon the water as upon a sheet of glass and brushed one slender hand across Diverus's eyes. Eyelids fluttering, Diverus turned away from Leodora and focused on the king above him.

"Ah, yes, and he's been to Edgeworld."

The king of Epama Epam tilted his head and looked past Diverus then, into the distance past the rows of columns. "No conflation of such piquant rarity is possible. This can be no mere matter of destiny." He rose, and Diverus leaned back his head to follow him. The king gave a flick of his wrist, and Diverus went floating deeper into the pool.

"What does that mean?" she asked.

"That we surely have something you need, and our quest now will be to discover it together while you're here."

Leodora started to climb from the water, but the king held out a hand to stop her. "No. Swim in soothing waters. Your Diverus is unsorcelled now, although neither you nor I can suppress his true feelings that have emerged. After a time the attendants will bring you robes, and then the feast will go on. Whatever there is to unearth, it shall be found in time." He walked then across the pool as across a solid surface, stepping up onto the lapis stripe and then out between the columns.

When he had vanished from sight, she stood on the last step and clutched the pendant. "Counselor?" she called to it softly.

"Truth was spoken," said the lion. "Economical truth." It went back to sleep.

She glanced around at the attendants, who remained well back, no longer pushy, standing cowed instead, as though she might charge out of the pool and hit them. She could not say why exactly she believed the king, but she did. She turned from them and dove into the blue depths and was not consumed.

Applause filled the Terrestre, but it was not so enthusiastic as in the past—at least, that was how Soter heard it. He got up stiffly from the stool in front of the curtained screen, and turned to Bois. "You did very well. Very well, in-deed." Bois put down the lute and bowed his head. He gestured at the exit from the booth. "No," Soter told him. "They mustn't see me. They have to think Jax is still working the puppets, and they've seen her, some of them." Bois tilted back his chin as if to say he understood.

Soter stepped into a front corner of the booth, where he drew back the cloth along the side of one upright and surreptitiously peered out at the dis-persing audience. Glaise and Orinda ushered them up the aisles.

Soter stretched, and his spine popped and creaked, and he groaned. "This is too hard on an old man like me," he told Bois, who shook his head in de-nial. "We can go out now, I think."

Orinda met them on the stage. "You did it perfectly—both of you."

"I'm sure we were adequate at best," Soter remarked.

"Far better than adequate, you foolish old man. She learned everything from you, which means you've as much skill as she."

He snorted, but Orinda would not let him refuse the compliment.

"She's more talented than any of us," she said, "probably all of us put to-gether, but her skill comes from a man who spends half his time arguing with her over what he thinks is best and the other half pretending he has nothing to do with who she is at all. You'd do well, Soter, to inhabit one of those roles and dispense with the other."

He wrapped one hand about his lower face and gave a small grunt that was part scoff and part chortle. Then he remarked, "All the same, what are we to do?"

She placed a hand on his arm. "We are going to hope they return shortly. If not, we're going to put on the show tomorrow as we did this one. In the meantime, we cast our nets farther. Bois and Glaise will cover the whole of the span and go on to the next if need be." The woodmen nodded their en-thusiasm and made to set off.

Soter said, "You'll want to contact Hamen and those underspan dwellers. They seem to hear of everything."

"That's a very good idea."

"Well . . . he seemed a decent enough fellow." He clasped his head in his hands. "I don't understand, Orinda. She's much too careful, too clever. If she went off to gather stories, she wouldn't forget the evening performance."

"Of course you're right. So we have to assume something important or terrible has kept them away, and probably against their will."

"Tophet's Agents . . . ," he muttered.

"Oh, surely not. Bardsham is long dead. What could Tophet want with her? Or with you?"

"She's his daughter. And no one knows for certain that Bardsham died. No one witnessed his death, no one hereabouts. What if Tophet doesn't know any more than we do as to the fate of Bardsham? Then he might think—"

"If that were true, Colemaigne would right now lie in ruin. We'd be dead and stone, every one of us, exactly as the governor described. That monster doesn't spirit people away. He punishes them without mercy and sups on their marrow." Her gaze slid side-to-side watching him, as if she looked for some sign of concurrence in his eyes. "Furthermore, outside of here, how could he recognize them? If he believed Bardsham were on the loose, he would be looking for a man he knows, not a young woman and her beau."

"Her beau?"

"Oh, dear, do you think I'm blind to love that runs as deep as that?"

"Nonsense."

She laughed gently, but with a teasing edge. "You know it as well as I. It's why you object to him so. You think to guard her even from her own feelings. It's time to stop doing that and let her feel. If you want to keep her affections, Soter, you have to let her take wing."

He stared into her eyes and his own grew hot. Orinda knew too much of him, nearly the truth of him; but he knew the rest and could never admit it to her. He nodded heavily and swallowed the anguish of tenderness. "I'm sure you're right about Tophet. But then there is *no* explanation, is there?"

"None as yet, my dear. None as yet." She linked her arm in his. "Come with me now. We should eat something before you exhaust yourself."

He let her lead him through the wings and the hallways. He felt quite suddenly a thousand years old and as helpless as a newborn. Where in all the world had his Leodora gone?

"I believe a story is in order," said the king.

Leodora, feeling warm and sleepy from the food and drink she had shared with them, drew her legs beneath her and smoothed the dark purple robe she wore. She asked, "And who's to tell it, sir?" then waved her hands about. "I have no puppets here."

A few of the dozen feasters smiled. They were all clustered close around the fire.

The king tugged on the sharp tip of his nose and became for the moment contemplative. Then his eyes brightened and he told her, "Hold your hands out thus." He spread his hands before him with the palms up.

Leodora imitated him. He arose and stepped to the fire pit, where he reached down into the embers. When he turned back to her, his hands seemed to be ablaze. He cupped them and blew into them, a visible breath as if the air had chilled about him. Opening the palms side by side as if reading them, he blew sharply once more and strode up to her. Then, leaning down, he parted his hands across hers; six flames tumbled onto her palms. The flames were colored greenish blue and didn't burn her hands at all. She moved her palms back and forth, and the fires slid upon them. She glanced up from the magical flames. "What do I do?" she asked.

"Now," said the king, "you pick a story and hold the image of the characters in your mind. Try it. Pick any."

She brought her face closer to her hand and concentrated. The most obvious character to imagine was Meersh, and immediately one of the flames swirled and grew, forming into a tall, gangly body in worn loose trousers and a vest, his nose hooked and crooked, his chin sharp, his eyes sharper, and his orange hair a tangle around his head. He looked at himself as if surprised to be there, then at his audience. He stepped to the edge of her hand and stuck his tongue out at them.

The members of the feast roared with laughter, even Diverus. Here was Meersh as only she could realize him.

With a delighted smile she gazed at the king again, and the figure unraveled and shrank to a green flame.

"There you have what will pass, I think, for puppets. Let us begin the storytelling."

She traded a glance with Diverus and was about to ask them if they would equip him with musical instruments to accompany her, but some instinct prevented her from mentioning his gift. She gave him a smile of reassurance instead. Then she focused on the flames, and settled upon one of the stories she had been performing on Colemaigne. The flame that had been Meersh coiled and shaped into the form of a man wearing a tattered cap, a striped shirt, and loose trousers that fell just below his knees. She looked up at her strange audience and began.

THE DREAM OF A FORTUNE

There once was a poor man who had no hope. His name is recorded as Loctrean, and he lived in an old, dilapidated house in the span of Guhnavra, which lay on a spiral far from here. He lived with his father and mother and sister.

His father was a dreamer, a teller of tales who was very popular at the local tavern because he always had a story and enough coin to buy his audience a round, and if they disbelieved his adventures, the free drink bought their complaisance.

The father claimed to have been a sailor on board the ship of the mythical Captain Sindebad, to have walked in exotic lands, seen impossible monsters, and sailed to the very edge of Shadowbridge and back. "Believe me," he would assure his audiences, "there is an edge of the world."

At home he told the same tales to his children, filling their heads with dazzling images, breathtaking adventures, and promises that one day they would all be terribly rich; but when he was off fishing, their mother would say, "The truth is, your father hasn't been anywhere at all. The only place *he's* sailed is inside his head." The children would have preferred not to know this, but they were children and at the mercy of the adults. Loctrean in particular wanted his father to be the adventurer of those wonderful stories.

His life might have gone on like that forever, except that one evening his father didn't return from the day's fishing, and no one knew at first what had befallen him. Eventually, other sailors found his father's boat and dragged it into the cracked and broken courtyard of the house. The keel had been shattered, a hole punched in it as if upon a sharp point of rock, and the sailors left it overturned there. Of his father they had found no sign. Loctrean overheard the superstitious sailors whispering that the gods had struck down his father for all the lies he'd told, and Loctrean burst upon them, shouting, "He didn't lie! He did travel far, he *did* have adventures!" But despite his defense, he was ashamed, though whether for himself or for his father, he didn't know.

It wasn't long after that before his mother succumbed to a wasting disease, a lingering, slow, and expensive disease. Paying for her medicine cost the family nearly everything they had. Before she died, she clutched her son close and whispered that she'd lied about his father because she was jealous. "He never took me on a single one of his adventures," she said, "even though I wanted to go. He hurt me, but he didn't lie to you." Now, she said, she was embarking on her own adventure at last. Then she closed her eyes and died.

In short order, then, he lost both of his parents and found himself suddenly an orphan with a sister to care for.

Loctrean inherited his father's house and the fishing boat, which is to say he inherited debt. The house fell into further disrepair. He couldn't afford so much as to replace the wine-colored awning over the door, which was too threadbare to keep even light rain from spilling through.

His father's boat remained in the courtyard. Its smashed planks grew so rotten that it would never be seaworthy again. He felt like that boat, as if a hole had been punched through him, never to be healed.

He could not repair the boat in order to fish, which was all he knew how to do, nor could he afford to buy a new one. There were a few fishing crews the span but none of them would hire him as they believed he was the same as his father, a dreamer who would be a danger to the others who sailed with him. Even the kindest of them explained to him that they couldn't take such a risk.

The only good news came when his sister married a neighboring grocer. The grocer made just enough money for the two of them and had nothing left over to help with the debts their father had left, but at least his sister was looked after, and Loctrean took solace in that.

He accepted that he was going to lose his father's house and there was nothing he could do about it. He determined that he must sell the property for whatever he could get, pay off all the debts, and use whatever was left over to start again somewhere else.

The night he made this decision, however, Loctrean's father appeared to him in a dream. "You must close up the house," said the vision, "but not sell it. Then travel to the span of Perla. There you will find your fortune."

"So it's true, you are dead," Loctrean said sadly.

"I drowned. It wasn't any fun."

"And how is Mother?" he asked.

"No longer in pain," his father's shade replied. "You were a good son to her. A good brother to your sister, too."

"Thank you," he said, and a longing to embrace his father welled up inside him. He wanted to reach out and hug the man, but in the dream he seemed unable to do anything but stand and observe.

"Never mind all that," his father admonished him. "Just wake up and go!" With that the dream ended, and Loctrean awoke.

Well, he thought, *I suppose it's no worse an idea than what I was* going *to do. I wish, though, I'd asked him to tell me one of his stories. That would have been nice.*

As instructed, Loctrean closed up the house, and with his remaining coins he set out for Perla.

Perla was an ancient town built upon a broad peninsula of land that jutted off the side of a span far removed from Guhnavra. It wasn't even on the shore; to get to it, a boat had to sail up a dark and forbidding river. Perla had a reputation as a dark place, surrounded by marshes and swamps, ghostly lights, and thieves who preyed upon the spans above. The air was tinged with the stink of sulfur long before the city came into view. Loctrean couldn't help but wonder why his father was sending him there of all places, or even how his father might have been familiar with it. Still, he could not imagine refusing to obey the wishes of his father's shade, and he booked passage on a ship that took him as far as the nearest spiral; there he had to sign on as a crew member to make the remainder of the journey. The captain of that ship worked him hard, too. He learned to tack and wear, to sound depths, and even to bake biscuits for the crew. There was no job aboard ship that he didn't learn before they had reached the mouth of the Black River.

The smell of the noxious city arrived long before they caught sight of it. Upon both sides of the river, strange lights danced in the mists. Some of the crew cowered at the sight of them, but Loctrean was unimpressed. He'd heard of far scarier things at his father's knee than bobbing lights in the fog. Besides, his father's ghost had told him to go to Perla, and so he remained confident that no harm would come to him on the journey. There was a reason he was here, and he must find it.

Once the boat arrived and tied up at the wharf, Loctrean took his leave.

Of course he didn't know what to do now that he had arrived. His father had not been specific at all about what to do once he got to Perla, only that he should go.

He walked the whole length of the city, and as anyone who's been there can attest, it's a long, narrow place, trapped between the swamps and woods on the one side and great hulking piers of the spiral on the other. Loctrean walked to the far outskirts of Perla without discovering anything. He was penniless and hungry, and had no idea what to look for or where to look for it.

A rain began to fall. First there was a drizzle, and then the skies opened up and a torrent poured down as if upon him alone.

An ancient, domed fane stood at the edge of the city there, on the last street before the city wall. Multiple rows of columns lined the front of the old temple, all of them gouged and pocked from centuries of bitter sulfurous rain. Loctrean hid beneath the roof that the columns supported, and while there he looked inside. The interior was dark and quiet and cool, filled with still more slender columns like a forest thick with trees. Small rugs were strewn everywhere. No rain dripped there. In fact, dust hung in the air. No one was praying or attending. He couldn't fathom to what deity the fane had been built in the first place—all icons and statues seemed to have been removed, or stolen—but it was dry and offered protection from the rain. He found a secluded alcove, curled up, and went to sleep. He hoped his father would show up again and tell him what to do.

Instead, while penniless Loctrean slept, a group of thieves crept into the fane. They had been coming there nightly for weeks. Each night they chiseled and loosened the mortar around a stone that, once removed, would give them access to a usurer's shop that abutted the old temple wall. The moneylender was a true fiend but known to be enormously wealthy. The thieves intended to kill him and rob him of his obscene fortune. The previous night they had succeeded in removing the large stone on which they'd been working for weeks, lifting it from the wall of the fane. Now they worked even more cautiously but urgently to remove the smaller bricks from the wall of the adjoining house. What they failed to take into account was the usurer's penchant for staying up late into the night to count his fortune. He had blacked all the windows where he kept the money so that no one could see inside. To the thieves it appeared that he'd retired for the night.

Thus the evil usurer, sitting in the very room they intended to plunder, was alerted to their intrusion. He blew out his candle and waited.

At last, the thieves removed enough smaller bricks in his wall to allow one man to slide through. Triumphantly, their leader insisted he should have the first look, and he stuck his head into the hole, only to find a cackling madman awaiting him, brandishing a scimitar.

When his feet frantically kicked out, his friends hauled the thief back into the temple only to discover that his head had been lopped off. Even as they stared in horror, the alarm was sounded. The usurer had rushed into the street and bellowed for the police. The thieves dropped the corpse of their leader and fled.

Poor Loctrean awoke to their commotion. He stumbled from his alcove just as the authorities arrived.

"Here's one!" shouted a deputy, and the police fell upon him and beat him senseless. Of the gang they found only the headless body.

They dragged Loctrean to the jail and threw him inside. He lay battered and bleeding upon his cot that night, and thought, *This is not what I came here for.*

The following day he was hauled before the chief magistrate. Bloody and bruised, he could only insist that he knew nothing of any robbery beyond what they themselves knew. The usurer of course demanded his execution on the spot, but that only infuriated the magistrate and swayed him toward more leniency than he might otherwise have shown his suspect.

"If I were a thief," Loctrean explained, "would I have waited to be captured, sir? Did you capture any others of this gang waiting in the dark? Any who still had their heads, I mean. Why would I have lingered?"

The magistrate sensed that he was hearing the truth. "What were you doing there, then?" he asked. "No one has worshipped in that temple for years."

So Loctrean explained his situation, his poverty, and how his father's ghost had appeared in a dream and advised him to seek his fortune here.

"You mean to say you sailed all the way from Guhnavra because of a dream? You're crazy, do you know that? Acting upon such things. I myself was visited just the other night in my dreams by a woman who told me she knew of a house where a great treasure lay buried."

"Did you find the house?" asked Loctrean.

The magistrate sighed. "You haven't been paying attention, have you? The woman and her treasure aren't *real*. In the first place, such a house doesn't even exist in Perla. It looks nothing like houses here. It was a square-topped place, with an old purple-striped awning and a rotted boat in one corner of the courtyard and a dried-up, broken old fountain in another. Crumbling old place, the sort of thing one sees only in dreams. Furthermore, and even more ludicrous, she insisted that the hidden treasure had come from the legendary Captain Sindebad. Well, I mean, *really*. It's a fairy tale, isn't it? Something recalled from my childhood no doubt and brought back by some turnips or bad beer."

Excitedly, Loctrean asked, "This treasure, where was it hidden?"

"How should I know that? I woke up, didn't I? Haven't you heard a thing I've said, this isn't . . . oh, never mind." The magistrate saw that the matter was hopeless. He had a simpleton here who could neither have robbed the usurer nor comprehended that the world did not operate via magical dreams.

"Listen, the best thing you can do, fellow, is go home and stop attending to these fantasies. Learn a trade. Establish yourself." He took out a small purse and placed two coins on the table. "Here," he said, "because we beat you and I'm certain you're innocent. Naïve, gullible, but innocent. Go home, my friend."

Loctrean thanked the magistrate and limped stiffly out of the police barracks.

He used the coins to buy part of his passage home on the same ship that had brought him. As before it wasn't enough, but the crew were happy to have him because his cooking had proved better than anyone else's. All the same, they taunted him. "Didn't find that treasure after all?" they asked. "No magic beans, no djinn in a bottle floating in that foul river just waiting for you?" He hardly paid them any mind, because he was fearful that something might have happened to his house meanwhile. However, it awaited him as he had left it, save for a few more rodents as tenants in the growing holes of its walls. The awning had finally split in two and hung down in shreds.

Loctrean entered the house and began searching everywhere. The woman in the magistrate's dream—surely it was his mother—had said that the treasure was buried, and he pulled up every stone in every room only to find dirt or sand or mice beneath. Exhausted, he went out and collapsed in the courtyard against the boat.

From there he found himself staring directly at the fountain pedestal. Hadn't the magistrate made mention of the fountain?

He got up, and even as he did, the stones beneath the fountain cracked, and it tilted slowly to one side.

Loctrean climbed over the retaining wall and into the dustbowl that had once been a shallow pond. He grabbed the canted pedestal and began wrenching it back and forth until it came away completely.

Pushing it aside, he stared into a dry hole where, presumably, water had once upon a time been channeled. He knelt and then lay amid the rubble and reached his arm down into the hole. His fingers touched the sides of a cloth bag. He caught hold of it and dragged it up onto the stones. It was heavy and thick, the neck tied with a cord. The outer layer of cloth had frayed, but there were at least two more layers beneath that one. He heard the coins before he saw them. When they spilled out, they were so big that he couldn't circle his fingers around them. They had strange writing on them, and faces of some other span's gods or emperors stamped onto one side. Loctrean had never seen any coins like them. One bag, he thought, must be worth a fortune. He lay on the tiles again and reached into the hole, and his fingers touched a second bag. He drew it out, and this one contained gems: rubies and sapphires, diamonds and emeralds. It was a fortune for a king.

Kneeling there in the dust he praised his father for telling the truth, even though no one had ever believed him. He *had* sailed with the mythical Sindebad. Here was the proof.

That night Loctrean had another dream. In it his father apologized for not telling him about the fortune years earlier. "I kept it hidden," he said, "because I wanted you and your sister to grow up unspoiled by riches, to know what it was like to have to work, to earn your way, the way almost everyone must. I wasn't supposed to have an accident."

After that, Loctrean saw both his parents from time to time in his dreams. His mother would tell him some incredible tale of the afterlife — how grapes grew as big as her head or animals talked — and his father would explain, "She's lying. It's nothing like that at all here, let me tell you."

Loctrean paid off his debts. He had the house refurbished from top to bottom, and hung a bright new awning over the door. He bought a fleet of fishing boats, but left his father's decrepit craft in a corner of the yard as a shrine. He showered his sister and her husband with gifts and ensured that they would never want for anything.

Eventually he sailed back to Perla on the very same ship, which he now owned. He cooked for the crew because by now he liked doing that. In Perla he gave the dismayed magistrate a generous sum in thanks for showing him compassion, adding, "Had I not listened to you, I wouldn't have found my fortune."

When finally he married, he doted on his wife, keeping her and their children happy every day—mostly by telling them fantastic stories of the glorious adventures of their grandfather, who had sailed to the ends of the world and faced every peril imaginable. And if the children didn't believe him . . . well, it hardly mattered, after all.

Leodora sat back and the shapes of the flames on her palms unwound from the figures of a family and back into dancing green fire once more.

Diverus watched as the gathered feasters pressed fingertips together in front of them and hummed as they bowed to her, their faces lit with delight, their red eyes glowing with rapturous wonder.

The king of Epama Epam said, "Ah, that was quite . . . exquisite." He waved one hand over hers, and the flames evaporated. "Your reputation is well earned, storyteller."

"Thank you," she said. "And your puppets are the most unusual I've ever seen."

"Yes, but what else would you expect from the world that threads all worlds?"

She laughed at that, then tilted back her head as she stretched. Overhead, the ocean sky had grown darker and the sparkling upon its surface turned to stars. "We've missed our performance," she said, mostly to herself, so that Diverus barely heard it. Her brow knitted as if puzzled by the indifference with which she realized this.

"Surely you can afford one or two," said the king.

"You don't know Soter," Diverus replied. He hid his concern, stretching as if he had just awakened.

"Perhaps not, but now as you say you've missed the performance, you

might as well settle in and enjoy our company. The night in Epama is
nascent, and there are too many stories you still want to hear. That I know for
certain."

She nodded in a dreamy way. "You *do* owe me some in return." To Diverus she added, "We can't very well leave without the stories, can we? If
we've sacrificed a performance, we deserve our reward."

"There, it's settled then." The king grinned. He called for wine.

Diverus scanned the faces about them, all of the sharp features crinkled
with friendship, smiles split wide to display teeth as white as clouds on a clear
day. Nowhere was there a member of the court not expressing unbridled joy
or radiating pleasure. It enticed, caressed, soothed, and he could not help im-
mersing in it as in the pool where he'd swum. Yet beneath the camaraderie
lay something undisclosed, something he was sure he would recognize were
he only able to clear his head and distance himself from them enough to de-
liberate. It was a disquiet he could not even express to Leodora. Something
essential was being stifled.

She, like a cat, stretched out before the fire, her eyelids heavy, her smile
soft and smug. She took the tall-stemmed glass of wine when it was handed to
her, sipped, and then said, "Tell me stories, then. Lots and lots of stories."

"Aeternalis," promised the king. The alien word reverberated through the
columns; and despite being on his guard, Diverus sank back and gave himself
up to their stories.

"She's dead," Soter bemoaned. He clutched his head in both hands. His ring
of hair stood up in tufts and swirls, making him look mad. He sat on a wide
settee painted so as to seem feathered, a prop he'd dragged from one of the
Terrestre's storage rooms to a spot beside the puppet booth. "It's from a play,"
Orinda had told him, "about a young queen who is sent to her doom by a jealous adviser."

"I would prefer to find no irony in that," he'd replied.

Beside the settee stood two small blue faience amphorae, most of their
former contents now residing inside Soter. "Everything I did to protect
her . . . all for naught. Lost."

Orinda sat facing him. In the light from the lamps at the front of the
stage she appeared both regal and grave in her long robe and gold sandals.
She had been forced to cancel that night's performance because of his un-

raveling. She didn't begrudge him the crumbling of his will. He was right to worry.

In the week since Leodora's disappearance, the audiences had fallen off appreciably, and she suspected that word had spread that the great Jax had vanished and left her troupe to cover for her. A night or two without a performance would not harm anything—the citizenry was too desperate for stories now—but if it continued much longer than that, who knew what would happen, or if the theater could open again.

"What about the street performer?" she asked. "Surely that was a clue."

"The stilt walker?" He pushed his hands over the top of his head, his chin almost against his breastbone, and looked at her through his brows. One of Hamen's people had stumbled upon the stilt walker at a street fair two days earlier. "She claims only that she spoke to the two of them, but that when she went out to tell everyone in the street that the famous Jax was among them, Leodora didn't follow her. She went back into that tunnel."

"The one to Sacbé."

"And they just disappeared there. Never came out."

"But surely that means they're *on* Sacbé."

"So one would surmise, yet nobody there that Hamen's folk spoke to ever saw her or Diverus emerge at the other end." His eyes closed. "No one. Whatever happened to her, I tell you it happened in that tunnel. In darkness. Has to have done." He grabbed for his cup of wine. "Gods, I am *cursed*!" Then he slumped sideways on the divan.

"That's not so, Soter."

He came alert angrily. "It isn't? The gods paired me with Bardsham, didn't they? I was doing all right on my own. I could spot a mark half a span away, size him up before he set eyes on me. I could tell you how much his purse would have and reel him right in. Practically had to stop him from handing it to me, every coin."

"You were a thief?"

"Thief? I was an artist. I could convince princes to offer me the jewels right out of their crowns."

"How?"

"By promising them more. *Always* more." He drained the cup. "Everybody always wants more." He lifted the nearest blue amphora and tipped it. When nothing came out, he grabbed the one beside it, which also proved to be empty. He glowered sullenly a moment, but then pointed at them and gave a mad laugh. "You see? My point exactly, isn't it?"

Bois was standing across the stage. Orinda gestured toward the empty jars, and he nodded and scurried off.

Soter watched it all, his head tilted.

"So, you were doing well when Bardsham found you," Orinda prompted.

"Oh, *better* than well." He broke off speaking, his brow furrowed. When he focused on her again, it was with a suspicious look. "I'm wondering, as you've never said, there's something I'm curious about."

"What would that be?"

"Why is it that, if everyone else who crossed the bastard Chaos's path was turned to stone, your two actors were only turned to wood and got to keep their lives?"

The question seemed to catch her entirely off guard, and a look of fear crossed her face before she regained her composure, forming a brittle smile as she tried to laugh away the question. "Why," she said, "distance, I'm sure. Some fluke, some accident of his attentiveness."

"Oh, no, I don't think that's likely, now, is it?" He sat up, now suddenly quite sober in his actions and his gaze. "Distance had nothing to do with it. People under the span were turned, too. Leodora saw them. There aren't any others like your two anywhere hereabouts, are there? Tell me, do *they* wonder how it is they survived, Orinda?"

"What is wrong with you, Soter?"

"I'm cursed by the gods, just as I said. Here I was thinking from the moment you took us in that you and I might share a bed one night, that we two might find one another's company . . . amicable. But my dearest Orinda, there's a nagging question no one has ever answered."

She cleared her throat. "What's that?" she asked, her voice barely louder than a whisper.

"Who told Tophet the Destroyer where we had gone? The Agents did come after us, to Remorva and then straight on to Emeldora. I wonder, as I always have, who set them after us in the first place? A lot of spans out there, a lot of spirals unfolding across the sea. Scattered islands, too. We were lying low, and then hardly showing ourselves. But they reached Emeldora not four nights after we did. No happenstance that."

"It must be," she offered, "that they asked along the piers, asked the boatmen, who would have identified a group such as yours."

"Boatmen along the pier would have had no cause to lie to them. But the Agents *never* came looking after Bardsham's little girl. Didn't know she existed. Wharf rats would have given her up, no reason not to. If they'd been asked. If there'd been a *need* to ask them. Someone who cared about the girl, though, might not have mentioned her, even to save two members of her own troupe."

"Soter—"

He held up his hand to silence her. He was wincing, as if pained. When he opened his eyes again, he didn't look at her but off in the distance at some memory. He displayed his hand with its missing fingertips. "He could be very persuasive."

"The Agents were going to kill them," Orinda explained. "Both of them."

"I've no doubt of it," said Soter. "The wonder is, really, that once you'd told them what they wanted, Tophet didn't kill 'em anyway." A crash followed upon his words, from the rear of the theater. Bois stood there, his expression an admixture of horror and outrage. The faience amphora he'd been carrying lay shattered on the floor, broken blue glass and wine like pooling blood. He turned on his heel and vanished into the wings.

Orinda cried, "No, wait, Bois!" as she climbed to her feet. She gave Soter one final helpless glance before hurrying after the wooden man.

Soter sank into a heap on the settee. There was no triumph in the learning of Orinda's complicity. His own overshadowed it completely.

"Cursed," he repeated. "As if it matters anymore."

Late into the night the storytelling unfolded. For every story Leodora told, she heard a dozen new ones from the people of Epama Epam. She learned of the Green Snake's terrible revenge, of the Milkbird that fed the starving, of the Armless Maiden and her hands of silver, of so many more stories that Diverus lost count and the details bled together. Each one seemed to carry her farther away from the desire to leave this wonderful place. In return she told them the story of the Fatal Bride and then how Meersh had lost his toes. As with human audiences, these people championed Penis at the end of it, while the flames danced merrily across her palms. Eventually, she admitted that she was surfeited with stories and one more would make her explode. Besides, she was exhausted, and she begged that they let her rest awhile.

The king commented that they had not yet determined what story she needed to hear, and that it was possible they might have to give her every story they knew in order to find it. It could take a long, long time.

Without hesitation, Leodora answered, "Then I'll stay here until the discovery is made."

This shocked Diverus. It was impossible she could feel that way.

The king took Leodora by the hand and led her and Diverus back into the forest of columns, turning to the side in the midst of them, emerging in front of a row of cerulean curtains. He parted the curtain directly before them. Behind it was a small chamber, the floor of it a thickly padded mat covered in blankets and pillows. A brazier to the side burned with a sweet, intoxicating incense.

"Here," said the king, "you and your consort may retire at *any* time."

"I'm not her consort," protested Diverus.

"As you say," the king agreed, though his tone suggested anything but agreement.

"Why do you think I'm her consort?"

Leodora tugged at his arm. "Diverus," she entreated.

"You must remember, I've seen your true self, revealed by the waters of our pool. You could not take your eyes from her. She was everything in your sight, she was your world, your intoxication. You displayed love of the greatest depth. Whether you wish to acknowledge it or not is of no consequence to me, but it ought to be of appreciable interest to you."

"Your pool was a trick, a magic."

"A magic that plucked upon your heartstrings. Not all tricks are necessarily lies."

Leodora curled up on the bed and pulled a pillow to her belly. "Diverus can pluck the heartstrings, too," she mumbled.

"Certainly yours," the king said. "Now rest awhile, and we'll continue."

Leodora only murmured, but Diverus met the king's genial red gaze defiantly. "What has to be done to learn the reason why we were directed here?"

"I assure you, it's a story you need, but I cannot tell you which one."

"Cannot or will not?"

The king smiled tolerantly. "Perhaps, when she awakes," he said, "we can take steps to identify it. I know, young man, that you think me scheming against you both. Please don't deny it. I knew it when first I met you, and the episode of the pool supports your suspicions. I cannot deny what took place. We have our scripts to live by as you have yours. Ours is a retreat from the world, and we must by nature try to draw visitors in. We thrive upon them. Had you both welcomed the nepenthe offered by our waters, we would not now be speaking thus, and you would be contented, happy, and at peace forever."

"But at the cost of our will?"

"Which you would not have missed." The king smiled. "Sleep now. You can doubt me more ably once you've rested." He stepped back and let the curtain fall.

Leodora was already soundly asleep. Diverus knelt, then lay down at her side. The brass pendant was draped across the pillow she clutched. He stared at it, wondering what it might tell him, and whether it would respond to questions that he wanted answered.

He sighed. Without awaking, Leodora reached over and put her arm over him. In her embrace, Diverus lay beside her but could not fall asleep. Her touch galvanized him. He stared instead at the pendant and resisted the desire to clutch her to him, sleep, and wake in the darkness of early morning, to make love. It was what her "consort" would do.

Had she entered the pool with him, even now he would be living out that desire, but it would all be a lie, and he didn't want her if it was a lie. It seemed to be the nature of this place—this Pons Asinorum or Epama Epam or whatever they called it—that every truth encompassed an untruth. Misdirection defined their nature, and what should he have expected of a world where the sea became the sky, flowing forever overhead? He needed one reliable answer—to know the nature of the cached lie underpinning all that had been explained. It would not come from the king or his people. They would act according to their script, just as the king had intimated—which Diverus took as another truth cloaking another lie. Leodora had fallen under the spell of stories and would petition to remain until the essential story had been told, assuming there was one. How long might they keep her here, promising to find the essential tale, trying another and another like sweets offered from a tray, each sapping her will a little more, until everything of her former life was forgotten and remaining here was all she would ever want? He knew this because what he had felt in the pool was not only to bind to her but to live here with her everlastingly, and while that spell no longer bound him, its memory served as sufficient tocsin. Having been under their sorcery and then released seemed to give him a kind of immunity, although that might be only temporary. He might go to sleep now and wake up as dazzled as she. He wished desperately to leave before that happened; but she would not go with him, and if he left her behind he would surely never see her again. She would never go.

She rolled onto her back, and the pendant slithered up the pillow, coming level with his eyes. As it did, its own golden eyes opened and contemplated him. He realized that Leodora could not have roused it.

He sat up. "Will you answer me?" he whispered.

"Naturally," it told him. "So long as you are in her dreams." Then it became inanimate again.

With great care, he knelt and worked the necklace and the Brazen Head over her face and up above her hair, but he needed to lift her head to release it altogether.

Slowly, he slipped his fingers into the tangled fall of her hair, edging them beneath the back of her head. Ever so slightly, he raised her head up. She murmured his name, and both of her arms circled his neck. At the moment he drew the pendant free of her hair, her lips met his. She kissed him deeply. He tasted the wine on her breath and the tip of her tongue. She let go of him and sank back. Her eyes had opened a little, and now rolled up as her eyelids closed. She moaned softly, body shifting, and then lay still, her arms and legs pushed apart as if open to him. He ached to continue, to follow her desire—if only he could trust that it was hers. Instead, he made himself roll away, with his back to her, and then lay still, the Brazen Head clutched in one hand. He waited while her breathing settled, softened, became slow and regular. Then he rose and crept out beneath the blue curtain. He peered in each direction. There was no one to be seen anywhere among the columns. He scurried across the cold stone floor and ducked behind the nearest pillar.

The liquid sky above was still dark and shot with stars. Firelight flickered from the distant feast and from torches beside the still pool of nepenthe.

Diverus stole from column to column until he had reached the far side, near the tiny door where they had entered. No one was about there, either. He crouched against a column in the last row and held up the pendant so that the brass head dangled before him.

"All right," he said. "Tell me."

The eyes opened. "Your deepest desire is to know if she loves you."

"I would hear of that, but not now. Not—"

"I couldn't tell it to you anyway," the head interjected.

That brought him up short. "What do you mean?"

"She loves stories. All else must needs occupy a second place."

"I don't care," he answered, and for that moment he believed it. "I want to know how to get her away from here. I want to know what this place is about and how to find out why we came."

"Time," it replied. "Time is no more."

"I don't understand you. How is time no more? Here? Everywhere?"

"Here *is* everywhere. Your eyes play you as false here as does your heart. The rising and setting of suns and moons is illusory. You cannot trust what you know. What you sense. What you want."

"I realize that," he answered impatiently. "Why do you think I'm holding you? Why do you think we're talking?"

The lion's muzzle flexed as if perturbed, as if it might shut its eyes again.

"*Please,*" he implored. "What's being withheld? How do we get away from here?"

"She needs one story for the battle to come, but be assured they will not serve it up until the day of that battle."

"And how long till that day?"

"Forever, if you remain here. This world is its own spell, enchantment concretized. They don't lie as you think of it, they merely act from the quintessence of that artifice."

He thought about that, about the pool, about her. It seemed a fine distinction that carried the same result. "If we're safe from this battle here, then why shouldn't we stay?"

"However long she remains, it won't matter. Her enemy will devour steadily everything else, encroaching span by span, until all but this interstitial world is lost, and no one who leaves it will ever return. Then you are as prisoners of nonexistence."

"How do *we* leave here, then?" he asked. "How do I convince her to go?"

The lion gave him a look as if it thought him imperceptive. "You seek escape from the wrong source, from inside their spell. Use your own formidable powers, Orfeo, if you want to change the script." Then it closed its eyes and was silent.

The name it had spoken shook him to the bone. He slid from his crouch and as he sat, the chain of the necklace slipped through his fingers and the pendant clattered to the stones, and with it the second object, which he'd taken off her accidentally, the two cords intertwined. It lay in his lap but he was oblivious.

In all the time that had passed, he'd not heard that name—not since before she had been wrapped in her winding sheet and cast into the water, a corpse that had taken his identity with her, snatching away the self she had gifted him with but that he could not hold on to.

His true name had returned.

A tickle about her neck woke Leodora, fingers in her hair. She opened her eyes and his bottomless black ones were right beside her, watching as if Diverus could not see enough of her, as if even as she slept he had watched; and she was reminded of a time she had done the same beside him.

She could not be certain what it meant, his closeness. Was it in the aftermath of some welcomed intimacy? But no, she still wore the purple robe from the feast.

The feast.

Her mind tumbled with a riot of images drawn from all the stories she'd heard last night: the clever Green Snake swallowing its larger adversary, the boar, with jaws that hinged impossibly wide; the melancholy maiden who sacrificed her hands to save her father and nearly lost her whole body as well; the girl whose feet were snagged by a seemingly innocuous loaf of bread that dragged her down into an infernal underworld; the king who turned all that he loved into cold metal; the conniving girl who drowned her elder sister to gain her sister's privilege only to have the sister's ghost return and denounce her through the strings of a harp. These and more clamored for her attention, too many to contemplate but still not enough, never enough. Stories filled her and she hungered for more, and they had them all.

"Are we starting again?" she asked.

"Yes," he replied.

As she sat up, his fingers threaded through her hair, and her pendant slid into the front of her robe; its chain caught around the back of her neck. His hand withdrew.

"I'm going to perform with you this time," he said. "Accompany you. I want to."

"It's my turn to tell them another then?"

"Your turn," he agreed. Then after hesitating as though making up his mind, he added, "We'll miss another day's performances if we linger." His eyes, almost sly, watched her.

"It's only another day." She would have missed a week, a month, if it meant more stories from these dark creatures.

He nodded slowly, as if she had confirmed something for him. "You'll tell them to let me play this time, yes?" he requested.

"If you wish." She rose and stepped over him, out the curtain and toward her passion.

Fire still burned in the feast pit beyond the columns and she started toward them without thought, drawn by what they promised. She looked at her palms, already imagining the flames dancing there, taking shape. They would want a story. Which one should she tell them? One they hadn't told her. Turning back, she asked which he thought would be the best.

"Tell them of how the zmeu stole the sun and moon."

"Isn't that one they told me?"

"It won't matter," he promised, and she tried to understand that.

When she reached the fire, it was as if the feast had never stopped. All the people were still there. The king rose to greet her, and her attendants scampered out from behind the columns to assist her as if she were old and frail and had forgotten her way. Diverus, in his green robe, shrugged off the hands of his attendants and sat next to her. He stared at her solemnly until she remembered his request and to the king said, "He's going to accompany me for the next story."

The king arched one brow. "Oh. You have another one to tell us."

"Yes."

"How does he accompany you?"

"On musical instruments."

The king leaned around her. The coils of his hair were sharp as knives. "He seems to have arrived without them," he said, and the feasters laughed.

"I'd hoped you would be able to provide me with something appropriate," Diverus responded. "You seem to be a musical people."

The feasters laughed again, and the king nodded. "You've read us well enough, young man. What would you play upon?"

"Oh, a harp would be nice. Anything else you might have. I'm very partial to the shawm as well."

"Multitalented, are you?" He gestured to the attendants to go retrieve what Diverus had asked for. "This should make for a very interesting telling then. Tell me, what story will you play out?" he asked Leodora.

"It's—"

"We can't reveal that," Diverus interjected. "It's more effective if it's a surprise."

She caught something in his voice, but she couldn't say what it was—some lilt she felt she ought to have known, which she might have identified if her head weren't spinning with stories. She lifted a goblet of wine and sipped while she waited for the next thing to happen.

The attendants returned with a small four-stringed harp and a lacquered shawm. The king turned from the fire with flames upon his palms again.

Diverus tucked the shawm in his belt and picked up the harp. She paused to watch him, recalling how remarkable his music was. It seemed to be an ancient memory.

He brushed one hand across the strings. His eyes closed and he began to pluck a dancing tune, a reel. It began slowly, softly, but his fingers moved faster and faster. The nearest feasters leapt to their feet and began to dance. They wore expressions of surprise, as if the desire to dance belonged to their feet, which hadn't told their brain. They pranced and stepped, skipped and swung about, spinning in time with a music that seemed to have taken possession of them. The king, although he restrained himself from joining them, couldn't keep from performing a small jig in place. Like his citizens, he seemed amazed, and his red eyes narrowed as he stared at Diverus, as if he thought he should be able to identify what was happening. Leodora wondered when her story was supposed to start.

Then all at once Diverus lifted his hands from the harp. The dancers swayed, stumbled. A few of them collapsed. Those farther away were laughing, thinking the whole thing a delightful jape.

Diverus inhaled deeply. His eyes opened. He looked at her and smiled as he set down the harp and picked up the shawm. Pressing the reed to his lips, he stared sharply at the king.

The song that emerged from the shawm was the very essence of grief. More painful than anything she had ever heard him play in the paidika where he had caused patrons to burst spontaneously into tears, it personified loss and longing, the threnody of an empty soul.

This time even the king collapsed beneath its weight. The flames on his hands hissed and turned to smoke. She looked around in wonder as people dropped to their knees and began to wail, to clutch at their bosoms, to claw at the stones.

Then at the highest note, Diverus broke off playing again. He drew the reed from between his lips, and surveyed them.

"Diverus, what are you doing?" she asked.

"I'm bidding them good-bye" was his reply. "Aren't I?" he asked the king.

The king pressed a hand to his breastbone, reached the other, trembling, toward them. "I—I—" he tried to say.

"Release her from the spell of this world of yours, or I'll play all of this tune and not one of you will survive it."

The king shook his head and Diverus put the reed to his mouth again. He raised the shawm like a weapon, taking aim. He played one simple verse and one of the four-armed attendants who'd pushed him into the pool fell dead beside the king, tumbling into the fire.

Diverus lowered the shawm. He stared at the king with disgust. "I know it's your world that enchants, not you. You merely act your parts, as you said, expressions of the enchantment. But you *can* shield the spell, as you did for me. You have that power, don't you?" When the king said nothing, he reluctantly lifted the shawm again.

"Wait!" cried the king.

Diverus waited.

"You have only to depart and it will pass, she'll come to herself again. We mean no harm, we only worship her skill. She is as a goddess to us."

"And to me," Diverus said. He kept the shawm but reached out and took her hand. "Come with me," he said.

The king called, "Tell me, please, who you are."

Diverus glanced over his shoulder. "My mother named me Orfeo," he replied.

The king's molten eyes enlarged with recognition. "We know this name and the skill bound to it," he said.

"Then perhaps one day you'll tell me of it," replied Diverus. "But that will not be today."

The king bowed his head and stepped aside.

Leodora witnessed all of this as if watching a play in some strange language, understanding and yet unmoved, untouched by the events and portrayals. She let him lead her from the feast, into the grove of columns to the heart of them where it was always dark. He let go of her hand and took the goblet from her other. He poured its contents on the stones and smashed the goblet. "Here," he said, and handed her the shawm.

From around his neck he removed a cord and on the end of it a small phial. She tilted her head. The green-and-black phial seemed familiar. Reflexively, she touched the chain of her pendant.

He tipped it and a drop fell from it into the wine covering the floor. After capping it again, he reached toward her with it. "I'm sorry, I took this while you slept."

She lowered her head as he slipped the cord over it, although uncertain why he was apologizing to her. At her feet, the wine rippled and seemed to reflect a different place.

"Come on," he said, and held out his hand to her as he stepped into the liquid. She reached out but handed him the shawm. When he tugged, she let go and he fell into the wine as if into a hole.

"Diverus?" she called, and leaned over the dark pool. "Diverus." It was dark below. As dark as a prison cell. She remembered Brodamante saying that from Palipon this world would look different. As she stepped into the pool of darkness, she wondered how.

Stumbling, she came up immediately against a wall of rough stone.

When she turned around, a creature with huge dark eyes, a long snout, and a woman's body clothed in rags was crouched in the corner opposite, watching her. A wig made of skinny black beads hung off her head, around her prominent ears.

The creature rose. She tried to speak, showing small sharp incisors and larger teeth at the sides of her mouth, top and bottom. Her words were strange, raspy, a language full of clicks and odd breaths. Leodora understood none of it. But when the creature stepped forward, her ankle rattled, and Leodora realized that she was wearing metal cuffs and a chain.

Behind her, a small barred window revealed a row of flat-roofed buildings with trellised windows some distance away and bluish with twilight. This wasn't where she'd intended to come at all. The woman said something urgent.

Leodora turned to leave, but no passage remained behind her. Instead she faced another stone wall, a dirt floor, and a small, thick door banded with metal. She was locked in a cell in a place she'd never been before, and Diverus wasn't there.

III

LORD TOPHET'S BANE

Diverus stood beside the broad wooden table on which they ate their meals at the Terrestre. The empty room lay dark save for one dim candle amid the debris of dirty cutlery, plates, and cups strewn across the table. It looked as if no one had cleaned up in days. He couldn't recall it having looked nearly so squalid the day before. No light came through the windows, which told him that it was night here. He said, "Leodora," and turned around, expecting to find her there. She should have been right behind him, but he was alone.

He realized there was a background din as of a large shouting crowd, and within it he made out cries of "Jax!" She must have manifested on the stage instead of here with him. Hastily he threaded his way through the wings, past ropes, past bags full of sand, dangling screens, and props of all sorts. The crowd's impatience was palpable—they weren't cheering her, they were demanding she present herself or start the show. From the shadows behind the curtains he peered past the rear of the puppet booth at a theater half filled with noisy, drunken miscreants. The various broken vegetables lying on the stage testified to their unruliness. By contrast, in one of the private boxes above the rabble, four faces watched the mêlée, unflustered by the clamor of the crowd, looking as if they could have waited forever for the show to begin. It was like watching four corpses propped up in chairs.

In the shadows of the wings opposite, movement caught Diverus's eye. Someone was working his way behind the backdrop and around the back of the stage, and a moment later Glaise appeared with his arms outstretched. He crushed Diverus to him.

"Yes, Glaise, I'm glad to see you, too," Diverus said. "Have you seen Leodora? Where's Soter?"

Glaise pointed enthusiastically at the booth, and Diverus plunged forward, but fumbled with the drapery at the rear corner until he found a slit and stepped through. "Lea," he cried, but she wasn't there, either. He thought he was alone, but then saw that Soter crouched on the floor beside the trestles supporting the undaya cases.

"Diverus!" Soter shouted. As fast as he could, the old man scrambled to his feet and embraced him. "Oh, lad, where have you been? The two of you had us convinced you were dead for sure. We looked everywhere, even turned out Hamen and all those people from the underspan, but nobody could *find* you." His expression tightened. "Where is she? We can't let her perform tonight. We've got to get her away from here immediately. You don't know what you've both blundered into, coming back now."

Overwhelmed, Diverus answered, "I thought she was in here. I mean, I hoped. The calls for Jax—I thought . . ." Agitatedly casting about the tiny chamber, he said, "I don't know where she is."

"Well, we have to stop her from coming on stage, you understand?"

"No, I don't. Find her *and* hide her?"

Soter put his hands over his face. "Oh, gods, this was inevitable, wasn't it? The moment we climbed those steps from Bouyan and set foot on Ningle I knew, I knew it must come to this." He turned to the front of the booth and cautiously parted the screen to peer out. Audience members called again for Jax, and something soft thumped on the stage beside the booth.

Behind Diverus two wooden hands pulled open the cloth of the booth, and Orinda stepped in past them. Glaise ducked in after her.

"Diverus, oh, my dear," she said, and hugged him. "Where have you been? Where's Leodora?"

"Oh, gods," Soter murmured at whatever he saw.

"Why is everyone so giddy?" asked Diverus. "I'm sorry about missing the performance, but we found a way to reach the Pons Asinorum and once there Leodora wanted to hear all the stories she could, and they enchanted her, and me, but we got away. At least I thought we did. We didn't mean to miss the performance, but they were going to keep us there forever." They stared at him dumbly and finally he said, "What is it? You all act as if you thought you'd never see me again."

Glaise stood with a hand raised to his mouth. Orinda answered finally, "You've been gone for *weeks*, both of you."

He blinked. "It was only the one night. A night and part of a day."

She shook her head. "Not here, it wasn't." Placing a hand on his shoulder, she added, "We sought you for weeks, Diverus, even onto adjoining spans. Bois is still gone looking, and Hamen and his people."

Without turning, Soter said, "He doesn't understand that they've found us, Orinda. If she comes back now . . ."

"Where is she, Diverus?"

"I don't know. She was right behind me," he said.

"She's not here?" asked Soter.

"I fear she isn't. Maybe I can find the stilt walker again, get another phial to open the dark waters—"

"No, that's *good*, don't you see?" Soter said. "She's in the world of the Pons Asinorum. They can't track her there. They'd never find her."

"I should go after her."

"That's for later, later you'll get her, once we're away," Soter proclaimed. He was scheming then, his eyes sharp but looking askance, as if calculating the details. "At the moment we have a final performance to give."

"But, Soter—" Orinda objected.

"The situation's changed, Orinda. With him here we can have a performance. He has the power to quiet them all. Don't you? You can put them all to sleep if we want. Right?" When Diverus didn't answer, Soter grabbed him by the shoulders. "You would do anything for her, wouldn't you?"

"Soter—"

"Yes, I would," Diverus answered with no hesitation.

"You love her." Diverus hesitated to respond and Soter shook his head. "It's all right. We both do, don't we? That's the thing that draws us and the thing that's divided you and me. Divided me inside myself." To Orinda, he said, "You're going to get away. You take Glaise, and Bois if you can find him, and get far away from here. We'll perform, we'll keep them riveted. They won't even notice your departure, and after, if he can lull them to sleep, we'll slip out and come after you, too."

"But Leodora—" Diverus began.

"You don't want her to be here right now," Soter said. "She's better off where she is, and you can go fetch her once we've escaped."

"Soter, you can't!" Orinda insisted.

"Can't I? We've been here before, Orinda. Or rather, you have. Glaise has. What do you suppose those creatures will do to him this time to get you to tell them what they want to know? If we were to flee and leave you here, you would pay the price again. Worse even than before."

She looked from him to Diverus with a sickened expression. "You're insane, Soter."

"Probably." He grinned and it made him look the part. "Now, you have to do one last thing. You have to introduce us. Introduce us like there's nothing wrong at all, and then take Glaise and go somewhere and hide. Go down below with Hamen's folk. Hide out until they've gone or *we* come find you."

She held her ground another moment, but finally acquiesced, pushing Glaise to turn him about and following him out the back of the booth.

Soter handed Diverus the mijwiz. "You like playing this double-pipe thing, don't you?"

"I am partial to it."

"Good. Good. Because tonight you're playing for your life. Maybe all our lives."

The principal problem was, the cell was utterly dry. The rough dirt floor had seen no water in a very long time. Near the prisoner, straw had been strewn about, not much of it but enough to absorb any and all moisture. Nowhere was there a container, a cup, even a slop bucket. The chain attached to her ankles allowed the prisoner to cross past the window as far as the opposite corner to relieve herself, and the noisome stink of the straw told Leodora that it hadn't been changed in a long time. The small window prohibited the flow of enough air to overcome the smell.

"I need water," Leodora explained.

The prisoner tried to communicate with her, babbling excitedly and incoherently for so long that Leodora thought the confinement had driven her insane. She had no experience of a place where the world didn't transmute naturally and the language become comprehensible. Finally, the long-snouted woman seemed to realize that nothing she said was making any difference, and she stopped. She tilted her head and stared at Leodora as if seeing her for the first time; this caused the black beads of her wig to clack and chitter. She gave her head a small toss and the beads shook again. She had human eyes beneath her prominent animal brows but the shape of the face was more like that of the kitsune, except that it had a surface of iridescent scales shaped like those of the Ondiont snake. In the silence, Leodora pointed to herself and said, "Leodora," then repeated it.

The prisoner placed her fingers on her chest and said, "Yemoja a Iunu." Her snout twitched. She seemed to be trying to smile.

"All right," Leodora replied. "Yemoja?" Then she pointed to the room, the door, out the small window. "Where?" she asked. "Where is this?"

The creature nodded in understanding. "Palipon," she growled.

"Oh." Leodora sank down then. Palipon: the prison isle. Its name, it seemed, transcended language barriers. It was the place where Gousier had sent the woman who'd tried to kidnap her when she was small. Nobody banished to Palipon was ever seen again. Nobody ever came back. Legend made it the original home of Death before Chilingana had called him forth by dreaming the spans. Whether or not that was true, she wasn't about to be trapped here.

Standing again, she went to the window. The light was fading fast, though she could still make out the flat-roofed buildings. They stood on a rise on the far side of a deep gorge. The drop from here to the bottom of the gorge appeared to be sheer—at least, with her face pressed against the bars she could see no obstruction below the window. She couldn't see them, but imagined there must be hundreds of windows like this one overlooking the dry and craggy drop. She stepped back with a sigh.

Yemoja spoke to her again, a series of growls and clicks. Leodora could only shake her head in incomprehension. She said, "The least I can do is try to get you unchained before the light's gone." She took a step toward her and Yemoja backed against the wall. "It's all right," Leodora said cautiously. She raised her hands to show them empty, then knelt. She had to press her lips tight and hold her breath to get close. Yemoja's whole body was begrimed, but her slender ankles were worse. The cuffs around them looked to have rubbed them raw, leaving them blackened, maybe putrid. Leodora's eyes began to tear up and she wiped at them with the back of her hands, then clutched at the cuff all but blindly. The cuff was hinged, the lock a small box exhibiting an odd cross-shaped keyhole. She grabbed hold of it and tried to pull the halves of the cuff apart, but finally sighed and gave up. There would be no removing it without a key.

She withdrew then to the window and breathed the night air until her eyes stopped stinging. She shook her head in exasperation, then withdrew again to the corner beside the door. There was nothing to do now. She needed both darkness *and* a pool of standing liquid. The darkness was here but she wasn't going to get the other until someone brought Yemoja something to drink, and she surmised that nobody would be coming tonight. Whatever meals were served, they had been consumed well before this.

"I need to get out of here," she said. A solution occurred to her then. She stood up and began pounding her fists against the door. "Obviously," she explained as though Yemoja would understand, "no one can reach the door, so anyone pounding on it is impossible. I just hope somebody can hear."

As if in response to that, someone shouted. Then other voices joined in, and the cacophony of yelling prisoners drowned out her pounding completely. To her discouragement, nobody came to see what the noise was about. Nobody cared. "And why should they? No one here can go anywhere anyway. If that gorge circles this place completely, then no one can escape very far." She did give up then, and glumly returned to her corner.

Across the small cell, Yemoja was being reduced to a shadow within a shadow as the last of the light faded.

Leodora drew her knees up and rested her forehead against them. "I have to get out of here," she said. "Right now, Soter will be yelling at Diverus because he came back without me, and so another performance was missed. Did I tell you we'd gone to the world between all worlds? That's what it is for all its formal names. It's full of sorcery, too, and hurled at you from every direction—everything that seems benign on the surface will trick you. I was caught there. Snared. I didn't even notice, because I wanted something and that's what that place does, it finds what you want and it entices you with it, giving you a little, and then more and more, until everything else you've ever been has been swallowed up in desire. They had stories, all the stories, and I wanted them. I wanted them so much, and if Diverus hadn't pulled me from there, I would never have left. Diverus . . . enchanted them with his own power. He has power, and a true name. I know his true name now. Orfeo."

Yemoja looked up sharply at that and repeated, "Orfeo."

"You know that name? I wish I could understand you. You probably have stories, too, from wherever you're from, stories I've never heard before, and I would like to hear them. I'm greedy, you see. I want them all, all the stories, because my father gathered them before me and I want to . . ." Her throat clutched and her eyes burned hot. She had to wait awhile to go on. "I never even knew him, but we're alike on this. And we both need someone to watch out for us, too. The only escape route from here is back through that world between worlds. Pons Asinorum. Fool's Bridge. It's a good name for it. But now I won't have Diverus to shield me. I wonder if they'll trick me again? Of course, I have to find that out, don't I? There's no choice. I have to go back."

Leodora talked on of nothing and everything, the way Yemoja had when she'd arrived. She babbled, soothed by the sound of her own voice, not telling a story this time, just talking about anything. Eventually the talking lulled her to sleep, where the Coral Man appeared to her in a dream as he had on so many nights; but this time his figure appeared less well formed. She recognized that as his song floated across the oceans, his body was wasting away, and she perceived a glowing knot in his chest, something orange and pulsing.

During the last story performance Soter had Diverus packing the puppets in the cases—all but the few he was using, and those he handed off one by one. The booth, they would have to abandon. "Perhaps we'll come back for it later," he told Diverus, "but leaving it standing might give us time to get away." What they were getting away from remained unspecified, but Diverus didn't argue.

Soter presented a Meersh story and the audience howled at the trickster's foolishness. Then, in the midst of their laughter, Soter swung about and gestured for him to pick up the piba and play something. "Don't put them to sleep. Make it lively," Soter whispered. "See if you can send them all on their way." Diverus nodded and closed his eyes. He plucked the first note and then his mind went blank.

When he next opened his eyes, Soter was patting him on the shoulder and saying, "Excellent. That was *just* what we needed." He turned from Diverus and lifted the lantern from its hook, but didn't blow it out as Leodora always did. He set it down beside a bottle of oil, and Diverus thought, *What an odd time to fill the lamp.* The undaya cases stood on the floor beside him, fastened and ready. Soter said, "We need to make certain Orinda's gone. Will you go and look? If she's still here, then you force her out. The same with those woodmen. Get 'em out, lad. Be sure they're all gone—it would be too terrible if they remained. Then you come back, we'll take the cases and go. All right?"

"Where?"

"For now, down under Colemaigne with those carters. We'll get a boat. Has to be a way down somewhere."

"I know a way. Through the leg of a tower, at the end of the span."

"Good, good. All right, you go. Stay to the shadows, though, out the back and don't let a soul out there see you."

"There's someone out there? I thought you said—"

"Please, Diverus. *Go.*"

Yet even as he pushed through the black fabric out the back of the booth, Diverus knew Soter was getting rid of him. He crept into the wings, and then scoured the back hallway behind the scrims and backdrops, finding no one, as he'd expected. Dutifully, he climbed the stairs and searched the rooms on the second floor, too. He entered Orinda's L-shaped room, which he'd never seen before. It was full of costumes and wigs, makeup and props, but deathly still. The Terrestre was empty.

Finally, he picked a ramp to one of the curtained balconies, walked down it, and with great care parted the drapes. He peered out. The pit and all the benches stood deserted. Whatever he had played on the gourd-shaped piba, it had driven the crowd away. Music contained stories, too, he thought. It could take people out of themselves the way stories did. It could transport listeners to rapture or to tears. It could . . . he shuddered then with the memory of what he'd done in order to rescue Leodora. He wanted to tell her what he realized about songs and stories now—how he grasped the power they both shared, how he needed to say to her *I love you* because he'd done something so terrible that the reason couldn't go unspoken between them any longer. But mostly he wanted to hold her, to tangle his fingers in her hair. To say to her . . .

A movement caught his eye, so subtle at first that he wasn't sure he'd seen it. Then out of the darkest recesses at the back of the theater, something flowed: four pale gray ovals, hovering above the floor, moving in unison like the segmented body of a snake. They slid down the steps and only as they neared the footlights did he make out that the ovals were faces—the faces he'd seen in the theater box. Cold, implacable, as unfeeling as stone, the pale heads streamed forward. It wasn't until they were rising up to the stage that he could see the bodies beneath the heads, bodies swathed in black, and he knew without a doubt that they were what Soter feared, they were the cause of his sending Orinda away, and of sending him, too. Even this far away and hidden, Diverus felt the terror of them. They threw it off like hoarfrost.

They moved across the stage and easily into the booth, one after the other, as if they could see where the slit in the material was, which he never could. The blackness of the booth absorbed them, but then he could see the tops of their heads as they collected in the middle of it. He realized that Soter could not be inside the booth at the same moment that it erupted in flames. The four sides went up as one, trapping the quartet inside. They whirled within the flames. They stretched their hands into the air as if imploring the gods to save them, and then one of them plunged back out, his body ablaze. He ran straight off the edge of the stage and into the pit. No one else emerged, and after a few moments the stage itself caught fire. Sparks rose in the updraft, and Diverus feared that the thatched roof was going to ignite, too. He dropped the curtain and ran back into the hall.

Soter had to be somewhere nearby. Somewhere in the theater with those puppet cases. He would never have let them burn.

Diverus bounded down the stairs to the first floor. Even as he reached it, Soter was climbing up the steps from the trap room beneath the stage. He'd made at least one trip already, leaving one of the cases by the door. Seeing Diverus, he gestured with his head to the large hemp bag beside the table. "Our clothes, and your instruments, Diverus," he said. "Can't do without our musician."

Diverus ran across the room and grabbed the nearest undaya case. He slung its strap over his shoulder and grabbed the bag, and then stepped aside to let Soter lead the way. "I doubt Orinda will be able to forgive us," Soter said grimly as he reached for the door. "The gods won't resurrect it for her this time." He flung back the door and stopped, filling the doorway. Diverus peered past his shoulder.

Outside, a pale bald head seemed to float in the darkness. It said, "No gods will resurrect *you*, either." Then it flowed nearer, driving Soter back.

The black-clad figure closed the door without turning. A short cape covered his shoulders, over a longer black cloak that swept the floor. His dead, unblinking eyes dismissed Diverus with a single glance before fixing on his target again. "Well, well," he said, a sly voice, "if it isn't the man who sells his friends. I never thought to see you again. How is the elf—what's his name?"

"Grumelpyn."

"That's right. Can he walk? He couldn't when we left him." The Agent moved farther into the room, and a vertical band of light from the fire on stage ran up him. One black eye gleamed in its deep socket like a star in the night sky. "So, tell me." He raised his hand, and Diverus glimpsed what looked like a blue-violet jewel against his palm. "Where is the storyteller called Jax?" The bright eye looked at Diverus again. "We had doubts, you know, as to the identity of this Jax. Surely, we said, the comparison to Bardsham was made up from ignorance—for who has seen Bardsham perform enough to say? I had convinced myself that was so. After all, I'm the authority on Bardsham's health. But now I've discovered you . . . and if you are here, then so must he be, too."

"No, he's not. You lot killed him."

"Oh, you know that for a fact, do you? I don't recall you were there." Then a slow smile of memory spread on his face. "But as it happens, so we did. However, it seems that Lord Tophet has come to the opinion there was a child, and again, here *you* are."

"What—" Soter cleared his throat. "What difference would that make to him?"

"The lord is of the opinion that a child of Bardsham's might pose a threat to him."

"How, for the gods' sake? Bardsham was no threat to him, either!"

"The how is not a matter I involve myself with. So I shall ask you once and only once more. Where is Jax?"

Soter looked back at Diverus and in the same instant swung the undaya case at the Agent. "Run!" he yelled. The Agent must have anticipated the attack. He sidestepped the case and slammed both hands upon it. The case pulled Soter off-balance, and he stumbled into the Agent. The hand bearing the jewel grabbed hold of his wrist. He screamed in agony. Diverus hadn't moved, hadn't run. Soter collapsed to his knees, but the Agent held on, and held his wrist up. "Stop it!" Diverus yelled. "Let him go!" The Agent considered him.

"Well?" he said. "Tell me what I know already."

"If you know, then why do I need to tell you?"

Soter, pooled on the floor, made whining sounds.

The Agent smiled but there was no humor in it. He released his hold and Soter's arm dropped. Soter curled around it, moaning in agony. "So Bardsham did have a son, heh? *He* was a small man, too."

"What do you want?"

"You. I want you to come with me now."

"Why should I do that? Why shouldn't I run as he said?"

"Oh, dear. Didn't you explain it to him, old man?" The Agent prodded Soter with the toe of his boot. "There is nowhere to run, boy. He should have told you that at the very least." Diverus sensed movement behind him. He turned, to be astonished by what he saw. The four Agents he'd seen cast ablaze stood there. Their bodies smoked, so charred and blackened that he couldn't tell how much of their costumes remained, how much was blackened skin, but their gray faces, smeared with soot, were the same, as humorless, hard, and smooth as marble. "Quick," the Agent commanded.

The four surrounded Diverus so quickly that he barely saw them move.

"You will accompany us now. We want those cases and that bag as well, all of it." The Agent turned, opened the door and walked outside.

They took hold of Diverus, and despite their condition, their touch was ice. He went with them without a struggle. Glancing down as he passed, he saw that Soter's forearm had turned as gray as dead coral. Soter looked up at him through tears and, trembling, gasped, "I'm sorry."

Diverus knelt to touch him, but the charred Agents kept him from quite reaching Soter. He said, "It's all right," though he knew it wasn't. It was his doom he was going to. At least, he thought, he would save Leodora from that fate—the thing they called Tophet.

Leodora awoke to a squeal of metal above her head: the hinges of the door as it swung open. She shoved herself up on one elbow, having stretched out onto her side during the night, but the door kept opening and she pressed against the wall, her head turned, eyes squeezed shut against the impact. Then the squeal stopped. She opened one eye.

Through the gap between door and wall, she watched a tall man step into the room. He carried a board horizontally and passed almost immediately out of her line of sight. He murmured something to the prisoner that sounded almost tender; then he laughed and Leodora knew it hadn't been tender at all. Yemoja snarled. The man said something else. When he went out, his hands were empty. He left the door ajar.

Leodora eased out from behind it. The guard had placed the board in the middle of the room. On it were a bowl and cup, and a lump of bread, and although the morning light coming in was gray and wan, she could tell that both bowl and cup contained liquid. The important thing was, the cell was dark. Yemoja said something to her, making no move toward the meal. She seemed to be indicating that Leodora should eat—a remarkable gesture given their circumstances.

Instead, Leodora went to the crack of the door and eased it back. It creaked again, and she ground her teeth at the noise. But nobody came to investigate.

Cautiously, she stuck her head out the door. She looked to the right down a long and dark corridor of rough stone walls and floor and a low ceiling. At the far end of it, two men were pushing barrows. Lanterns swung from the handles of the barrows. The first man took a wooden shovel and entered a cell. A moment later he came out with a pile of straw balanced on the shovel, which he threw into the barrow. Then he shuffled closer along the hall. The second barrow contained a large mound of straw already, and that was being tossed in to replace the old. Between her and the barrows but nearer to her stood a board full of pegs against the far wall. On the pegs hung what she guessed were rings of keys.

She looked in the other direction, where the corridor was perhaps a third as long before reaching a dead end. A cart stood in the darkness, so close that in two steps she could have touched it. It contained stacked boards like the one in Yemoja's cell, all of them balanced upon the bowls of the morning meal.

Shortly, the tall guard emerged from the next cell along, and she drew her head back in. She pressed to the wall and listened to the sound of him coming back to the cart, then wheeling it farther up the corridor. It scraped and rumbled along, and then stopped. Keys jingled and another door creaked open. She glanced out. He had gone. The men at the other end were moving slowly, steadily closer.

She counted until the guard reappeared. He pulled another board off the cart and walked across the corridor to the next cell, spent a moment fumbling the keys, and then went in.

The instant he did she was away. She walked briskly down the hall, pulled the purple robe tight around her, and kept close to the wall. With every step she expected someone to yell, but nobody saw her. Nobody paid her the slightest attention. She passed a narrow doorway into a stairwell, but kept going until she reached the board on which the keyrings hung.

There had to be dozens of them. She scanned them for a key to match the lock on Yemoja's ankle. It was easy to spot, replicated as it was at least a dozen times over. Duplicates, so that multiple jailers could work in multiple cells at once. It didn't matter if all the locks were the same, not if you were chained to one.

She lifted one set of them and pressed it against her robe to keep it from jingling. She turned around. The guard with the food cart was picking up another board. He glanced toward her, paused, and raised his head. She pressed hard to the wall and slid along it. Reaching the stairwell, she stepped into it, then stood and counted to ten before carefully peering into the hall again. The tall guard was carrying another meal into another cell. He hadn't seen her after all in the corridor's gloom. She ran back to Yemoja's cell.

She knelt before Yemoja. It took only a moment to fit the key into the slots and open the cuffs on both ankles. Yemoja babbled something and Leodora hushed her, then listened. Nobody came to the door. All the noises in the hall were from far away.

She realized she'd been holding her breath, and sighed. "All right, now," she said. "Just wait a moment." Then she took the cup from the board and carried it to the corner where she'd slept. The sun was rising outside and the cell was already too light. She needed darkness. There was only one way to get it.

Turning, she reached out to Yemoja to take her hand. Yemoja complied, and Leodora drew her to the corner. She poured some of the contents of the cup onto the floor, and it was immediately absorbed in the dirt. "That won't work," she muttered. She got the bowl and set it on the floor at their feet. It was too small, too contained, to qualify as a pool of water. She glanced back at the board. It was certainly larger. It would have to do.

She carried the board to the wall and set it beside the bowl. Then she took out the phial. "Now comes the hard part," she said, and picking up the bowl she gave it to Yemoja, then gestured to indicate how she wanted it poured out onto the board. The long-snouted creature whuffed but said nothing, and finally nodded.

Leodora looked back out the door. She watched the guard lift another board from his cart and walk into a cell. It was now or never, she supposed. She grabbed the door and dragged it open.

It squealed on rusty hinges, the sound seeming to fill the whole prison. She dragged it back until it cast the corner in darkness. "Now," she said and dipped her head at the board. Yemoja poured out the contents of the bowl. It was a dark, watery soup and it floated on the board long enough for Leodora to spill a drop from the phial onto it. Distantly, she heard someone yell, but she stayed focused on the rainbow colors swirling across the water, expanding as it ran off the board and onto the floor.

Taking hold of Yemoja's hand, she watched for the dark liquid to form shapes. After a moment, she could see people distantly, black hair and blue skin. "There!" she cried and leapt into the pool with Yemoja following.

They sprawled onto a hard dirt floor and she thought, *It didn't work!*

A pair of sandaled feet strode up to them. Expecting the guard, Leodora raised her head to find the king of Epama Epam standing over her and holding a silver chalice.

"This is quite unorthodox," he commented.

"Perhaps so," said a female voice behind her, "but she rescued *me*."

The king gasped, and Leodora realized that the voice belonged to Yemoja, which she now understood as if they spoke the same language. She got to her knees and glanced back. The woman had turned greenish black, and her eyes burned orange. She was tearing off the rags that clothed her.

"Goddess," said the startled king.

"Oceanus," she replied.

The surroundings bemused Leodora. Everywhere, the walls were old and made of rough stone, the ground was dirt, and it seemed as if everybody on this street lived in flat-roofed houses like those she'd seen through the bars of the cell. "This can't be right," she said, but no one was listening.

"This girl's been here before," the king was saying querulously. "She disrupted everything, refused to enter the pool of true desire, refused to accept the offer of our eternity, and what's more, her companion—who also escaped, I might add—caused the deaths of *two* of us in making his exit."

"Really?" The goddess's orange eyes considered Leodora anew. "Good for you," she said. "He really is a bastard, you know."

"Goddess—"

"Oh, shut up about your petty issues. Would you care to hear instead how mortals caught *me*, trapped *me*, and put *me* in a prison where the guard clutched at me every morning? A dry, dusty prison without any moisture? Without any way out and none of you knew where I was nor came to my aid? Prison, where I wasted away for more than a year, subsisting on the tiniest cups of liquid that hardly deserved to be called water? Living in my own filth in a space the size of one of your glorious pots?"

"We couldn't have known."

"Indeed not. *She* rescued me from there. So you will afford her every courtesy, help her with everything she needs from now until eternity, and you will not so much as grumble or try any slyness at all."

"Goddess," he importuned.

Yemoja touched her shoulder. "Leodora. Oh, yes, I know you, and I know why you're here. So does he. Epama has something you need, a story you must hear before you can leave. It was why you were sent to us in the first place by another demigod." She shot the king a severe look, and he hunched up like a child. "Oceanus ought to have told you that story before, but he's an inveterate trickster and a liar by nature and would withhold what you require until you're driven mad by the need and then give it to you as if the whole matter is your fault."

"I'm insulted," said the king.

"I doubt that's possible," she replied.

Leodora dusted herself off. "I have to go back to Colemaigne. They'll think I've died by now."

Yemoja shook her head. "You must take what he has for you. You dare not refuse it."

"Can I . . . can I go back first and then return for it?"

The goddess considered Oceanus. He shrugged. "It would seem you can do whatever you like."

"Indeed, she can, but she is best advised not to refuse this gift here and now."

Leodora considered this and finally nodded. "All right, then. A little longer. I would like my clothes returned to me, too." She turned to the goddess. "Thank you."

Yemoja laughed. "You save my life and thank me. You're too good for your own world, child. Come. Let's swim and feast and hear what he has to tell you. Then you can return to your Colemaigne equipped to face whatever it is."

They walked down what seemed a dusty corridor identical to the one in the prison where she'd stolen the key to free Yemoja, but the door at the far end of it opened once again upon the many-pillared palace with the deep blue pool and she knew that, no matter the outward shape of this place, this was its core, the center of a maze she was learning how to thread.

Many hours later, alone in the dark of that same dirt corridor and dressed in a freshly laundered tunic, she poured a goblet of Oceanus's best wine upon a metal platter and a drop from the phial into the wine. She held in her mind the image of her booth in the Terrestre, and this time stepped through without any misdirection. Her destination, however, was transformed beyond anything she might have anticipated.

She stepped down onto the stage of the theater . . . and nearly fell through it into the trap room. Half of the floor, including the part where the puppet booth had stood, was gone, burned away, and the edges around the gaping hole were charred and blistered. The back wall and two of the balconies had been destroyed, leaving one of the doors to the wings standing inside a frame without a wall around it. Gone, too, was one of the uprights supporting the roof, and most of the thatch overhead, which now leaned precariously to the side. Given the damage she could see, it was a wonder the whole place hadn't burned down. The stink of smoke still tainted the air although the fires were long cold. The remaining floor of the stage had buckled. Boards had popped up or split, probably from a combination of intense heat fought with buckets of water. Standing puddles remained under the last two rear balconies, causing her to think somewhat incongruously that the stage must not be level.

She looked down into the trap room below, full of unidentifiable debris. She saw no bodies, no sign anyone had been on hand when the fire began. The blaze had done its worst damage where the booth had stood and she couldn't escape the conclusion that it had begun *in* the booth—the lantern, perhaps, falling off its hook, spilling oil and flames all in a moment. Had it already happened before Diverus came back? It must have, else the embers would still be glowing. After all, it had been only a day since they'd parted company. Surely he was near.

After circling the hole, she walked to the rear and around the surviving door into the back wing. The various screens there had been raised high to avoid the fire, a move that had probably saved them. She walked through the crossover hall to the side of the theater left intact. The floor creaked underfoot. The heat had warped the boards.

The opposite wings, redolent with smoke, looked to have been saved. She turned to climb the stairs at the back, and there stood Orinda at the top. They saw each other in the same moment.

"Oh, thank Edgeworld for hearing my prayers!" cried Orinda. She flew down the stairs as on wings and clutched Leodora to her, saying, "You're alive after all," by which time she had burst into tears. "We thought you would never find your way back. Diverus didn't know how to go after you."

"He couldn't. He gave me the phial. But what happened? How did the fire—"

"There's much you need to hear, and none of it good, I'm afraid. The fire is the least of it. Come with me, he needs to see you."

"Who?"

"Soter. He hoped you would return in time. I think his conscience would never be clear if anything had happened to you."

"A lot *has* happened to me, but his conscience wasn't involved. It wasn't his doing. Why do you say—what do you mean *in time*?"

They came to one of the rear rooms in the hallway, one she hadn't seen before. It was, by comparison with the small chamber she had occupied, opulent. There were racks of costumes, a shelf lined with wigs, with shoes and boots, with makeup and mirrors. Bois and Glaise stood at the back of it, looking worried until they set eyes on her. Then both of them beamed with rapture and jumped to her. She hugged them, but even as she did she was turning to see what lay around the corner of the room that they had been guarding.

He lay on the bed. The top of his head faced her, his thin hair pushed up by the pillow, and even from that view she recognized him.

Soter rested with his eyes closed and his breathing shallow.

"Oh, no," she said, though she'd had sufficient warning to guess. "The fire?" she asked.

"No, dear heart," Orinda replied. "He started the fire—in the hope of escaping."

"Escaping. I don't understand."

"Who is that?" Soter asked. His voice creaked like dried-out leather.

"It's me," answered Leodora. She pushed around Orinda to circle the side of the bed.

Soter's feeble gaze followed her. Tears ran from his eyes. "Oh, you're all right then."

She sat on the edge and reached to take his hand. She noticed only then that his arm, lying straight by his side atop the covers, was as chalky white as the Coral Man.

"I don't understand," she said again. "How did this happen in a few days? Where's Diverus?"

"It's not been a few days," Orinda explained. "Before Diverus returned, a month passed. We'd exhausted every effort to find you. Bois and Glaise traveled to other spans, we'd interviewed the stilt walker you spoke to and the tunnel seigneur as well, who swore you'd never crossed from here to Sacbé. Hamen and Pelorie and the rest all scoured the piers to learn if a ship had sailed you away. There wasn't a trace."

"There wouldn't have been. We didn't tell anyone, we didn't know we were going. But a month?"

"Diverus said the same—only a day to you," Soter rasped, "an eternity to us."

She looked from him to Orinda. "Where *is* Diverus?"

"My dear," he said wearily, "you have to listen to me now."

"First, tell me what's happened to Diverus?"

"They took him."

"Who did?"

"Soter." Orinda said his name anxiously.

"Orinda, my time is short now whether I speak or not. Better that she know everything than wonder ever after." His rheumy eyes met hers. "The truth was kept from you for your own good as well as mine. If you'd never wanted off that damnable isle—if you'd had Tastion and married and had babies and become part of their village . . . but I should have known that wouldn't happen. Not with your family history. I cursed Gousier for all this, but maybe it had to be. You'd never have lived inside anybody's proscriptions."

"No, I wouldn't, but—"

"Give us a drink then, and I'll tell you what you need to know, everything of Bardsham and Leandra. And Diverus."

There was a tray on the floor with a clay pitcher. She poured him a cup of wine. When he did't take it from her, she realized he couldn't move the stony arm. She reached under his head and pulled him up enough to drink from the cup. As he tilted up, the cover slid down and she saw that the paleness of stone colored his chest, blending back to flesh just beneath the collarbone. *The most important thing*, Shumyzin had tried to tell her, so long ago atop the tower of another span that it seemed like a memory of a dream. The sun that gave him life had been pushed aside before he could finish. And here it was, the demigod's petrifaction but a harbinger of this moment in time, like an echo thrown ahead of the sound that made it.

He drank and then pressed his head back. Seeing the look of despair and recognition in her eyes, he wheezed, "Hardly any of me left, is there? Another day in your Pons Asinorum, you'd have missed me altogether." He smiled, as if acknowledging that his approaching death were mere japery. "Now listen," he said, "and afterward you can hate me as you see fit."

SOTER'S TALE

"I hated your mother, Leodora. I hated her and did all I could to be rid of her. That's the truth and now there's no point in keeping it from you. I'm your friend, whatever you may think. I've always looked out for you. Always, child. More'n your uncle ever did or would have done. But I believe I share with him that hatred for his sister.

"I'd had Bardsham to myself for so many years, you see. There were hundreds if not thousands of indiscretions, assignations, and peccadilloes in that time, on every span probably. Bardsham and women . . . you wouldn't have thought it to look at him, scarred and rawboned as he was, but he had such charisma, such presence, that when he spoke to you, it was like the gods were gifting you with his attention. Like you were the only one in the world who caught his eye."

Leodora swallowed and said, "You were in love with him, weren't you?"

Instead of answering directly, he replied, "He always came back to me. Asked his dearest companion to dust him off, dry him out, and protect him from the woman who'd mistaken a dalliance for a proposal. As it was with that woman on Vijnagar who'd have left her husband for Jax, and you not even encouraging her—that's how it was all the time with your father. In love with him? Pathetic, I suppose. But nobody gave a toss about Soter except him. Nobody else scraped the dirt off and saw the lonely wretch below. He loved me and I loved him and that's how it was.

"Until she came along.

"Whatever his power, Leandra gave it right back. He wanted his little affair. She turned him down. He plied her with gifts, jewelry, costumes. He tried to seduce and tempt her. She said no, and sent the things back untouched. His performances began to flag. Audiences noticed when he cut back to two tales, and then one, and they actually stopped coming. Stopped paying. They thought it was ego. He didn't really notice. I'd never seen him like that. Nobody'd ever shaken him up, not in all the years we'd traveled. He was like your emperor in that kitsune story you like so much.

"Leandra had been nicely accommodated by somebody. She didn't need gifts to get along. She had come to the show and found what Bardsham did to be exquisite, that's what she said and the way she said it I knew she felt the same as me. She'd come back again and again. And she'd seen him beguiling the barmaids and the patronesses. She knew what he was like—more Meersh than little thief. And she had that about her, too. Cut from the same cloth, they were, neither one conforming nor obeying the rules. She knew better than to give her heart to him or he'd be after the next conquest before she could roll over. Turned out she was a skilled dancer. She'd trained, that lithe and supple beauty, with that flame hair you inherited. So I made her a proposition and hired her on as a dancer to entertain between acts, because I couldn't think of another way to fix it so he'd go back to work. I hoped at close quarters they would discover they hated each other and we could move on. Though I didn't get my wish, he did start performing again then. He had a reason to now. The audiences came back, filled the halls and theaters again. Soon enough I knew how it was going to be. The Red Witch and the World's Greatest Puppeteer. He never looked at another woman again. I think he stopped seeing 'em. He stopped seeing me, too. Didn't need me now to protect him from himself. I was just another member of the troupe, with Tahman and Grumelpyn. Well, I bore it, didn't I? And nobody so much as asked if I could.

"That was our sea change as a troupe. We moved on, and one day Leandra was pregnant and the dancing between acts stopped once it became obvious. I thought a baby would keep her away, in the wings, and I'd have him back. A little. Was that so much to ask for? He doted on you, though you don't recall, and he coaxed your mother into working herself into shape again for the dancing. Fuller hips but no one complained about those. She danced barefoot between tales, she took to doing some of the voices in them, and to the world we must have seemed the happiest family on all of Shadowbridge. The troupe what had everything.

"Your mother never stopped trying to get rid of me. Anything went wrong, any place didn't have our lodging ready, she went after me for it. Only fair, I guess, since I did the same with regard to her, trying to make him see her for the petty, jealous creature I thought her. She'd been a kept whore when we found her, hadn't she? I could always remind her of that, and make her twist with anger. Our war, hers and mine, because we both loved him. Ain't that laughable. I think it was the two of us drove him into his cups most of the time. Him and Tahman and that elf, they'd sit and drink and watch the two of us go at it like *we* was the married couple. Like it was a show put on for them."

"But what happened?" asked Leodora. "What happened in Cole-maigne?"

"The story changed is what. We'd come to this very theater and the crowds were huge. Your father's ego, it must have been as big as the sun resting on the horizon. Gods, but he was revered.

"And then one night I noticed a couple of creatures in one of the boxes out there, watching us. They were hairless, humorless things, like you'd get if you bred the moons Saphon and Gyjio together. Orinda and Burbage conveyed the hearsay that they was archivists from the Library itself, and didn't that inflate your father's ego still more. Nobody knew then or now what the rumored archivists look like, see. It made a good story. Bardsham's reputation had brought them—that we had no doubt of. They carried with them a glorious jewel they called Tophet's Eye. It's the *sort* of thing you'd call a spectacular jewel . . . at least one that had brought bad luck, Tophet being a far-flung name for the god of Chaos."

She asked, "Why don't I know the stories of him?"

He winced as if pain stabbed into him. "You don't know the tales because I kept those from you. I replaced Chaos in every story with some other god or demigod's name. I didn't want you to know that name ever. It was never to be spoken on Bouyan. Your grandfather, your uncle and aunt, I was shielding them, too. What they didn't know, they couldn't ask after. It seemed then the only way to be safe."

She nodded with understanding, and he went on.

"Third night there was five of them in that box, all of 'em as pale and cold as marble, and by then the chatter that the Library was come to canonize Bardsham was irrepressible, all over Colemaigne. After our performance they appeared backstage, immediately approached Bardsham, and announced they represented a great and powerful lord on another spiral who would pay an unimaginable sum for us to come and give an exclusive performance for him. The entire troupe had to agree—they were quite specific about that. Well, we'd done the like before, and for far less coin than this secretive lord was offering. It was too good to be true and I said as much. Of course, Leandra and I were fighting, so if I said it was a bad idea, she was bound to say it was brilliant and we must leave at once. Bardsham, drunk on booze and himself, didn't need coaxing anyways. At that point his vanity was as wide as the Adamantine Ocean. I'm sorry, child, and that's the whole truth of him.

"He was for it and that was that. Now, you, a baby, weren't going to make no voyage like that. Or maybe it was your mother having a premonition of what waited for us. She already had a nurse looking after you—Bois's sister, I think it was. You stayed here with her and Orinda. We sailed willingly off the edge of the world.

"I suppose we sailed for a week or more. Went right past spirals and beneath spans, and soon we were far outside anyplace we knew or had ever heard of. Mostly those Agents kept to themselves, but more than once I saw one of them with that blue jewel, holding it up as if trying to peer through it to see Leandra where she sat. Then one morning we woke up and the ocean was a darker color as if it was full of wine, and the look of those places we sailed beneath was dark and silent, 'cept for the birds perched about, watching us. It was like we'd sailed into another world or into the past, to the places in that tale of Chilingana's you tell, before any people had come. Whole spirals seemingly awaiting their tenants, that's how it looked. Then finally we hit this sargasso of dead calm, a whole surface of violet and black weeds that should have tangled us all up but didn't somehow. My misgivings had grown all the while, as had Grumelpyn's, although our hosts had given us no cause to worry. They'd fed us well and let us be, and more importantly they kept Bardsham merrily lubricated. Tahman, too, when he wasn't seasick. Always smiling they were, those hairless things, but not a drop of humor in it. Too late then even if everyone else had agreed with me and been willing to turn back. We didn't know it but we had passed into some other place.

"We reached our destination that day. It was a great curving span near the end of a spiral. The span and the whole spiral as far as we could see in either direction was gray and dead. Not a soul in view save where we anchored, and then they were like our hosts, cold and somber. Pale as skulls. The span itself was in worse shape even than Ningle, as if neglected for centuries. The Dragon Bowl of it had broken apart, and the beam and one little curved slice of that bowl just hung there in the air.

"They hauled the cases up for us, onto the surface of the span, and save for a coterie of staff, there was nobody about, just hundreds of statues in various positions, many of them crumbling, old like the buildings. His palace though was low and long and gleaming, and it ran half the length of the span. More dour, pale people greeted us, led us to our rooms, left us.

"By then even Bardsham admitted this was a mistake and not worth the money. What foolishness. He proposed we give our performance, collect our treasure, and leave as soon as possible. We still didn't know who our benefactor was, or what he was. We were still hoping he was just a demented recluse. But in order to pretend that, you had to deny that the world looked and smelled wrong, you had to pretend not to see that the birds flying past were not a kind of bird you knew, and most of all you had to overlook that the creatures waiting on you weren't terrified out of their wits.

"We set up the booth in a great hall of the palace. That night Bardsham performed Chilingana's tales, and the Fatal Bride, and finally 'How Meersh Lost His Toes.' The lord was delighted by the stories. He sat across the hall from us, in an enormous carved throne with an odd drapery hanging before it that kept him in the shadows. When he emerged, one of his attendants always stood before him, bearing a pole on the end of which was a huge mask—of hammered gold, and bigger and broader than a human face, with a serene expression. So we never saw his true face, even as he proclaimed the first performances captivating. His fingers, though, were so long and slender that they looked like they had extra joints, and his hands were the same color and substance of that jewel the Agents had carried with them, as if it had been cut from him. He insisted on having his own personal musician play along with Tahman. It was an old blind man who sawed with a bow upon some wretched stringed instrument with a long neck and one peg in it. He was in fact quite good, provided you liked the one song he knew. He played while your mother danced between the tales, over and over and over, the same tune, slow, fast, whatever was called for, but always the same. I've only heard that tune once since then: the first time Diverus played for me. You remember that? That was why I raged at him. It was the most vile thing I could have heard. How could I think it was an accident? I thought Tophet must have sent him after me. I know that's not true—I know it now.

"Anyways, we played for this hidden madman. The world is full of eccentric kings, lords, and emperors. It's where all your stories come from, isn't it? We decided he was just a little bit more demented than most. His span all but a ruin, a city of ghosts. Who wouldn't be mad living there? Then one of his staff, who was helping us, let it slip that he was *called* Lord Tophet. That jewel was named after him. Grumelpyn, who heard it first and told the rest of us, said, 'He thinks himself to be the god of Chaos.' Well, so long as he paid, we weren't going to care. We kept reminding ourselves that another performance or two and we were off back to Colemaigne and much richer for it, and he could think whatever he liked. But it was about to come clear that we'd been taken there under false pretenses.

"The second morning I was sitting outside his palace when two of his entourage approached to tell me that their lordship wanted to speak with me, and I assumed it was about payment, as I took care of that sort of thing. They led me to his private chambers. Quite lavish, they were. Polished and shiny, marble and smooth reddish wood everywhere, and not a hint of decay. His lordship was still abed, and as with the throne, a gauze surrounded the bed, obscuring him from view behind its shadows, and the servant with the mask on a pole stood beside it. I'd concluded by then that he was deformed in some manner, cruelly shaped by nature or a curse. He was eating his breakfast, and I wondered why he'd felt compelled to bring me in before it was finished.

"The moment I arrived he remarked to me, 'I know you despise that whore who travels with you.' And whatever I had ever thought about Leandra, it took me a moment to understand that he meant her. His voice . . . it was like a hive of furious bees, and perhaps that caused me to have to sort out what he'd said.

" 'Whore,' I repeated, like I didn't know the meaning of the word.

"He clarified by saying, 'The common dancer. I wish for her to remain behind when you leave, which you may do now at any time. As I'm informed of your hatred for her, I thought it best to apply to you. I want you to arrange to leave her behind. I don't care how it's done. Give her to me, take your fortune, and depart.'

"I babbled something about how she was Bardsham's wife, but that relationship didn't matter to him, either, nor should it matter to me if I hated her to the degree he believed I did.

"I listened to him and gods forgive me I thought about it. I blamed her for our being there. That much was easy to justify, but not enough to warrant what he asked. Bardsham would have killed me on the spot if I'd suggested it. I was about to try to explain this to the madman—for now I knew he was truly insane—when the door to his chamber opened and two of those gruesome Agents came in. Between them, they were dragging Tahman. He'd been thrashed and beaten, his shirt shredded, sopping blood. His mouth was swollen up, his face all bruised. He saw me and his eyes pleaded and hoped. He tried to say something, and I saw that some of his teeth had been knocked or pulled out. Before a word of explanation was spoken, I knew what had occurred, and under my breath I cursed the stupid bastard.

"Lord Tophet announced, 'Your drummer is a thief. He attempted to steal from me earlier this morning. I promise you untold wealth and you respond by sending a thief into my private chambers to rob me.'

" 'We didn't send him,' I said. 'We didn't know.'

" 'Oh, but you *knew* he's a thief.'

"I said, Yes, of course we'd known about that forever, and then added, 'But we didn't suspect him to be so infinitely stupid as to rob you.' Until that moment, I believe Tahman thought I was there to rescue him, to bargain for his freedom.

" 'Yes, that is accurate, I think,' said Tophet, and he parted the curtain and stepped out to confront Tahman.

"The servant with the pole and mask didn't move to cover him this time, and I saw him clearly. Cloaked in a green robe, he was, his hair long and black. The face—truly it is the face of Chaos. It's almost indescribable. Horrible. Not because of any deformity or scars like I'd thought, but because it was hundreds or thousands of faces all flowing through each other at once. Faces of agony, of terror, of more pain than can be withstood by any of us. Tahman screamed at the sight of him, because that slithery face was intent upon him alone. The lord rolled back one sleeve, revealing more of that gleaming purple arm. 'There is a single punishment for theft in my world,' he explained, and then he grabbed hold of Tahman's wrists. Tahman twisted, kicking out, but was held in place by the two Agents while the color drained from him and the grayness rose up his arms, his whipped torso, his neck, his face. It must have taken mere seconds but it seemed I stood watching that unspeakable progression for hours, and at the end of it Tahman's face slid across Tophet's writhing features and was sucked into the worming mass, and Tahman the thief, the fool, was an eyeless thing of stone like the hundreds we'd encountered upon our arrival. Not statues at all, they were the former citizens of that span—whatever it had been before Tophet claimed it. His body seemed to swell with vigor as he turned to me. 'One less division of the spoils now,' he declared. 'Two, if you give her up.' He cast off the robe and his attendants came flocking to fit him with costume and wig for the day, but beneath it was that horror of a visage ever in motion until the mask moved up between us again.

"He gestured my dismissal. 'Now I will have your boat prepared,' he said. 'We'll see you off in the morning. I expect you will explain to your comrades why this one can't play. I'll stand him in the dining hall should they need further prompting. Your thief makes your job that much simpler, doesn't he? This could happen to any or all of you, and for me it would be simpler to execute, but I've no wish to deprive the world of its Bardsham just now.'

"I took from his words that he *wanted* this story performed. He wanted the world to know he existed: Tophet the Destroyer, the god of Chaos, did not reside in Edgeworld, but rather walked the spans of Shadowbridge with us.

"The Agents who'd brought in Tahman took hold of me and dragged me away.

"None of this could I keep from your father or the troupe. Tophet didn't really grasp the bond at the center of a theatrical troupe, even when they war with each other.

"Unbeknownst to me, he'd already met with your father and your mother. Your father, he'd entertained late into the night, and as was Bardsham's custom he'd hobnobbed with his lordship, who had wanted to hear only one thing: What stories did Bardsham know of people who'd sold their souls? He'd asked him to list them all, every story he'd ever heard like that, and your father of course obliged. He saw no harm in it. And as he knew literally hundreds of such tales, it meant he got to continue enjoying Tophet's cellars while he rattled off every one. In the end, it seemed that Tophet had been satisfied with that recitation, and had sent him to bed.

"We were more surprised to find he'd also made overtures to your mother. She'd rebuffed him, no surprise there, but she'd known that wouldn't be the end of it—she had too much experience of men who thought themselves powerful and desirable. She just didn't know where it was going to come out next. And do you know what she did?"

Soter leaned forward though it cost him in pain. "Your mother told us to go, the three of us, to leave her behind. She wanted to save you. To save him. I think she knew what was coming if we didn't comply. As is said of the gods, the best you can hope for is that they don't take notice of you. This one had fixed on her, and that was that. Your mother . . .

"Bardsham, he wouldn't hear of it. 'Are they providing us a ship?' he asked and I said they were, Tophet claimed it was being readied. 'Well, then, we'll take it,' he said. 'Not tomorrow at his lordship's convenience, but tonight, after our performance.' He told Grumelpyn to find out where it was moored, but to be careful not to end up like Tahman.

"And that's what we did. Bardsham gave one of the best performances of his life, like he was in the grandest hall, in front of the very gods of Edgeworld themselves for an audience. It was so fine that Tophet had to toast him, hail him a genius and all that. For once your father's excesses and ego came in handy. He matched that monster drink for drink—he'd taken his measure the night before while babbling away—and he drank him into oblivion. When Tophet finally collapsed and had to be carried to bed, Bardsham retired, too, unsteady on his pins and having to be helped to his room. Of course he wasn't half so drunk as he feigned, but it convinced the staff, which was what we wanted. Grumelpyn had mapped the palace for an escape route to the quay below. Nothing was secured—they weren't used to having to guard things. We found our boat, loaded with bags of silver. Bardsham dumped most of that into the harbor to lighten our load. We were away and gone within half an hour.

"Then it was sailing halfway round the world and us not knowing where we was going for most of it. We'd stop on a span and ask where we were, use the silver we'd kept to provision the ship and buy anyone's silence—at least we hoped as much—and then we sailed on. I suppose it should have come as no surprise, but we *were* surprised to encounter a few people on those nearer spirals who'd fled the spans that Tophet had taken over. Whether they recognized the silver coins, or maybe just our furtiveness, I don't know. They told us he'd been moving across the face of Shadowbridge slowly, for centuries, like a great devouring juggernaut. A sucking louse in no hurry to kill what it lives off. No one knew where to run to next. Maybe they prayed he would just go away.

"We sailed on and never saw pursuit, but they'd no idea which way we'd gone and neither did we, and they thought we would be drafting deeper, slowed by the weight of our abandoned fortune.

"Eventually we reached familiar waters, the Adamantine and a span we'd played on, and from there we were able to make our way back to Cole-maigne, coming into Sacbé, one span below it, at night, in case the Agents were there ahead of us. They didn't know about you. We collected you right away along with what belongings we had, bid Orinda farewell, and sailed on to a span called Remorva, way down the far end of another spiral, well away from our usual circuit. After we'd hidden there a couple of weeks, there was no sign of anyone coming. We thought maybe we were safe. Just to make sure, though, we put two more spirals between us and Remorva before we tried performing again, settling in Emeldora. That copper-faced kingdom had never seen our like before. They had pantomime but no tradition of pup-pets, and Bardsham was a wonder to 'em. Leandra, though, stayed hidden. She didn't dance any longer, and Bardsham performed simple, unembel-lished stories, the way Peeds had taught them to him when he was a boy. That's what he called himself there, too: Peeds. It was a small place. You couldn't have packed but a dozen people into it. Two weeks we were there and no hint anyone was hunting us. It looked like we'd rid ourselves of them.

"Then one night while Bardsham was performing 'The Armless Maiden,' I went outside and they grabbed me. Tugged a bag over my head and when they removed it, I was on board a boat and in front of me was one of those hairless gobshites holding up a gold mask on a pole. This one didn't look serene, either. It was a mask of rage, of fury, and I knew who was sitting in the shadows behind it.

" 'We had a bargain,' his voice buzzed at me, 'and I'm going *well* out of my way to allow you to fulfill your part of it.' He suddenly closed the distance between us and took hold of two of my fingers. It didn't last but a moment, but I cannot describe how much it hurt, the two fingertips turning to stone in his gelid grip. Pain sliced right into my bones, all up my arm like you'd run a blade to split my marrow. I thought I must have screamed so loud the sky cracked. What this feels like now, creeping up me like a vine, is nothing com-pared with that pain from him directly. He pushed the fingertips he'd taken onto the floor and leaned past the mask, so close that I could see every wriggling snake of his face, all the shifting hollows around his eyes. 'You'll get her for me this time,' he said. They'd already come to Colemaigne and destroyed half the span looking for us, though we didn't know that then. He'd drunk up half the lives there, finally settling on Burbage's theater. But Burbage was dying from something else already and so Tophet's threats didn't move him. Instead he had his Agents torture those two decent fellows standing at the end of my bed. Bois and Glaise. You know what he did to them. He could have destroyed the whole span, but gods are chimerical, who knows what—"

"He's not a god," Leodora scorned.

"Oh, Leodora, you don't *know*, you haven't faced him."

"What god chases a mortal woman across the world?"

"In stories, girl—"

"*Only* in stories, Soter. Nowhere else." She drew a deep breath. "What happened, then? What did she do? Did she give herself up?"

Soter tried to look her in the eye, to hold ground one final time against her ever-challenging sureness, but he finally lowered his gaze. Blanched tendrils crawled like worms up his neck as she awaited his answer. He squeezed his eyes against the pain. Tears leaked from the corners.

"No," he said at last, then gasped a breath. "I gave Leandra up. Out of my own terror. I'm a coward, Leodora. I gave her to them. I betrayed everyone. I made up a story, led her outside, and they took her. She looked at me . . . like she'd foreseen it all and had already accepted it. Like she was forgiving me. That was worse—infinitely worse—than if she'd spat on me."

"My father?"

"Asleep after his performance. Exhausted. By the time he came around, they were long gone, and there was Agents left behind to keep him from ever trying to leave Emeldora again. Two of them with another boat. He knew I'd been the one, sold him out. I couldn't work up enough bile to lie to him. He made me swear to protect you, keep you away from them, keep you off the spans. Whatever happened, you were my responsibility from now on. Then we hatched a plan that used poor Grumelpyn as a decoy. We couldn't tell him. Sent him down to our own little ship with one of the undaya cases. It was empty, but he didn't know it. He was to make ready to sail back to Remorva. Of course those Agents went right after him. They must have tortured him awfully—Scratta said as much—but we'd told him nothing so he couldn't tell them anything they wanted to know and I suppose they kept at him and at him, and meanwhile Bardsham had stolen their boat and gone after your mother. I never saw him again.

"Someone, a mangy fellow, recognized the undaya case quayside and brought it to me. The boat was gone, he said. I paid him and gave him some money to give Grumelpyn but for all I know he kept it or drank it and never even looked for Grumelpyn. For all I knew there *was* no Grumelpyn any-more anyway. I didn't dare look for him myself. I had to look after you. If any-thing had happened to me, there was no one. I hid on Emeldora with you a full month before I bought a boat and sailed to Ningle. I knew that if either of them lived, your parents would know to find you on Bouyan. I buried my guilt, what I'd done, and it would have stayed buried but for your ambition and that damned coral ghoul Tastion found."

"The Coral Man—"

"It's your father, girl! Come back to haunt me, to plague me for all I did to him. To *her!*" He sobbed, and when he inhaled, his chest crackled and the tendrils slid into his jaw. "Oh, gods, it's coming for me."

Leodora pushed him back against the pillows. "Soter, the Coral Man isn't Bardsham," she said. "He's not my father."

He focused on her again. "What do you mean? Of course he is!"

"No. That's your *story*, that you've told me now. The truth is, he's part of another story, one that you stumbled into once and that I've now been given to know. But you have to tell me, where is Diverus?"

He shook his head, a gesture of pain and denial. "Gone. The Agents took him. Came for you and found him. He's like your mother—he gave himself to them to save you, told them he was Jax."

She clenched her jaw and doubled over, her head touching the cot. "Did they . . . did they do the same to him?"

"No," he said. "Took him is all. They won't harm him till they're in front of Tophet. They acted as if they expected to find Bardsham in the booth."

"How could they think that? They killed Bardsham."

"I don't know, Leodora. Maybe because they saw me. But they've found out about Leandra's child, and they think Diverus is him. Is you. That's why it was 'Jax' all the time, why it had to be. You understand?"

"Where are the cases?"

"They took those, took his instruments. Everything."

"Then the Coral Man's on his way." He stared at her without comprehension. "You and me," she said, "we've become part of his story. It's like Shadowbridge itself, Soter—yours, mine, Bardsham's, Tophet's, Orinda's—all these stories, they're all coiled together, braided."

"No," he said. "He came to me. He *haunted* me! Look what he did to my arm!" He lifted it to show her the sucker mark where the Coral Man had grabbed him, but the mark was gone.

She shook her head slowly. "Your guilt haunted you, that you'd tried to bury on Bouyan. When you returned to the tales to give them to me, I think you made it manifest. You've haunted yourself, Soter, all along. Back on the island, too. Those weren't my parents' ghosts. They were never there."

Miserably, he looked up from his arm and stared at her. Then he began to cry, keening for the burden he'd carried for so long, which had made him mistreat Diverus and lie to her, and had twisted his every decency into an act of diversion and mendacity. He sobbed, and the anguish seemed to speed the effects of the jewel's poison. The veins in his neck went powdery white. Suddenly he took one ragged breath and his back seemed to bow up. He looked at her with eyes that knew the time had come. "Forgive me, sweet child," he said.

"Soter." She fell across him. "You taught me everything," she whispered to him.

He made a small dry sound, and it was as though the venom surged up into him. She felt the change and drew upright. The face below her was as blank and dead as Shumyzin's at the top of a tower so long ago that it felt like years. Upon the bed lay a lifeless statue.

The Brazen Head opened its eyes, and softly it iterated, "Time is that which ends."

She sat alone on top of the southern tower of Colemaigne. This one sported no statues, just the pennants seen from the street, hanging listless now. A storm had passed, its clouds scudding away across the sea in a single line, leaving her bathed in late-afternoon sunlight, all too reminiscent of Vijnagar where they'd all been alive, and surrounded by puddles of water. She knew she should go, but could not compel herself. Her thoughts churned through everything she'd shared with Soter—starting with all the tales she'd learned to perform, the people and traditions she'd defied on Bouyan; the gods and demigods who'd intervened along the way, and the avatars and tricksters she'd encountered; ending with the quiet musician she'd rescued from a randomly chosen paidika, who had now sacrificed himself for her. Closing her eyes, she could see Soter as he held up the figure of Meersh in his hut, dazzling her with the revelation of who her father had been and what powers might be hers. From then on, it was a jumble of events, disconnected and disparate, that had brought her here, and Diverus—what *was* Diverus? Did she love him? She wanted to but doubted the authenticity of her own feelings. What did she know of love, whose reliable examples were all from stories. Soter had perhaps loved her most, but he'd feuded with her at every turn, lied to her, tried to rein her in. It didn't feel like love. Dymphana, she supposed, was a better model, but a surrogate one, and yoked to a bastard upon whom that tender word could not find purchase. Tastion? He'd been unable to distinguish love from lust. And what did Diverus have on his side of it? A mother he'd invented, conjuring her as a merwoman and a sphinx long after she was gone—fantastic illusions that couldn't be credited. Not one reliable example between them, yet they proposed to love each other because they'd gone together to a place where the truth of the heart was revealed. He had acted on that to save her.

Soter had known Diverus loved her without the pool of true desire, because he'd recognized what he was jealous of. He'd seen Diverus look at her the way Bardsham had looked at her mother and had done everything he could to stamp out that passion before it caught fire. Soter had known so much and hidden so much more. In the end, he'd been protecting her from her own heart. Now that was over, the shield gone.

She sat, gazing out to sea, and grief grew tangled in the complexities. She could have awakened the Brazen Head and asked for advice again, but she had no desire for riddles now, no interest in clever puzzles, and anyway she wanted no one's advice anymore.

Soter had always been. He was a permanent fixture in the world, dependably grouchy, as adamant as she was recalcitrant. She'd no concept of what a world without him was like, but one thing she did know: She would be damned before she gave up Diverus, too. The gods could hang themselves if they thought she would sit by and allow it. As she'd said to Soter, while they thought they were forging their own, they had all become characters in a different story, one belonging to a seemingly lifeless husk, which Soter had mistaken for Bardsham's body and ghost. They were like bees carrying pollen

from one place to another, from an island, across spirals, to its proper destination, although it might well be to death that she was delivering. Bees acted
out of their own needs. They didn't realize that flowers would bloom as a result. Were the patterns of the world as capricious as the gods or merely in-
scrutable? *There* was a question for the Brazen Head to answer sometime.
Some other time.

Now it was time to go.

She got up, and even as she did, one lone straggling gray cloud let loose a
few drops of rain on her.

Then out of the turret at the end of the bridge a figure emerged, and she
was astonished to recognize Orinda in a violet mourning gown.

Soter's body lay on the cot back in the costume room of the theater. No
one knew what to do with him now. The theater itself was closed until further
notice. Somebody would have to send to Sacbé for wood to repair the stage
and the galleries—Colemaigne had none. Probably it would fall to Bois and
Glaise to do it.

Orinda took in the view as she approached, her face encased in a violet
veil. Only her eyes showed above it, and Leodora realized it was her poise that
had identified her. "I have never been up here before," she said. "I wasn't
aware it was accessible. You can see everything, can't you?"

"You can see a lot."

"Sometimes a different perspective helps."

"How did you—"

"Glaise followed you. I think he was worried you might do yourself harm.
I knew better, but still I didn't want you to go." She hesitated before adding,
"We'd hoped you might stay on with us."

"I can't do that."

"Of course. Your puppets are gone."

Leodora asked, "Did you love him?"

The eyes widened, stung and unprepared. Orinda raised a trembling
hand to her mouth, hidden though it was. Her eyes looked inward awhile before she spoke. "I suppose I must have. He whinged a good deal, and was un-
necessarily harsh to you, but he always brought me in mind of Mr. Burbage,
and of the best times ever this theater knew. And now you go, too, and that
will be the last ember. The fire dies and I've no energy to kindle it afresh.
Gods come to the rescue just so many times, I think."

"Love makes no sense."

"Nor ever has, dear. The theater is full of examples."

"He named that puppet after you, didn't he? There was no figure in any stories with the name Orinda."

Above the veil, Orinda's eyes teared and she squeezed them closed until she had fought back the urge to give in to sorrow. "Where do you go now?" she asked.

"Back through the Pons Asinorum again. From there to . . . wherever it is Diverus has been taken. I'm not certain where that is, but I know now who lies at the far end of it."

"Nothing can be in this world certain but uncertainty," Orinda proclaimed. She reached out and grasped Leodora's arm. "Return to us," she said in words laced with fear. As she had already given an answer to that, Leodora said nothing and, when Orinda let go, she stood her ground. Orinda turned and walked quickly back into the turret. Above the crenellations, she gave one last look out across the ocean, then descended.

The sun hugged the horizon now, and the puddles on the rampart were dark enough for her needs. She straddled one and took out the stone phial from the recesses of her tunic. As she let one drop fall, the Brazen Head animated. It watched the drop splash into the puddle and the reaction ripple out to the edges.

"You're wondering why you have to pass through Epama Epam like a gateway each time," said the Brazen Head.

"I was, that is, yes."

"Well, you *don't* have to, you know. You can go where you want to go directly from here or anywhere so long as that fluid holds out."

"Then why wouldn't I?" she asked.

"Direct doorways open both ways, and what lies there can then come here. The continuum of Epama serves as a buffer."

"You might have said earlier," she scolded it.

"You might have asked." It closed its eyes. It might not have been Soter, she thought, but the Brazen Head shared enough of his traits that she would never forget how he'd vexed her.

She stepped forward and sank as if into the great broad tower.

It was night and the sea-lane of Epama Epam was deserted. No one awaited her arrival this time. No one was celebrating her return. She supposed that by the perverse rules of this place, as she was neither a traveler to be tricked nor someone to whom they now owed anything, she was of no interest to them— not so much unwelcome as dismissed. At least physically it looked like Cole-maigne again instead of the dusty prisons of Palipon.

Nevertheless, she didn't intend to stay long this time. She walked the street in search of a puddle of water, but could find no moisture on the stones. She went to the houses lining the lane and knocked on doors, but there were no answers. No one was about and no lights shone anywhere. It was as if everyone had gone someplace else. She recalled glimpsing the monstrous pa-rade from Hyakiyako and wondered if all manner of unnatural things sooner or later must thread through here. By whatever name, it connected to every-thing else. The goddess had called it the world mountain, although Leodora could see nothing anywhere in Epama Epam that qualified as a mountain.

She finally abandoned the houses, crossed the lane to the railing, and peered over.

Below, stars twinkled back at her from a black tapestry of sky. The effect was not so unnerving as it had been in the day. Night made it seem a reflec-tion, as if an impossible liquid sky didn't lie above. "A dark reflection," said the Brazen Head.

She glanced at it but it had already gone back to sleep—or had she only heard it in her mind? How far away the undersky lay she couldn't be sure. Darkness made it appear terribly close. She climbed over the railing then, and stood on the narrow ledge of hard, glistening street over what seemed to be a bottomless gulf. She drew out the phial on its cord, uncorked it, and poured a single drop into the night sky. Then she stood craned over the rail, expecting . . . something. The drop, she concluded, must have fallen forever without reaching anywhere. It wasn't *really* a reflection. She would have to go back to the houses, maybe break into one to get what she needed. She didn't like that idea much.

Then as she drew back, ready to climb over the rail to safety, the stars below rippled. She craned her head back and stared. A pure darkness un-wound from directly beneath her. Swiftly it blotted out the stars. Nothing showed in it but a huge emptiness: She had not fixed upon any destination. But she didn't know the destination; didn't know how far along the journey the Agents might be; didn't know where Tophet might have moved to since Soter had seen him. Nothing in the confession had told her where the Destroyer might be now. How much more of Shadowbridge would he have devoured while she grew up on her little island? How many years remained before he banqueted in the long house of Tenikemac?

Meanwhile, the darkness absorbed all. She could not wait.

Taking a deep breath, she stepped off the ledge and into the sky below that was no longer sky. "Diverus," she said, and fell. She held him in her thoughts, his face in the darkness ahead, remembering him with his eyes closed as he played some tune that snatched him away, his fingers delicate upon the shawm. Down and down she fell, knowing all the while that it was up, that everything about this journey was inverted, and that she was drifting down so slowly because there was no surface below to pull her to it, no wind, no sense of motion save that the blackness where the stars had hung expanded and engulfed her. Then it was as if she passed through a membrane.

Her feet touched and she bent her knees to take the compression of landing, even though it was gentle. She settled in a crouch like a tumbler, coiled to spring and roll if need be. Rising up, she found herself inside a small room with a low ceiling through which it seemed she must have passed without any sign. A pad lay on the floor for a bed, and upon it were empty shackles. These were a prisoner's quarters, then.

Light spilled in from a small porthole in the wall, and that combined with a sense of motion told her she was on board a ship.

The view through the porthole was of a shifting gray fog behind which towered sheer walls, so high that she couldn't see the crest from there.

In turning, she kicked something that clittered across the floor. She picked it up—a flat reed set in a piece of wood that penetrated the center of a thin disk. She turned it in her hands, not recognizing it immediately. The reed had been scraped unevenly, and the whole piece had obviously broken off something larger. She realized then that she held part of the shawm that Diverus played. It looked as if someone had stepped on it.

She glanced at the bed again, imagining him shackled there. They had kept him a prisoner in here, and the mouthpiece of the shawm had acted as a magnet to her, even though Diverus was no longer here. She had arrived too late.

She opened the door and entered a corridor leading past other small rooms and out into a galley strewn with clay pots and jugs, bottles and cups. Curiously none of these things looked used. The bottles, full of wine, were corked and wax-sealed; the uneven darkness of the pots suggested use, but it must have been long ago. They were dusty now. The door on the far side of the galley led her onto the deck of the ship.

The rails and masts were lacquered black. At the stern, red bulbous lanterns hung like two extinguished eyes off a wing-shaped taffrail. The place she had just emerged from was a foredeck house. A ladder ran up the side of it. She climbed high enough to look across the top. A curious waist-high cylinder protruded from the center of the foredeck, looking something like a capstan, but at a location that made no sense.

She climbed the rest of the way up and went to it. Recessed in the top was an elaborately etched brass plate. She traced a finger across the black lines in it, which fanned out from a second, smaller pocket in the lower half of the plate. Other, curving lines intersected the rays, and at the top of the circle was a kind of gnomon on a swiveling needle. The small niche at the bottom was empty, but it seemed intended to hold some object smaller than her palm. She rubbed her finger on the projecting gnomon, then pushed at it. The ship abruptly canted, and she pulled her hand back. The ship settled against the jetty again, and its lines went slack. Whatever it was, the device exercised control over the ship. She left it and walked to the prow.

The ship had sailed into a channel of some sort. The high walls loomed everywhere, curving out of sight in both directions, suggesting that they'd sailed into a giant's labyrinth. The ship was moored at the end of a jetty, one of three that lay like huge fingers upon the glass-like surface of the water. Two additional boats were tied up at the others, and the three jetties led to a single pier running along another stretch of wall. She could make out the zigzag of steps leading up, up into the fog.

She reached into her tunic, clutched the Brazen Head. "Where are we?" she asked.

The head yawned, showing its fangs. "At an end," it replied, as cryptic as ever.

"Might you unravel that?"

"All spirals," it told her, "come to an end. This is one such. Called Calcaria once upon a time, but no longer."

"The end of a spiral," she said in wonderment. Soter had told her that all the spirals on Shadowbridge began or ended in a helical span, which was why they were called spirals in the first place, but she had never reached one before. Spirals stretched far across the oceans before coming to an end. She imagined the nautiloid shape enclosing her, and wondered where the ship had entered the maze and how far she might be from where she'd begun.

"You are halfway across the infinite," the head told her as if she'd asked it aloud. "Given the nature of infinity, however, I'm sure that's not helpful."

"And where is Diverus?"

The lion's brow creased. Its gold eyes shifted away from her. "He is above. A soul in torment. Another displaced." The eyes rolled back to her again. "Act wisely and take care to be Jax." It became still again.

She held it a moment longer to be certain it had finished riddling. She gnawed awhile on what that was supposed to mean, and finally reached into her tunic and pulled out her domino mask. Wrapping it around her face and the top of her head, she tied it firmly in back, tucked her hair into her cowl, and pulled the cowl up. She didn't know why the pendant thought it important, but she knew better than to disregard its advice.

She left the foredeck, then stepped up over the rail and down a plank to the jetty. Even from directly below, the end of the span seemed to rise up forever. All the same and however far, that was where she was going.

If the span that had once been Calcaria looked like anything at all, it looked like her first glimpse of Colemaigne, but in far worse condition. Here a powdery shale covered the surface and billowed with each step she took. The buildings, however they had once stood, were decomposed into gritty heaps that made it seem she walked through an antediluvian graveyard of enormous creatures, their bulk decayed and deformed into mounds over skulls and ribs and long, broken limbs. And everywhere beneath these grotesque heaps stood the statues. She knew too well how these statues had come to be, and what they really represented. The citizens of this span had been round-eyed and long-snouted creatures, reminiscent of Yemoja but with longer, thinner snouts, inhuman round eyes, and crested foreheads. Weaving through their various silent poses, she mourned not merely their obliteration but the eradication of their collective story of themselves, a world of tales that would now never be heard.

The only sound on that windless span was her feet crunching through the ruins. Unlike Colemaigne, nowhere here did any pristine structures remain, and no live creatures lurked among the groves of the pale dead.

Then somewhere in the middle of the span, she turned a corner and stopped, amazed.

There, as if grown from the debris surrounding it, stood a stepped ziggurat of the same grayish white hue, except that this shape gleamed. Its curved edges were smooth and hard. Against the gloomy backdrop of fog the structure seemed an illusion, a place where the lowering clouds had congealed. Barely visible from the ground, a bluish dome capped its heights.

A great rectangular arch had been cut out of the lowest step of the ziggurat, an entrance that could have accommodated the Agents' abandoned ship in the harbor.

In no doubt of her destination, Leodora walked into the ziggurat. No torches or lamps were visible, but the walls themselves gave off a glow, a phosphorescence that she'd seen before in sea creatures at night. The entrance became a ramp. She had no choice but to ascend, though her legs were already tired from the climb onto the span. She found it odd that the ramp took her up without any access to lower levels, of which there surely had to be at least three or four. Instead it rose steadily until she reached a landing that opened upon a chamber so vast she couldn't see the far side of it. Ahead, light poured down from the blue dome she'd seen. It made her feel that she was moving through water. She thought of Oceanus and his pool of the true heart, but this was nothing as benign.

Furniture and objects lay scattered everywhere—benches, rugs, draperies, hookahs, filigreed trays and stands, painted amphorae, faience bottles, and real statuary—a treasure hoard taken from spans too numerous to count, the final remains of whole worlds devoured and destroyed in Tophet's passing.

Directly under the dome stood a dais covered on the sides she could see by gauzy curtains. Shapes moved behind the curtains, although she couldn't tell what they were. She drew nearer, but a movement on her left caught her attention. For a moment she didn't know what she was seeing. Then as it dawned on her she gasped. Swiftly she wove her way around the various furnishings and toward the object, the impossible object.

Her first impression had been that the thing was a tall mirror. It stood on a pedestal of granite. Reflected or held in its surface was a room virtually identical to this one, filled with treasures, but not quite the same ones or in the same place. Within the field of them, an image of herself wandered. The image wore a gossamer white gown that left her taut but scarred belly exposed. A jewel-studded collar circled her throat, but the jewels could hardly compete with her flaming red hair. Coming nearer, Leodora saw that this near twin was barefoot and wore bangles with tiny bells around her ankles. A heavy belt of garnets pulled the skirt almost obscenely low on her hips. The image did not match her own movements as she worked her way to the mirror, and when she stood directly in front of it, the image looked out past her, as if scanning a distant landscape, but then did approach, walking right up to the glass until they were almost face-to-face and might have been watching each other had the other's forlorn gaze only found her. She felt as if she were peering into the future, perhaps ten years from now if those years served to take a heavy toll on her, deaden her features, kill her spirit. But by then Leodora knew the truth.

"Mother," she said, the word spilling anguish. For a horrible instant it seemed that the image heard her and stared into her eyes. She pressed her hand to the glass as if she might reach through it, but Leandra's eyes did not see the hand, or her; and she recalled the man who had come upon her lying on the beach of Bouyan and cried out "Witch!" in the misapprehension that Leandra had returned. Now she understood that in a sense Leandra had. "I can see you," she told the image.

"She doesn't hear," said a voice behind her. Even as she started to turn, two of Tophet's Agents grabbed her by the arms. A third, the one who'd spoken, eyed her menacingly. "What manner of creature strays into Tophet's realm?" he asked.

Her heartbeat pounded and for an instant reason left her; she felt undone. Then it was as if all the terror fell away: These creatures had taken Diverus, and a surge of anger doused her fear. She answered him: "One who resents being misrepresented by fools."

The Agent massaged his chin with thumb and forefinger. The one gripping her left arm asked, "What's she mean, Scratta?"

"What we already know—that the old man lied to us, and we're set about torturing the wrong captive."

Her heart sank. "Torturing?"

"What else are we to do when the boy can't provide Tophet with any stories other than his own? And it's a paltry thing at best, one for the weepers— a mother turned into a mermaid, the boy abandoned and sold into slavery, into supper for some demented afrits. I expect by now he's told them how he was rescued, but it's evident he's not withholding, he really doesn't *know* any stories. Does he?"

"He's only a musician," she said.

Scratta smiled flatly. For a moment his eyes looked away from her, looked at some internal discomfort, and she suspected he was taking stock of the trouble he was in, having kidnapped the wrong person. Then he came back to her. "The lord is not going to be pleased. Although your presence may ameliorate." He pointed at the curtained dais. "Take Jax to him now."

"What? This one's Jax, too?"

Scratta almost tried to explain, then sighed. "Yes, this one's Jax, too. Take her to the lord."

The two dragged her past Scratta. From behind he taunted, "You're no clever *boy*, are you? Jax, the masked storyteller—you had no choice, did you, but to hide your real self. Why, on some spans, they'd have thrown you into the sea."

They dragged her through the treasure trove to the dais. Closer, she saw that what she'd taken to be more statuary was in fact a line of the round-eyed and long-snouted natives, lushly appareled in a rainbow of surcoats and coathardies, the females adorned with heavy wigs. They watched her dragged past them, never moving, their expressions an admixture of silent horror and supplication—but what were they begging her to do? Free them or cause no trouble and give in? At least, she thought, he hadn't killed *all* of them, though they had been transformed like the Agents into something other than their original substance. They might have been standing there like that since the day Tophet arrived and took their span.

Behind the curtains, behind the dais, the treasures thinned and the space opened up. One group of figures clustered in a semicircle directly under the dome, its blue cast distorting their intent in its soothing color. In their center was a high-backed throne.

A three-sided puppeteer's screen had been set up before them, its white square burning like a blind rectangular eye. In front of it, hanging from chains, was Diverus. His body, as naked as when he'd entered Oceanus's pool, ran with sweat, and he was babbling, his tormented words falling over themselves as if he couldn't keep up with what he had to say even though it was nonsense.

An Agent stood just behind him beside a brazier. He held a set of tongs

from which something long and paper-thin dangled. She twisted in the grip
of her captors as she recognized that it was skin.

The Agents hauled her around the end of the semicircle. More of the natives in their forced finery stood there as if watching a play. Some of them
were weeping silently, their terror palpable. At the midpoint of the group,
upon the throne, sat a figure in a dark robe that might have been green under
other light. To the side of him a naked and ice-pale bald female held up a
pole that was like a gibbet. From the crosspiece at the top of the pole hung a
golden oval mask portraying a sun god's cherubic face. It was at least five
times the size of a human face, a sun disk. The attendant herself was either
blind or else had eyes that were utterly black. From behind the mask, a voice
said, "What is this, Scratta?" It buzzed like a hive of hornets.

"Lord," answered Scratta. "I believe I have solved the puzzle of Jax."

Behind the mask, he drummed long fingertips on the arm of the throne.
They were shiny, of the same blue as the dome overhead. "That's good,"
Tophet replied, "because this one has passed the point of making any sense,
and all we can do is finish stripping the surface off him for the mere pleasure
of doing it, not in order to learn anything." Another pause. "So what is the
puzzle's solution?"

"*This* is Jax, Lord." He turned, and the two behind him dragged her forward.

"Well. Is that right?"

She didn't realize he was asking her until Scratta raised a hand as if to cuff
her. "Answer him."

"Yes," she said. "I'm Jax. The one you're torturing is my musician and I
would like him back intact, if it wouldn't be too much trouble."

The laughter began low, sounding as inhuman as his speech, like metal
grinding against metal, ending finally in the words, "A female puppeteer.
That's unheard of, isn't it?"

"Lord, *we* have never encountered one to bring before you. Storytellers,
yes, but not a puppeteer, much less one compared to—" He faltered.

Tophet seemed not to notice. "But how did she escape your attention,
Scratta?"

"Lord?" Scratta asked, the word rimed with fear.

"She had to have come here on your boat along with this useless creature.
How did she elude all of you?"

"I don't know, Lord. We saw no sign of her."

"Perhaps your eyes are going in your dotage, hmm? I may have to consider that it's time you were freed from your position, Scratta."

From the way he stiffened, Leodora could tell that *freed* didn't mean anything as pleasant as it sounded. "I shouldn't care to leave your service, Lord Chaos."

"Mmmm," Tophet answered equivocally. "So Jax has come to rescue a musician. I'm impressed you didn't flee. Most are disinclined when they receive my invitation."

"I suppose that's why you lie and promise them great wealth?"

"Who have you been talking to?"

She shrugged. "I was told you were looking for a storyteller and that you pay handsomely for a good performance."

Tophet shifted upon his throne. "Where would you have heard such a thing?"

"From . . . oh, what was that name?" She seemed to be asking Scratta, who gave her an anxious look. "Oh, yes, now I recall. Bardsham."

The entire group became a diorama in blue. For moments, no one moved. Only Diverus made a sound, whimpering, half out of his mind. She desperately wanted to go to him, but knew they would both die if she did. She had to stand her ground.

The buzzing voice of the Lord of Chaos slashed the air, dismissing her claim: "Bardsham is long dead. He told you nothing."

"Yet your Agents here sought that name in seeking me. How is it they were thus confused?"

"It was your *skill* that confused the masses. They compared you to him. Bardsham was thrown from a span just like this one. A great height, wasn't it, Scratta?"

"Thrown? Not turned into stone like all the others?"

Chaos rose up. "Why am I explaining myself to a *puppeteer*?" he shouted. "Scratta!"

"If I may," she interjected and waited until the tension dampened. "You requested a story, a proof from him"—she pointed to Diverus—"and he couldn't provide you with that."

"Your musician. You said."

"I did. Allow me to recompense you with such a tale. It will make up for his inability and satisfy you that I am she whom you've sought." With a gesture at the undaya cases, she added, "You've kindly provided me my puppets, too, so I will give you a tale to hold you rapt and you will give us safe passage come morning."

Tophet the Destroyer chuckled. "I've seen hundreds of your kind, and most of them you'll find strewn among my possessions—the ones we haven't left behind. You are brazen for someone so young and untested. You had best hope your talents match your presumption."

"Lord." Scratta filled that single syllable with all his misgivings.

"Yes," Tophet answered and likewise in a syllable dismissed those doubts. "I'll have her shadowplay now. What is your concern in it? You failed even to collect the right individual, tricked by an old sot."

Scratta bowed his head. He looked at Leodora from beneath his brow. His lips stretched in what might have been a retributive smirk. "Yes, Lord," he answered softly.

Leodora didn't move.

"Well?" Tophet asked.

"My musician?" she said.

"One of you get him down."

"I'll need water for his wounds. Wine for him to drink."

"Brazen," he said again, and she unconsciously wrapped one hand around her pendant to keep it from speaking up.

"I don't *have* to perform. We might instead take a meal with all your friends, Lord Tophet."

His fingers squeezed the arms of the throne. "Do you appreciate at all to whom you speak in this manner?"

"I'm well aware," she said.

Another pause followed, and then he sighed. "You remind me of someone, girl, who defied me even though she drowned in fear. Why don't you remove that mask and show us your face?"

"Perhaps after my performance, and you can show me yours."

Diverus, lowered from the chains, collapsed on the floor. They had torn three strips the length of his back. She could hardly keep from screaming at the sight of what they'd done to him. He babbled softly with foam and vomit on his lips.

"I doubt he'll play you any tunes today," Scratta said to her.

"Maybe not, but he won't suffer any further because of me."

The pale Agent shook his head slowly. "The day is long from over, storyteller."

"You're wrong," she argued. "The day's nearly done." She carefully took hold of Diverus. His eyes fluttered open and focused on her a moment. He breathed her name and she shushed him. If Scratta heard the name, he didn't respond. She held him to her, raised him to his feet, and then supported him while they shambled around the broad puppet screen.

An attendant delivered a goblet, a bowl of water, and a cloth. Leodora directed him to place them on the performer's stool under the burning lantern that cast the silk screen in glaring light—too much light. She eased Diverus against the stool, where he stood leaning, his legs trembling but holding him up. She walked back into view of Tophet and his terrified audience, and struggled to remove the lid from the larger puppet case. Then she pulled it around the side of the screen. The second one she lifted as it was and carried out of sight. She stood the case on end directly in back of the lantern, where it threw a long shadow across the polished floor.

She took the bowl from the stool, rolled the cloth in it and then washed his face and mouth, soaked the cloth again and squeezed some of the water over Diverus's back. He cried out, then hung his head and muttered, "I'm sorry, I'm sorry." Again she hushed him. Then she turned away with the bowl and crouched down and poured the rest of the water in the stripe of shadow cast by the puppet case. A few moments longer she knelt there, her back to Diverus.

She set aside the bowl and stood. Beside her, the other puppet case lay open. Glancing down, she found that the figure of Meersh lay on top of the pile. She picked it up and carried it to Diverus.

"Hold this," she told him. Then gingerly she wrapped her arms around his waist and guided him to the standing case.

Either he realized or saw what she intended and tried to struggle. "No, Leodora, no," but she covered his mouth with her hand.

"Epama Epam," she said. "Go into the pool. The goddess will help you. She's called Yemoja."

"No. I have to—"

"Do it, Diverus, you'll die if you don't. You're dying right now. And someone has to look after Meersh." She lifted him, and he hadn't enough strength to defy her.

She pressed her lips to his, tasting his sweat, his pain like cold fire. "Goodbye, my love," she whispered in his ear, and then let go.

The moment he was gone, she pulled the case aside and laid it down.

There was only a shiny puddle of water on the floor, a many-colored oil sliding snake-like upon its surface.

She opened the second case. The flat-piled puppets waited for her to bring them to life. She crossed to the larger case.

"What is wrong, storyteller?" called Tophet the Destroyer. "Can't get your musician to play?" Then, "Where is my story?"

"It's here," she answered. From the larger case, she took out the puppets and set them aside, then reached in and tugged the ribbon, lifting the lid on the secret compartment.

A hiss of surprise escaped her. She took a step back.

In his cavity in the case, the Coral Man had turned to dust.

Kneeling beside the open case, she sorted through the puppets but kept staring at the powdered coral. In the middle of it something black sparkled in the lantern light. She turned from the puppets and dusted the thing off. It wasn't very big, a knobbly fused lump like a clump of beach sand that had been struck and transformed by lightning. She smiled grimly. Her last lingering doubts of the Coral Man—doubts she had kept even from Soter—had been banished.

Rising, she carried a piece of setting with her to the stool.

"I want my story!" yelled Tophet like an angry child.

"Here, then," she replied, and she hooked the flat strip of scenery onto the screen. It cast the shadow of a rough surface, representing a span, any span, all spans.

"This tale," she announced, "took place long ago and far away in the season of the monsoon on a span called Dyauspitar."

There was a commotion on the far side of the screen.

"Dyauspitar sat low, a curl hovering just over shallow marshy water. Gnarled and twisted trees grew on either side of it in incalculable numbers, and the people harvested the wood for their every need. The buildings were made of strips of this wood woven with great skill, houses like giant baskets that could flex and bend against the terrible winds that came with the season of monsoons."

While she spoke, she lifted up a handful of the dust and threw it at the screen. It burst like a cloud into the air, and as it floated between the lantern and the screen it created an illusion of soft rain. Then she took the goblet of wine and flung the contents across the screen, and the sky burst crimson.

"Stop!" cried Tophet. "Stop it now!"

She only lifted another handful of dust and flung it into the air above her-self. Then she grabbed the strap of the large undaya case and hauled it, empty of puppets, around the screen in front of the throne.

"You will not tell that story!" commanded Chaos.

"Why?" she asked. "It's the one you've asked to hear, time and again. From every single storyteller you kidnapped and killed—all of these petrified forms surrounding us—you anticipated that story, the only one that ever concerned you. Bardsham with his tales of Meersh, of girls who gave up their arms for their fathers, of brothers who fought over magical gifts out of a Dragon Bowl—you didn't really care about any of those. There was only the one, and nobody knew it. But you put them to death anyway, just in case. As someone said to me not so long ago, how many stories we keep is the secret everyone wants to know."

She tipped the box and poured the dust of the Coral Man across the floor, into a large ring. Setting it down, she stepped into the ring and sat down, cross-legged.

Tophet was on his feet, and the blind attendant had somehow lost her sense of things, had forgotten him. His true face glared at her over the golden mask. As Soter had described, it was a gruesome war of expressions, a horrible roiling, writhing coil of slaughtered features.

"Dyauspitar was home to a priesthood," she continued, "dedicated to the god Dyaus, who had once been a celebrated sky god, until a collective of demigods struck him down for his excesses and drove him into the sea. That span, according to legend, was built along the spine of Dyaus, which kept the waters shallow there. The truth is, the ousted god embraced his submarine exile and gave himself a new name: Oceanus.

"I doubt you knew that, but it hardly matters, for this tale doesn't concern him anyway."

"You will stop now, storyteller."

She stared at his terrible face and replied, "I think I will begin now." She pushed back the cowl, caught the thong in her hair, and unwound it. Then she clutched the mask and dragged it from her face.

At the sight of her, Tophet sat down upon his throne again. From behind the gold mask his voice emerged: "I don't have to stay for this."

"You can't leave. You've breathed in my dust, and you'll stay put now for the story you've ensured no one could know." She gathered another handful of coral dust.

"Leandra." His voice cracked.

The name cut her and angrily she flung the dust at him, but when she spoke, her voice was calm and controlled. "On Dyauspitar when a child reached the end of his childhood he endured a ritual of passage where his soul was removed for three days from his body and for three days he lay dead while his soul entered an animal selected by a class of priests known as enchanters. And when the spirit of the boy was put back in his body, it was mixed with that animal spirit and he was a man. This was the ritual of manhood and it had gone on since Dyaus fell. It was so perilous that the priests who could perform it were few.

"Our story concerns one of them, whose name was Auuenau. He'd come to the order early, an orphan, and his training had begun well before he was ready to pass through that ritual. He was better versed in the mysteries of the enchanters than most of his elders. He knew, for instance, that one member of his brotherhood guarded a cache of scrolls containing the secrets of Dyaus, which had been found floating upon the water after he fell. In them were secrets of life and death and eternity. Had the archivists of the fabled Library of Shadowbridge known of its existence, they would have taken the cache from Dyauspitar to protect the world. Even the gods of Edgeworld would never have bestowed such knowledge upon any mortal, else risk the destruction of the world.

"Auuenau coveted the hidden knowledge, and for years he collected hints, clues, and inadvertent comments that knit together to lead him to the scrolls. They were concealed in a rough stone kist in the order's ossuary.

"He was careful to present his interest in the ossuary as an expression of reverence. He tended to the bones of his forebears. One by one, however, he removed the scrolls, replacing each with a blank, until he had them all. He hid them in the cistern inside his house.

"The house was filled with seashells and coral and desiccated sea creatures that he'd collected, some shells so large that it took two hands to lift them. He shared the small house with an apprentice under his tutelage, and out of fear of discovery he had to limit his examination of the scrolls to the times when the apprentice was absent. Thus he read with the intention of memorizing every detail of every spell and ritual. In those texts he found the source of the enchanters' power to remove the soul at puberty. The grander shape of the simple rituals he had learned was explicated, and soon enough he had the means to expand upon the limited powers granted the enchanters—to cleave body and soul completely, achieving true immortality. No one can say what might have happened if he had accomplished this as he intended, unhindered. Unnoticed.

"On Dyauspitar when the monsoon arrived, everyone retreated to their houses and remained inside until the storm abated. It was called the Month of Cold Rice. To go outside during the monsoon was to risk disappearing forever. Although ropes were strung from end to end, and looped around bollards down the main avenues, these were no guarantees against the screaming winds and the crashing waves. Let go for even a moment and you would be blown into the trees or over their tops and out to sea. Only a fool ventured out during the monsoon. As the storm began, Auuenau sent his apprentice out on a fabricated mission to the far end of the span, from which he could not possibly return before it struck. Thus safely isolated by the storm, Auuenau assumed he could achieve what he'd read in the scrolls.

"To begin he had to score a specific and intricate pattern into the woven floor of his house. Drawing it first with a stick of charcoal, he discovered that it took up almost the entire space. He had to tear up his bedding, and shove aside tables and cushions. His collection of shells and dead sea creatures he piled up in the corners. Then began the task of carving the pattern he'd drawn, using a mallet and small chisel. This proved to be exhausting. It took him days to chisel out its symmetrical curves and whorls. All the while the storm pushed the walls and roof so that the house seemed to breathe in and out like a living sea creature itself, with curved window eyes and slatted ribs.

"At last he completed it. He rested, he couldn't say how long, for the monsoon made everything dark, everything the same, so that night and day melted together. But finally he stuffed the scrolls into the front of his tunic and began to walk the pattern. At various points he was to stop and recite certain text. Most of it was in arcane languages he did not know the meaning of, forcing him carefully to sound out the words, the phrases. What the scrolls failed to mention was how enervating each recitation was, as if at each stage some part of him was siphoned off. He found that he could not go any farther than the first two stops upon the pattern that first day. Having arrived at the second branch, he had to retreat, his legs barely holding him up as he backed carefully along the line he'd walked, and out again. Then, in the corner, he collapsed, sleeping as if dead.

"Hours later, perhaps the next day, when he awoke, he entered again, finding that he could pass the points where he had already recited from the scrolls. He entered deeper into the pattern, making it through the third and fourth stages before he had to withdraw again and rest.

"The storm never let up. It shrieked and shook the house, and the walls and roof continued to flex. By the time he entered the fifth stage, the outer darkness seemed to have entered the house and penetrated him as well. He could feel the blood in his veins going gray, then black. It seemed he'd been walking this pattern for eternity. There were places along it, so the scrolls claimed, where a wrong step could suck him into nonexistence, into some other world, or turn him inside out. He couldn't remember how many times he'd backed out and come back in, how many times he'd passed out from exhaustion, nor when he'd last eaten. The swirling pattern of spirals was no larger than this room, this hut, yet it seemed to have expanded to the size of Shadowbridge itself. As he cleared the tenth and final stage and dizzily walked toward the center, he sensed a second self beside him, an umbra in his shape walking at his shoulder. Precariously he stepped, balanced on one leg, and then set the other foot down in the center of the pattern.

"He had arrived.

"Auuenau glanced sidelong at the dark self sharing the center with him. It hadn't gone away, but turned and looked back at him with blackness for eyes, and in the blackness stars sparkled.

"He stood, waiting for something explosive—for the fabric of space to tear apart, for the gods to unveil themselves and embrace him, for the sense of cleaving, for anything to tell him that the transformation had occurred. There was nothing. He dangled in the wedge between wholeness and split. The thing hadn't happened but hung on the brink. Exhausted, he fumbled for the final scroll again, peeled it apart, and read. What had he forgotten? Nothing. He was sure of it. He scanned the text, his vision blurring. He rubbed his eyes, stretched the scroll out again. And there, amid the warnings of dire consequences awaiting he who failed to follow the path to the end, *there* was the final opaque phrase that had to be recited from the center of the pattern. He laughed at his simple foolishness. Then he read the lines, whatever they meant, in whatever language it was.

"The darkness closed in from all sides. It circled the pattern, pressed down from above. The shade beside him began to spin. He watched tendrils drawn out of him, pulled into the whirling thing, which grew smaller as it spun faster. Warmth left him, beginning in the core of him and withdrawing to his extremities. Behind it came a sharp chill, like the touch of marble. When the last warmth left him, the tendrils vanished and the spinning form compressed still further, until it was a small flickering thing, hard, burnished and knurled. He reached out to close his hand around it . . . at which point the door to his house flew open.

"The head of his order stood there, clinging to the sides of the door, and clinging to him was Auuenau's apprentice. The apprentice let go one hand and pointed. 'See?' he cried.

"Auuenau, standing with an unfurled scroll in one hand and the pearl of his soul gripped in the other, could only shout, 'No!' Even as he said this, the room changed. The chaos of the monsoon was pulled through the doorway and into the pattern. It sucked the hapless priest and apprentice with it, whirled them like dolls around the pattern and straight at him. He watched them scream as the forces of the storm and of the magic he'd unleashed tore them apart, shredding skin from bones and grinding the bones to dust. He howled and the dust of their deaths poured into his open mouth, down inside him, filling him. What was cold as marble became as jagged as fishhooks within. The floor beneath him was disintegrating. The pattern itself turned to blue crystal, flowing out from him. Still he clung to the twisted pearl that was his separate soul. The scrolls had made it clear that he could not leave the pattern so long as he held on to it, yet he dared not let it go with disaster unfolding about him. He stretched his arm across the pattern, and the only thing he could reach was a nautilus shell in the heap of those he'd collected. He dropped the pearl that was his soul into the shell, listened to it rattle through the chambers and into the center.

"He found that he could move then and walked quickly back around the pattern. He tucked the shell into his robe. The other scrolls blew and tumbled about the room. He dashed to grab them as he balanced on the path, but they were being torn apart, too, and he managed only to snatch shreds. The knowledge contained within them was lost forever. Even had he wanted to, Auuenau could not now undo what he'd set in motion, which his apprentice had disordered; but he did not want to undo it. His very substance had by then become Chaos, and what was happening around him was his doing.

"He exited the crystalline pattern and from the doorway watched as it began to unthread, the scored boards torn loose and drawn down into the center. Then the floor outside the vortex broke apart, whirling around it. Shards of crystal gashed him, embedded in his flesh. The woven walls of the building shredded and fell in, every moment the great whirlpool growing, expanding as if unappeasable. Auuenau remained in the avenue for only a moment before the storm seized him and yanked him off his feet. Instinctively he clutched a guide-rope, but in doing so he let go of the final scroll, and it flitted away on the wind.

"The surface of the span of Dyauspitar cracked beneath him and collapsed into the maw of the whirlpool. Like the dark form that had arisen beside him, that core seemed shot with stars.

"He dragged himself along the rope, and the darkness circled after him. The rope came suddenly unmoored and flung him into the air, all the way to the opposite side of the span. He struck the rail, doubled over it, but hung on. Below lay a skiff, anchored and storm-tossed. As the span shook apart, he leapt over the rail and down into it. It was half full of water and he fell, but he untied the lines and with a long pole pushed away. The edge of the span split behind him and the wind threw flinders at him. Between the piers the water swirled, capturing the collapsing fragments in its force, sucking them in, and like a fire fueled by new wood, the whirlpool expanded across the water.

"Auuenau tried to pole his skiff away, but he couldn't. The thing had caught him, and helplessly he began to whirl around it, faster and faster, riding the crest but certain to follow everything else down into the star-shot blackness of eternity in the maw of the pool.

"He comprehended suddenly what would satisfy it. As he clung with one hand to the side of the skiff, he tore the small shell out of his robe as if tearing out his own heart. He stared at the striped nautilus and understood that he and the whirlpool were of one substance now, one purpose shared. It was his shadow self, rapacious and unappeasable unless he gave it the one thing it wanted. He lifted the shell, and the pearl rattled inside it. He grinned sickly, and that was the first moment when he felt the faces of those he'd absorbed moving across his own—the features of the monk and his apprentice.

"He tossed the shell over the side and into the mouth of the maelstrom. He didn't even watch it vanish, but set down the pole and lay back to let events play out.

"The whirlpool devoured his soul. At once it shrank beneath him.

"Within moments Auuenau's skiff was circling a patch of foam, of nothing, of water indistinguishable from any other. Of the span of Dyauspitar all that remained was the ridge of rock that had supported it, the spine of Dyaus. The rest, all of his brethren, all of the people, were gone, absorbed, the fuel that fed his immortality.

"He, the embodiment of Chaos, began to laugh. He looked at his hands, his arms, his skin transformed into something harder than flesh.

"Light rain sprayed over him, but the winds had ceased their howl and sun-speckled clouds floated overhead. Even the storm had been sucked down into the horror of the force he'd unleashed. Lying back in the skiff, he let the currents of the ocean take him wherever they would. He was deathless and fearsome now. He needed a new name for his new self, and by the time he reached another spiral, he had one, extracted from ancient legends, the name of a god: Tophet the Destroyer, the Lord of Chaos. Thus Auuenau became a god, and no one the wiser save for a real god whose span he'd destroyed."

She reached into the dust and picked up the gnarled burnished pearl in her fist.

Casually, she added, "If you like I could repeat the whole tale for you with puppets," she said. "It's better with puppets."

When he said nothing, she gathered herself up and walked to the throne. No one tried to stop her. No one moved at all. The golden mask hung before her, his last protection.

"When you had Bardsham's puppet cases brought here—you didn't know that, did you? That these are his?—when you did that, you brought the very thing you feared, not just the story of it. Your tale, like the whirlpool in it, comes full circle. After all, you never were a god."

She went around the mask. He sat defiantly, but his head was tilted away as if in fear of her. His robe had fallen open, and she saw that his body was covered in spurs and sharp splinters of bone that had pushed out of his skin. She stepped up to the end of the throne, between his knees. He reached out suddenly, triumphantly, and grabbed her wrist. She winced, stiffening at the frigid pain that burned to her marrow. But then suddenly the flow reversed and a charge ran out of her fist into him.

His fingers leapt free of her and he bucked violently with a great cracking gasp.

She opened her palm and the knobby black pearl was gone.

Tophet's head began to vibrate from side to side faster and faster until she couldn't distinguish the awful features anymore, the millions of faces blurring into a smudge upon the air. The blur flung off sparks that spun through the room. She recalled the story the Ondiont snake had told her of the bride of Death, who had captured souls like tiny lights; and of the brothers who were turned to rock with a final wish to be worshipped; of the thousand stories of people who wished for something before they understood the price of it.

The sparks flicked and vanished, flicked and vanished, around her, past her, through her. They pitted the gold mask behind her where they hit it until it became as thin as mesh. And when the last one burst forth and died, the body of Tophet stopped moving. The indurate form had become a dried husk, a gaping mummified thing without a face.

She stepped back from the corpse and brushed against the huge mask. It fell, slipping past her shoulders as she turned to see the figure of the attendant stumble and release the pole on which it hung. The mask bent when it hit, and slid across the floor like a leaf skimming a pond. The pole clattered after it. The blind attendant caught her balance against Scratta. He in turn rocked to and fro and then fell, shattering when he hit the floor. All around Leodora, the Agents of Chaos had become stone that within moments had begun to crumble away. The force that had knit them together was gone.

Her hand where Tophet had grabbed her was burned white as if covered with powder, but it hadn't turned to stone. She looked at the people around her, the survivors of this span, who were too fearful yet to believe that the Destroyer was really gone. She stepped down from the throne and walked away, out from under the dome, and by the time she passed the curtained dais she was runnning, weaving back through his trove of treasures until she reached the mirror. In dread she approached it, hopeful that the magic behind it had been banished; and yet her heart swelled when she discovered it had not and her mother still agitatedly filled the frame.

"Why didn't she go?" she asked as she touched the pendant.

The Brazen Head awoke. "His magic was cast in the glass, independent of him, as with the dome. Magic needs magic to be undone."

"How do I set her free? I can't leave her this way."

"What is she?"

"My mother."

"But if I say your mother is long dead, then what does she become?"

"I don't know. A reflection."

"A reflection," he repeated. And he fell silent again.

She stared around her, turning in a circle, then looked up through the dome and shouted, "You knew all along! All of you! Shumyzin! Cardeo!" Her voice echoed through the vast chamber and came back to her unanswered. The most important questions were the ones they never asked.

She gripped the phial. It had to be nearly empty. The drop that had rescued Diverus had taken forever to spill from it. She couldn't pour the last drops on the upright mirror and couldn't tilt the mirror on its stony base. Instead she held out her hand and tipped the phial over her palm. Two drops splashed out.

For a moment she hesitated. The air filled with distant cries of "Jax!" as if the crowds from the Terrestre were clamoring for more; but she knew it was the survivors of Calcaria, freed and seeking after their savior.

"Good-bye, Mother," she said, then she wiped her hand over the glass, smearing the reflection from top to bottom. She stepped back and the image in the mirror rippled and faded. The mirror turned black.

"Diverus!" Leodora called, and she stepped through the darkness.

THE PUPPETS OF BARDSHAM

There is a span on Shadowbridge called Calcaria that claims it has Bard-sham's original puppets. The span is terribly ancient, so old that its Dragon Bowl has long since fallen into the sea, and most of the span is composed of uninhabited ruins. The puppets, however, are on display in a museum that is a great towering structure like no other on the span, and which lends cre-dence to the story they tell there of how the span fell into ruin. The people of that span—tall, slender creatures with prominent snouts and eyes like black marbles—tell a story about how they were once imprisoned there by a fiendish god named Chaos, and how the ghost of Bardsham's wife came out of a mirror and destroyed him with a story, leaving the puppets behind as a tribute to those who'd suffered under his yoke. The mirror from which she emerged is a dull and unpolished thing that no longer reflects. It is also on display there, beside a pocked and damaged mask that they claimed was the face of Chaos.

This local tale would be dismissed were it not for the puppets themselves: Bardsham is not known to have performed on spirals anywhere near Calcaria, and in truth most of those other spans are dead ruins, too, peopled only by

statues, the cause of their abandonment likewise attributed to the same shattered god. The puppets, however, are quite real. Detractors of the story point
out that there's no puppet of Meersh in the collection, and we all know that
Meersh was Bardsham's signature figure. Of course, the people have an explanation for that, too: that Bardsham took his puppet with him when Chaos
had him thrown off the span into the sea. It's a perplexing story to be sure.

On the other side of the world, far across the Adamantine Ocean, the
spans sing stories of a girl puppeteer, who followed in Bardsham's footsteps
but was even greater than he. Some say she was his daughter, and others that
she was a goddess who healed the span of Colemaigne. What happened to
her is not known. At the height of her powers, she stopped performing. Many
there are who believe she and Bardsham were so skillful that the gods of
Edgeworld whisked them away and they live now as immortals for the entertainment of the eternals. Stories of her—of a puppeteer called Jax, who came
from an island and brought Colemaigne back to life—are now performed far
and wide in pantomimes and puppet shows, recitations and comedies. No
one really knows for sure any of it, but, then, not all mysteries are explained.

PHOTO: BETH GWINN

GREGORY FROST has been a finalist for nearly every major award in the fantasy field, including the Hugo, Nebula, James Tiptree, Theodore Sturgeon Memorial, International Horror Guild, and World Fantasy awards. He is the author of six previous novels, as well as the critically praised short-story collection *Attack of the Jazz Giants & Other Stories*. Greg is one of the Fiction Writing Workshop directors at Swarthmore College. He lives in Merion Station, Pennsylvania. His website is www.gregoryfrost.com.